The Claimed Queen

E.M. Jaye

Contents

Dedication:

To my husband and daughter. Without you, none of this would be possible.
Also to my supportive family, who allowed me to start this journey.

Geldon Language Pronunciation and Definition Guide

Abiciant—(Ab-iss-e-ant) Rare sublineage that allows the weaver to channel their mental energy upon another and control them.

Animare—(An-a-mare) Term of endearment given to a mated male from his female. This term is the highest form of respect one mate can give to another.

Aninare—(An-a-nare) Term of endearment given to a mated female from her male. This term is the highest form of respect one mate can give to another.

Aniun—(An-ee-um) One of the six great, or main, lineages, this is the control of the power of water. Warriors gifted in this often exhibit calm personalities.

Atelean—(Ate-lee-on) The family name of the founding Gelder ancients, once the most powerful family in all the galaxy.

Beb—Term of endearment used in the Star language, usually reserved for a couple that are in a romantic or sexual relationship.

Belator—(Bell-a-tore) The power name of the high warrior king, belator appeared upon the king when he came into maturity.

Bellum—(Bell-um) Term that refers to securing something, commonly used as a multilayer weave that allows a room to be locked securely.

Caeli—(Say-lee) One of the six great, or main, lineages, this is the control of the power of air. Warriors gifted in this often exhibit joyous and carefree personalities.

Cerum—(Sear-um) Word that designates a ceremony of great importance.

Chakkas—(Cha-kas) Invisible points that run throughout the body that channel the energy of the cosmos.

Cognata—(Cog-na-ta) Familial relations that means cousin.

Deim—(Dem) Curse word, profanity.

Erain—(Air-ens) Race of aliens that thrive on the pain, suffering, and death of all races other than their own. They attempt to commit genocide on any planet they come across. Normally impulsive and historically prone to fighting among each other.

Fiefling—(Fef-ling) Curse word, profanity.

Hael—(Hail) Sublineage that gifts the weaver with healing abilities. Gelders who are strong in this line commonly become medical doctors. Those gifted in *caeli*, *vim*, and *simul* often possess strong gifts in *hael* as well.

Ignis—(Ig-nis) One of the six great, or main, lineages, this is the control of the power of fire. Warriors gifted in this often exhibit passionate personalities, and are commonly quick to anger.

Itumnis—(It-um-nus) The fountain from ancient Gelder, known for its eternal life.

Lacieu—(Lass-ce-o) The one original lineage, known as the lost line. No one alive is thought to possess a gift in it.

Massa—(Mass-sa) Title of honor to a warrior who possesses mastery in a lineage.

Medate—(Meh-date) Form of medi*tatio*n that only the most disciplined warrior can perform. It allows the weaver to access every fragment of information they have ever come across, even something that they did not consciously know they observed. Performed incorrectly it can destroy the mind of the warrior who attempts it.

Memien—(Mem-ee-in) A physical manifes*tatio*n of power, it can function as a power source and can protect, attack, or provide energy to the weaver.

Merate—(Meh-rate) Lighter form of medi*tatio*n that warriors who are adept with mental skills can achieve.

Myo—(My-oh) Meaning my or mine.

Praesidium—(Pray-seed-ee-um) A group of six warriors who are masters in their lineage that are pledged to protecting their pledge holder.

Ratshult—(Rat-shult) Derogatory name.

Scimaar—(Sim-mar) A blade used by the Gelders in battle.

Starskies—(Star-skees) An alcoholic beverage that is so potent even a Gelder can become inebriated.

Tatio—(Tat-tee-oh) Unique mineral that is necessary for Gelders to be able to weave their power.

Terra—(Tare-ah) One of the six great, or main, lineages, this is the control of the power of rocks and minerals. Warriors gifted in this often exhibit stoic personalities, and are commonly levelheaded and serious in nature.

Chapter One

Ellie

The view out of my small, dirty window is staggering only in the sense that it is utterly unremarkable. The picture that is showcased by this dirty glass is the same one I have looked at for the past twenty years. I may have moved to this new, but somehow even smaller, apartment after finally leaving my parents' hovel, but you wouldn't know it by the view.

Run-down buildings stretch as far as the eye can see. The old and dilapidated tarmac roads are barely recognizable due to the damage they have suffered. Lining those poor abused streets are countless barrels that are home to small bonfires. The only source of warmth any of us who live here have access to. Having air that is either heated or cooled on command is a luxury only those in Area Five or above are granted.

The sky is a dreary gray—you would mistake it for smog or clouds, but you would be wrong. It is ash, floating down from the wreckage above. Our horizon is a deep, blood red. A reminder to all of what life on our world has become.

Scared.

Dependent.

Dying.

Only a fool would ignore that sky, walk past it and never once think of the billions who were murdered. I am no fool. Every single day I am plagued with the thoughts of what we have suffered and I will never forget the horror that has become our normal.

And so I stare out my dirty window in my dingy apartment and look out on a day that on the surface seems exactly like all my other days. It seems wrong that a day that feels so momentous to me is not marked by something. Anything at all out of the ordinary that would symbolize that it is indeed special. Or just something to say this day will be different than all the rest.

This particular day feels so significant to me that I can't shake the feeling that the view outside is wrong. The scene I see from my window should reflect the turmoil I feel inside. Maybe if it did, the *people* outside would realize that things have changed. Deep down in my gut, I feel different, as if I am standing on the precipice of something great. Or possibly horrible. I feel as if something is amiss—the portrayal of life outside my window is so incongruent with the conflict burning inside of me.

Today is the day that I have been both anticipating and dreading for twenty years—it is my Claiming Day. Just thinking of it causes my arms to tingle and gooseflesh to appear. We have a Claiming Day every year, but this is the first year that I will be participating in it, as I turned twenty just today; the day that I came into this world is forever marked by the suffering of women worldwide.

My mother tells me that the day of my birth was a sign from God that I would be nothing but trouble. It is just one more reason my birth brought her pain. Not only did my father abandon us the day I was born, but since that fateful Claiming Day, not one single woman has been claimed. Not one. Twenty years ago today marks the day that we stopped paying our fee for our salvation.

I doubt that she really believes my birth is somehow the cause for the lack of claimed women, even she is not that daft to think I am in anyway significant. That I could somehow have a role to play in this world. No, I am sure it's just a way for my mother to cope with the loss of my father's affection. Well, one way. The other was marrying the horrid man that I am only permitted to speak to in public. Apparently, it would appear odd to others if it was common knowledge that I am not allowed to talk to my stepfather. In private I am to be invisible, neither seen nor heard. The few times that I failed in that regard were met with swift and painful punishment that I will remember until the day I go to my grave.

So I have lived most of my life never speaking to my mother's husband, as if I would even want to. That vile man has taken great pleasure in abusing me for as long as I can remember—starvation and beatings being just two of his favorite punishments. I would never intentionally seek his attention. I suppress a shudder as the memories of his more creative punishments come rushing at me from where I keep them locked away. I close my eyes and let myself fall into my own mind. My refuge. The one place I can retreat into where no one can hurt me.

Slowly, I slip away from the world around me, letting everything fade away. I may not physically go anywhere, but that doesn't bother me. I am no longer surrounded by dirt, garbage, and death. Instead, I am just floating in an inky sea of blackness. The peace that settles over me is so profound I struggle to express it with words.

I once tried to explain this process to my sisters. I only wanted to show them how to handle their own pain. I attempted to instruct them on how to seek shelter within their minds, but they never understood what I meant. If I were smarter, perhaps I would be able to share with my sisters how to do this. But, alas, I am just plain old me. Not stupid like my mother claims, but by no means smart either.

I enjoy floating in my mind for a little while longer before I grab on to those cursed memories of pain and hunger and I picture a little box. I force those thoughts into that box and lock it as tightly as I can. Then I let myself bask in the bliss of my own private world for just one more moment. Then I slowly bring myself out of my meditation, open my eyes, and am greeted with the same scene as before.

Except there is more activity out on the streets below. It won't be long now until the ceremony begins. I wonder if I can avoid going home afterward. My mother wanted me to drop off the money to her then, but perhaps I can delay it until tomorrow.

Claiming Day is a day that affects everyone, especially my mother. She becomes violent, angry, and resentful. I have yet to sit in that abandoned arena, full of trepidation, waiting to see if this year is the year that I will be claimed. If I will be the woman who will never see her family and friends again. Taken from all I know and love to pay our debts. Waiting in those cold seats to see if I will be the one who is to be whisked away from our planet, never to return.

I have been told, repeatedly, that it is utterly terrifying to sit and wait in that crowd of young women. My mother hated the claiming ceremonies and had no qualms about sharing her horror. She filled my childhood with an alarming amount of vulgarly depicted stories featuring young women dragged down the aisles by large alien males. Describing the distraught women who began screaming and crying when their names appeared on the board.

She rejoiced in embellishing the stories with her own perspective, outlining how at least the women who were sent to their deaths were the boring and stuck-up ones. Harping about how they slighted her, then colorfully outlining the agony she imagines they went through.

But, I believe I took a completely different lesson away from those stories than what my mother intended. She wanted to instill fear in me, but all she did was increase my distaste for her and women like her. We are duty-bound to be claimed. That is the price we pay, and even if we don't like it, our survival as a species depends on it. So women who try to refuse a claiming put us all to shame. And a woman who takes pleasure in another person's pain is sickening, even if that woman is my mother.

Though I cannot refute that I am similarly plagued with apprehension over my imminent Claiming Day. But, for me? There is an entirely different issue that is fueling my anxiety over this annual ritual our society partakes in. I am afraid *because* no one has been claimed. The fact that not one, not one single woman has been claimed in twenty years sends bile to the top of my stomach, threatening to erupt any moment. Because all I can think is... why?

Why have they stopped claiming us?

We earn protection by giving up our women. This is the only thing of value we have to offer our much more advanced protectors.

Is there something defective with us that prevents them from taking us?

Will they ever claim a woman again?

What happens then?

What do we do when they no longer want us?

I look out the window into the sky and see the burning remains still visible from the last attack from the Erains, my eyes slowly following the softly falling ash. We are hopelessly outmatched—if we lose the protection that the Gelder warriors provide for us, there is nothing left to save us. We will all perish. An entire species wiped from existence like they were never there. Just gone.

This will be my first of many claiming ceremonies. And for every year to come, I will have to be plagued by this uncertainty all over again. My mind is awash with a million questions, all that I have no hope of ever answering.

Whatever happened to the women who were claimed before my time? What will happen if women continue to fail to be claimed? Is there an expiration date on the security we are given by our Gelder protectors? If they do start claiming us again, what does that mean for the poor soul who gets claimed?

For my entire life, I have been overly curious. As a citizen of Area Three, I had specific roles I could choose for my occupation. With my passion for discovering the answers to questions that many never asked, I fell naturally into a love of history. Luckily, I wasn't Level Two or One, or I would never even have been educated in the field of history let alone earned a position at a respected department specializing in preserving our past.

In my job as a historian, I specialize in the celebration of time before the Purge War, as well as the remembrance of the Purge War itself. There are dreadful facts stuck in my brain about that horrid time period. Most people refused to study the war, but I have always been drawn to it. I know exactly how many humans perished when the Erains first attacked a century ago. I refuse to ignore their memory just because it is painful.

We were utterly unprepared to face a threat from the skies. Billions died in mere hours. If not for the treaty, billions more would have died. Our entire existence would have been wiped out had we not agreed to an alliance with the Gelders. Their demands may have been unorthodox at the time, but the choice was simple. If giving up our lives to uphold the treaty is what we need to do, I am willing to make the sacrifice. The alternative is too bleak.

As much as I try to deny it though, I too am worried about what it means to be claimed. I know every woman who has ever been claimed; I dedicated most of my youth to the sole purpose of determining what becomes of these claimed women. Scouring every available text for clues about their fate, with very little success. I know of their lives before the claiming but after that? Nothing. It's like my mother says, it's as if they were dead. There one day, gone the next.

Most of my people prefer ignorance, but not me. I can never feel safe when I do not have all the facts. So once I realized their fate was beyond me, I turned my research to discovering why they claimed who they have. Looking for a connection between the women claimed.

But again, I was met with failure. After all my research there were no patterns to be found. Some are younger, some are older. Some are rich, some are poor. Some are small, some are large. The only connection is their age range, twenty to thirty. No order of any kind, let alone one that explains why they suddenly stopped taking us. Or predicts who will be next. It could be anyone, a woman living anywhere on the planet.

In my world, we stand as a planet, as a global race. There are no countries anymore. Nothing like what I read about in the Old Earth. Here, on what we now call Earth Nueva, there is no racism against your fellow human. Honestly, it is not needed, we just chose other things to judge each other by. Why bicker over race when there are so many more things to discriminate against?

Over a century ago our entire species faced annihilation. That really puts things into perspective. I imagine a woman a century ago, who had no idea that we are not alone in this galaxy, might have thought it mattered where you were born. That where your mother was when she pushed you out gave some sort of bearing on who you would be as a person. But really, when we are just lowly, defenseless humans out of all the galactic species, we have to stick together. Regardless of what piece of land you were born on.

Now that we are aware of the vast and diverse forms of life in our universe, it is almost laughable how little we matter. Compared to nearly every race that Area Ten, the ambassador, and his cabinet members, have begun trade with we are behind in medicine, weapons, technology, and nowhere near equal in space travel. Now we have read about some other primitive worlds that exist out in the cosmos, but we have no contact with them here on Earth Nueva.

A sound of a door clicking shut vaguely registers in my mind. An exasperated sigh, followed by a small chuckle can be heard before a voice I know all too well speaks up. "Honestly, I knew I'd find you here are this window. I don't know why you are so worried, Ellie. No one has been claimed in our entire lives, and it is doubtful that we will ever see a claiming," Marilee says to me, snapping me out of my reverie. Her hand pulls me away from the window.

Marilee is my best friend. We have known each other since we were children. She is a gorgeous, tough, self-assured woman. Her auburn hair is always effortlessly tamed, compared to my own tangled mess of wild blonde hair. Her body is a work of art, full of tall, lean muscles, while I am small and frail. Her green eyes blaze with inner fire, while my blue eyes are lackluster.

She fears no one and doesn't let anyone tell her what to do, while I have always been a follower. Doing everything that is expected of me. I often wish I was more like her. My whole life has been centered on doing what my mother asks of me, and even after twenty years, I cannot manage to stop trying to earn her approval. When deep down, I know she will never give it.

"Trust me, you are worrying over nothing. The call for claiming is simple. Last year all we did was go to our assigned waiting areas, wait for the global call, look at the display and see that there was no one on it, and go home," Marilee says to me.

Marilee is one year older than me and went through her first calling last year. She mistakenly thinks I am so worried because I fear that I will be called. Honestly, the thought of someone claiming me is laughable. I am painfully aware of my own shortcomings, my mother has made sure of that. I know I am nothing special, so I don't think our protectors would have any reason to claim me. Who would want me?

She, like many others, believes that the Gelders have merely decided to forget about our part of the agreement. They think that somehow the most dominant species in the galaxy simply forgot that we must allow as many as one hundred of our women to be claimed by them annually. Perhaps some think that we are merely of no more use to them, so they don't claim us anymore.

They all seem to have forgotten that this was what we agreed to do in exchange for their help. It is our payment for their protection against the destruction of our people. Everyone else seems to think that we should just be thankful, but if you pay attention to the agreement, you would be very concerned about this turn of events. Everything in this world has a price, and eventually, the bill will come due.

They used our weaknesses and our desperation to force us to agree to the terms they wanted. We did minimal negotiating. How could we? We had nothing else they wanted. Mark my words, the Gelders have a very particular reason for drafting this treaty, and I am sure it benefits the Gelders, not us humans. Not that I fault them per se. They have flawlessly protected us since the agreement, protection that we desperately needed. They have lost soldiers in the battles, giving their lives to save ours. We need to pay our debts to them.

"Marilee," I say her name with a sigh. Hesitant to start this conversation once again. "I just feel that one day soon we will find out why they have stopped claiming us and I don't think I want to be there when we do," I tell her, attempting to explain my feelings of apprehension. "Or worse, what we now must do to earn their continued protection."

"Oh, Ellie, you worry too much." She gives me her standard reply, complete with an overly exaggerated eye roll. How she can be so unconcerned drives me crazy, but like always, I avoid confrontation and let it go.

"Regardless, it is almost time," I say to distract her and end our discussion. "We should get going to the arena. The ceremony will be starting soon." As hard as I try to keep my worry from my voice, I hear it when I speak and how my words tremble.

I have no desire to go down this path, something is going to happen. I just know if I step out that door, it is the end of something. I can feel it in my bones. I just don't know what it is going to be the end of.

No use delaying any longer though. With a small nod to each other, Marilee and I gather our things. All eligible women are required to bring something that we wish to take with us in case we are claimed. Once claimed you are immediately taken away to be prepared. No heartfelt goodbyes or lengthy packing allowed.

We are permitted to bring only two possessions: one item of our choosing and one item to give as a gift to the Gelder who claimed us. I have my objects packed already in a small tote, as does Marilee.

I am so pleased with my small closet-sized apartment. I just moved in last week, but it has already become my sanctuary. I moved out later than most, even though I obtained a job early since I give over half my income to my mother and stepfather. It took a while to be able to afford even this small place. But still, to live on my own is the purest form of pleasure I have ever known. Sadly, it is the only pleasure I have ever known. Well, that and my riverbank.

As I lock my door, I cannot help but feel a sense of finality in the action. We leave my small apartment and head over to an old stadium that used to house sporting events before such frivolous pursuits were banned.

Imagine, being paid to play a game. That is definitely a thing of the past. Games of any kind are not permitted in public places or common areas. It was outlawed decades ago, one of the current ambassador's first laws when he was appointed.

This old stadium is the assigned area where all the other eligible women who are of Area Three class or lower in our geographical zone are to meet for the global call. I try to shift my focus to the frivolous chatter of Marilee to help calm my nerves. She is talking about a dress she wants to buy or something like that, but I am struggling to maintain focus. Anxiety keeps rushing in, interrupting my thoughts. Before I know it, we have arrived.

At the stadium, we will be joining the five thousand other eligible women in our social class that live in our geographical area, along with over fifty thousand women of different ranks. As a lower-middle level area class, we are one of the larger areas. Of course the lower the grade, the larger the group. The lowest class is enormous, comprising over eighty percent of our population. With every level, the numbers get smaller and smaller. The top-tiered levels are minuscule in comparison.

As we walk into what once was a massive stadium and follow the directions to where our area meets, I can't stop the feeling of dread. I am apprehensive about what it will mean if someone is claimed today, or possibly even worse, what will happen if yet another year goes by with no claimed women to pay our debt. Both outcomes are terrifying thoughts, only time will tell which is worse.

Danion

Excitement courses through me, filling my body with anticipation. Today is the day, finally after all this time. Twenty years I have been waiting. As the strongest of our people, I feel the pull of my mate more intensely than others.

Gelder warriors, male or female, know their mates on sight, and in rare cases, they can feel a mate calling to them before they ever lay eyes on them. I felt the pull of my mate the second she entered this world. Felt her soul calling to mine across the millions of stars. Never before has anyone sensed the bond so early and over such a vast distance.

It has been an immense struggle to prevent myself from caring for her as is my right. It is physically painful for a warrior to ignore the call of a bond, but I had no choice. Each mortal world that is a member of the Pact Worlds has specified regulations on how we can claim their women. Earth required us to wait until their women were mature, and I agreed at the time. To forsake the treaty I myself wrote would weaken the legitimacy of all of our agreements. Even worse, it would be dishonorable.

So I have not been able to watch over my mate as I desire. Instead, I have been forced to remain a silent protector, providing for her what I am able to from afar but never genuinely guiding her. I understand the reticence of these mortal races for placing a restriction on the age their women are claimed, no matter how frustrating it has been to me personally.

In truth, it has not been an issue before, waiting to claim women until they are of a mature age. Most warriors do not feel their mate as I have felt mine. If we did as they feared, take children from their parents, then it would indeed make us monsters. But we would never do this, not to the other half of ourselves.

Once mated, our entire focus is ensuring the happiness of our mate. This is what I long to do for my Eleanor, but the humans have prevented me from doing so. They have no comprehension of what a soul mate actually is. Not allowing me anywhere near her, or any contact with her of any kind is akin to torture. My only intention was to interact with her, and learn her hopes and dreams so that I can make sure she gets everything she ever wanted.

That is the gift a mate gives to her warrior, a purpose for all eternity. A gift that I am very anxious to finally meet, and a gift that fewer and fewer warriors are experiencing. No new claimed women have come from her race since her birth, and the other mortal worlds have not produced a new mate in over a century. Undeniably the unknown cause of our lack of mates is as distressing as it is worrisome. Without mates, we have no children, and without children, we are at an end.

I know the claiming of my mate will bring change to my people. Hope to a dying race.

My mind turns to the ever-present mystery that is causing our slow but inevitable death. Over the millennia, I have watched fewer and fewer of my kind be created until eventually, we reached where we are today. Not one new Gelder has been born in over five hundred years. We continue to lose precious warriors in battle, and our numbers decline every year.

We are indeed a dying race.

I must save my people, failure is not an option. I will save us. I know that my mate can help me achieve our salvation. I have led my people for more centuries than I can count. I have sacrificed all I have to keep them strong and have done deeds that my mate will most likely not approve of to ensure my both people's happiness and their safety.

I find myself smiling. It seems strange that I will now have to think about how my actions will be viewed by another. It has been quite a long time since I have had to be concerned with such thoughts. My parents died long ago, and there has never been anyone else whose opinion mattered to me.

No one dares question me now. The last one who did was over five hundred years ago, and I quickly made him see the error of his ways. He was no challenge at all. Thinking about our battle brings a humorless smile to my face. I cannot remember the last time I was challenged by a worthy adversary, or come across anything of interest. My existence has stretched on for so long that I am feeling...empty.

But a mate, that is a different matter. She will fill my empty days with joy once more. She will be the perfect challenge. One, if I am honest, I am very eager to experience. The few mated pairs I have encountered have all shared a deep connection, a common goal that has solidified them as a joined pair. I have always envied this connection. Desired someone to keep the loneliness at bay. Someone to share the never-ending years with. Someone to share the burden of protecting not only my people but the entire galaxy.

"I bet you are glad today has finally arrived, eh, Danion?" my cousin Golon asks me. He may be one of my closest friends and one of the two beings I trust completely, but I detest him acting as if he knows my thoughts on a matter as personal as a mate.

For well over two thousand years he has been perfecting the ability to needle me. Taking quite a bit of pleasure in trying to spike my temper. He needs to know he cannot predict my actions, let alone my feelings.

Regardless of the fact that he is actually quite good at it. He doesn't need to know that.

"And why would I be awaiting the arrival of this particular day?" I take care to keep my voice void of emotion. This game is one we have played many times before, him trying to impose his will on me, and me fighting to maintain the upper hand. I may be King, but that means nothing to him.

"Come now, Dane, don't try to pretend you are unaware that today marks your mate coming of age. There is no need to hide the relief you feel now that you can finally be released from the restrictions that the agreement to the Earth race kept you bound by." He sounds exasperated and slightly defensive. Good. He is unsure of my position, it's now time to further unnerve him.

"Golon, I have dedicated my entire existence to my people. For thousands of years, I have selflessly devoted everything that I am to those I rule. Not to mention the billions we protect. A mate is just another responsibility, one I will shoulder just like all my others." I take special care to make my words sound empty. Golon may be the most intelligent being alive today, but he has a lot to learn before he can make predictions about me.

But in truth, I counted the days until I could finally claim her. Of course, she had to be born of a race where we negotiated a restrictive treaty. When I brokered this treaty, it did not seem like such a compromise, since so few Gelders ever find a mate. We did not even know if there would be mates among them; the Earth beings were primitive people.

It was understandable that they feared the mating rituals of our race. Being so un-evolved is not their fault, it is just how they are. They see lust where there is only love and see sinful thoughts where protection is the only goal.

They were, and still are, incapable of grasping that mating is so much more than a sexual experience to our people. Once a warrior has bonded, he devotes himself to the happiness of his mate. It is not unheard of that we bond before adulthood, but a sexual bond is such a crass and disrespectful way to describe a mate to a Gelder. Often sexual aspects do not become a part of the relationship for years, sometimes decades, depending upon the rate of maturity of the female species.

And due to the humans' failure to comprehend and trust our intentions, they insisted on unneeded restrictions. This happens with virtually all of our mortal wards, so I felt no reason to fight them. If I had known my own mate was to be born to them, and that I would know of her immediately and be forced to wait twenty Earth years, I might not have conceded this point so readily.

Though I admit, it is exceptionally uncommon that I have found my mate so young. I knew of her as soon as she was born. In all of our history, there has only been one documented instance of this happening before, with my father and mother. But they were on the same planet at the time, not light-years apart. My parents had an exquisite bond, and I have long craved to share my existence with a mate as they did.

So yes, I am quite anxious indeed to claim her. To care for her, feed her, clothe her. I simply want to provide for her. Share thoughts with her. Know her dreams. Her fears.

I am not strictly lying to my cousin; she *is* another responsibility. But in no way is that responsibility unwanted. She is the sole purpose for my existence, and it is all I can do to sit here and patiently wait for her to be brought to me.

"Sure, Dane, act as if this is nothing to you." Golon says with a scoff, " Regardless, I thought you might like to know that the claiming ceremony is about to begin. Best we hurry to not miss your responsibility."

As if I ever would.

Ellie

I look around at all the women in my stadium section. New walls are sectioning off the open area in the center as well as up between the seats. There are five thousand women in here that come from my own level, but thousands more that are members in other areas. We are not to interact with members in the other area classes unless it is in a professional setting and cannot be avoided.

All these women are here due to the laws that require us all to enter the claiming pool at twenty. I know that I am merely a face in the crowd. A crowd of single women, all between twenty and thirty years of age.

The only way to get out of the claiming is to age out. When I was young and scared after another rant of my mother's, I used to contemplate getting married so that I would never have to enter this claiming draft, but the laws require all human females to remain unattached until she reaches maturity. If you marry in secret and then are claimed afterward, the human union will be dissolved, and the human man left behind forfeits his own life.

Needless to say, once I learned of this I never thought about marriage again.

So here I am, doing everything that is expected of me and waiting to find out who will be claimed this year. Despite Marilee's assertions, I can't shake the feeling that this year is different. Someone will be claimed, I can feel it in my bones.

On the projection at the front of the arena is a three-dimensional display of a rolling script. It explains what is expected of us women to maintain the treaty, as well as a copy of the agreement that saved us from extinction.

Welcome our lovely eligible females! You have finally met the age of maturity. I am sure you are anxious to give back to your society by ensuring we continue to receive our much-needed protection against extinction that an interstellar war would bring upon us.

As a reminder, you are representing humanity during this claiming ceremony as well as any activities and events that will follow, if you are so lucky to be claimed.

Let us remember why this claiming ceremony exists:

Over a century ago, our skies lit up with fire. The wretched Erains came to destroy our entire planet.

For no reason, they hate us.

For no reason, they kill us.

For no reason, they seek to torment us.

They purely wish us dead and gone.

They would TORTURE you, RAPE you, or KILL you for no reason other than that you are a human. They are fanatics who believe only Erains deserve life. They outmatched us in both weapons and defenses. Over the course of one day, we fought them on our own. Within that day, over two billion souls were lost. Then suddenly all the fires stopped, the death toll halted, and the Warriors of Gelder emerged. They held off the Erains and met with leaders across the divided globe to strike a treaty.

The treaty reads as follows:

Our people, the Warriors of Gelder, will fight on behalf of all Earth people and defend their planet to ensure prosperity is returned. We will continue to do so against any and all foes, not limited to only Erains, for as long as the treaty holds true.

We will admit Earth as a member of the protected realms as a Pact World. No race can attack a protected domain without first combatting with the Gelder. The conditions are few but rigid. They must be met without argument or Earth will be forced to face the wrath of their enemies alone.

1. All humans must come together as a species. There are no country borders allowed. Since the Purge War involves the entire planet, the Gelder warriors will only help if Earth unites as one species.

2. The Gelders require Earth miners and all resource collectors to submit any and all minerals and resources to be first evaluated by the Gelder race prior to being utilized by Earth dwellers.

3. Every annum, all females who have reached the age of maturity, agreed upon to

be the age of twenty Earth years, must submit to being evaluated for claiming. A maximum of one hundred females may be claimed per annum by the Gelder. Earth dwellers are not allowed to question a claim in any way or they will forfeit the benefits of the treaty for the entire planet.

We are all familiar with the treaty agreement. We are all prepared to uphold the treaty for our people.

My feeling of dread increases as I read agreement number three. This one has always disturbed me. Why do they claim us? Why must we be "mature" first? Why will they not tell us why they want us? And why do we never hear from any claimed women? The list of questions goes on and on inside me. While someone being claimed might have never happened while I was alive, it has happened before, and I have heard the stories.

The rolling script is interrupted on the dais as a very beautiful, yet older, woman walks on stage. Her hair is pulled back in a severe top bun, and she is dressed gaily in bright pink. The color is striking against her tanned and flawless skin. Her face is done up impeccably, almost doll-like. She definitely does not appear like any other woman in our area.

She steps on a small circular platform in the center of the stage. As she settles on the platform, it begins to slowly rotate. With the walls up each area only gets to see a very narrow portion of the stage. As she slowly turns, each area will be able to see her. As she turns to face us I see her smile a brittle, fake smile at all of us.

"Welcome, ladies." Her voice booms out over the crowd. Amplified by speakers I cannot see. "We are officially beginning our one-hundred-and-second claiming ceremony. I am sure you are all as anxious as I am to see if there is a lucky lady in the crowd." Her voice is too sweet, too high. I suppress a visible cringe at the thinly veiled sarcasm in her tone. "I am Lady Annabeth, as I am sure many of you know. And if you do not, shame on you for not doing your due diligence in educating yourselves of your betters." She pauses to sneer arrogantly at the women in the front rows. "I have presided over the claiming ceremony for this area for over thirty years." She pauses once again to look around the room as if this should impress all of us. "In exactly three minutes the projection will appear with the names of any claimed women and the area and district number she is in. If that area is yours and it is your name, you will stand up and walk to the front of the aisle. From there we will prepare you for what will be expected of you in your new life."

"Don't worry so much, everything will be fine." Marilee looks at me worriedly. She eyes my hands gripping my tote so hard that my knuckles are white. I give her a tense smile.

Despite how confident she is I cannot shake the feeling something is about to happen. Something big. Something life-altering.

"It is time, ladies. Please bring your attention to the screen. It will transmit the Gelders' claimed women in a manner of moments," Lady Annabeth announces calmly.

The screen in the front is counting down from 10. It will be fine.

8

7

Everything will be fine. Marilee is right, I'm worrying over nothing.

3

2

I am sure tomorrow I will wake up in my tiny apartment, laughing at how foolish I was.

1

The screen flashes a final time and then reads...

Claimed females:

Eleanor Sette—Area Three, Section Forty-Two.

Chapter Two

Ellie

No. No, it is not possible. I blink, and when that doesn't change anything, I blink again. I can't believe what I am seeing. There is no way that this is possible. That screen does not say my name. It does not say my name. Maybe if I repeat it enough times, I can make it so by sheer willpower alone.

"Miss Sette, please stand and come forward." Lady Annabeth seems shocked. Confused even. I do not think she was expecting any claimed females either, let alone here in her area. Marilee looks at me with dawning terror.

"Ellie...what...I am so sorry." Her voice wavers, she is visibly grasping for words." I...I will miss you. I love you." Her words seem abrupt and empty, but I know she is as shell-shocked as I am. This will be the last time I ever see my best friend.

"Please tell my parents..." I actually don't have anything to say. We have always been strained, and they will see the results live. They will see my name as the claimed one and will know they will never see me again. They will probably be happy.

"Just tell them goodbye. And that I am sorry about them losing my income." I know the money will be a harder blow to them than losing me. And then I remember something urgent. "But my sisters—Marilee, under my bed there is a trunk that you have to make sure they get. Please, Marilee." My brain is finally processing everything, and I need to ensure they get my gift to them. She nods mutely.

I hug Marilee, tell her that I love her, and woodenly stand up. Thousands of faces shift to me the second I stand. All of them wearing dazed expressions varying from disbelief to terror. From the sea of bewildered women around me, I know that Marilee was not the only woman thinking no one would be claimed today.

I feel like I am in shock myself. I knew something was going to happen, but I never suspected I was going to be claimed. I slowly make my way to the aisle, avoiding the shell-shocked faces of the women in the row next to me. When I emerge into the center lane, I am filled with determination. I am not going to let down my people.

The safety of our entire planet, our entire race, our entire species depends on our cooperation. *My* cooperation. Maybe some women could live with the guilt of killing their whole world but I could not.

Dutifully I follow the security detail to the front of the room, passing row after row of silent women. I realize that no one in this room has ever seen someone claimed. I am the first in twenty years. Why me? The looks of horror are beginning to scare me, so I avert my eyes from the other women and fix my eyes forward. I am led silently behind the stage and into a small room. The security officers bow, turn, and close the doors. I hear a distinctive click as the door is locked.

I look around and see no windows or other doors. I see only a small, sterile room. It is all white with one white couch and one white coffee table stationed in the center. There are two straight-backed wooden chairs, also painted a stark white and adorned with similarly colored cushions across from them. The lack of color gives the room a sinister atmosphere. The rest of the room is completely bare. No paintings, no vases, no decorations of any kind. It gives me an uncomfortable feeling. Never in my life have I ever been in such spotless surroundings. Not a single speck of dust can be seen in the room.

I cannot hear anything. Nothing but my own breathing. It is so quiet in this room I imagine I can listen to the very sound of my blood pumping through my veins. My anxiety grows with each passing moment. I have no idea how long I will be here. I begin to force my breath to come in long, deep pulls instead of the rapid panting that my anxiety-driven state was causing.

I throw myself deep into my mind in an attempt to calm myself, I separate myself from this cold, sterile room and allow my consciousness to float in the safety of my mind. Finally, I am able to bring myself under control. I tentatively lower myself to the edge of the couch. Careful not to disturb more of the room as I am just by being in here.

If no one is going to come to talk with me quickly, I am at least going to be comfortable. I look around in an attempt to distract myself, but it proves to be impossible. The trepidation I have been fighting all day starts creeping in all over again. My emotions have been on a roller coaster since I saw my name on that screen.

It seems such a simple thing, my name. It doesn't seem possible that a string of letters could be the cause of what is to come. But it is. My name on that screen symbolizes the end of my life as I know it. I have not even stopped to think about what this might mean for me and my future. Now as I sit here, I can't do anything else but ponder my uncertain future, and I only worry more.

I wonder if I even have a future. For all I know I am going to be a sacrifice for our alien protectors. I wonder if I will be sold into slavery. The list of possibilities is endless, and each one is worse than the last. I am trying to stop my mind from running wild, but with nothing else to do in this room I can't control the fear. So I just sit and worry. And sit and worry some more.

After what feels like an eternity, I hear the door unlock. Lady Annabeth and five men enter the room. As I stare at the men, I see tattoos peeking out under the collars of their tight-fitting brown shirts.

It takes me a moment, but I recognize them as Gelder warriors. I recall in my history lessons that all Gelders have markings that cover their torsos. It is reported as a retelling of all of the kills they earn in battle. It seems to me that it's a very bloody diary of all their sins. I quickly divert my eyes to Lady Annabeth.

"Welcome, claimed! I tell you this sure is a surprise. It has been so many years since we have had a claimed woman. Now, let us get down to business because we are sorely pressed for time. There are no real steps here. My job is to get you ready to depart as quickly as possible. Speed is the only real requirement." She is speaking quickly, almost to herself, not even making eye contact with me as she continues to talk in quick succession.

"Normally we have about twelve hours from the claiming to get you to your Gelder male, but I have been informed you are expected there in only three short hours. It will take you two and a half hours to travel there, so you are already behind schedule." Lady Annabeth is barreling through her speech as if I am not even here. It appears like she is talking to herself more than me.

I can barely keep up. My mind is racing with questions, but one is screaming louder than all the rest.

"What do you mean, my Gelder male?" I interrupt her. She does not seem pleased with my interruption. Her words are decidedly colder when she begins again.

"Well, the male who claimed you. When you are claimed you are claimed by a specific male. Now that is all I can tell you. Before you try to interrupt again I cannot tell you more because I do not know more. It is usually communicated to me who you are claimed by so that I may prepare you for your future life, but this time it is not being revealed. I can do nothing at this point. However, I really must say that your manners would be best improved.

"Whoever your new owner, oh I am sorry, I mean Gelder male"—she has a cruel smile on her face, and I know that her slip of the tongue was no accident. I am being sold into slavery. I will be given to an owner. She continues as if she said nothing—"will be none too pleased with interruptions I am sure. You need to give serious thought to how you are behaving. If you do not please your Gelder male, you risk the entire treaty." I have not been able to hide my shock at her revelation, and she looks very pleased with herself.

"Now, I am sure we wouldn't want that, would we?" she asks with a little smirk. She reminds me of the girls I went to school with. I guess some girls never outgrow the need to be cruel.

"No, Lady Annabeth," I answer her, even though I don't think she was really expecting an answer.

I can tell she wants to scare me with her words, but finally knowing what being claimed means makes me so much more relieved. I find the unknown expectations much more frightening. My biggest worry is that by some action of my own, I will cost Earth Nueva its protection. Now I know as long as I listen to everything this mystery Gelder male tells me to do, I can be sure that my planet is not left defenseless. I can hear my mother telling me how much of a disappointment I am and how I can never follow directions but I can. I know I can.

"Now, it is time to get you prepared for getting on your way as we have very little time. Unless you have any more interruptions?" She stares at me pointedly. I shake my head slightly. "You will need to change your attire. You are so horridly dressed right now it is insulting to my eyes. Take this and please change. If it is not in the parcel you are not to wear it. Understood?" She stares at me again with a look of disdain. Once more, all I can do is move my head.

I'm not at my fault for my attire, it is what all the women in our area wear. I glance down at my coarse linen chemise and wraparound skirt. They are a dull beige color and fraying in several places. Cloth is very difficult to come by this low down on the social ladder, I only have two outfits and they are a little old, I admit. They may be a little more worn than Marilee's or other women's clothing, but I do not stand out too much from other members of my class.

I glance at her wardrobe though, smooth silk in that brilliant bright color. The material clinging to her as if it was made for her, it probably was I realize. Compared to her I do look like a poor street urchin. There is nothing I can do about it now, she already judged me and it appears I am to change anyways.

She stands, "We will leave you to change in privacy. Please knock on the door when you are ready. And please do hurry." The last bit is said with such scorn I am left with the impression that she thinks so little of me she doubts I can even manage the simple task of changing on my own.

With those final words, Lady Annabeth and the Gelder males file out of the room. The Gelders all give a small, respectful bow in my direction on their way out. It appears that the rumors of the Gelder manners were not exaggerated. I look at the clothing box and take a deep breath. I open it and look inside. And gasp.

Well, this is not what I expected.

It is an elegant creation of silk and gemstone. There are tiny jewels sewn into the bodice. It almost appears to be created out of small stones sewn together rather than the jewels being on the material itself. It is the very deepest blue, with what I am guessing is sapphires all over.

My knowledge of gemstones is laughable, so who knows if I am right. The upper chest and arms do not have material, but they are actually covered with transparent white lace. It looks so delicate and elegant. It will cover me from neck to ankles but is sheer in just the right places to leave little to the imagination.

The dress is the only thing in the box besides a pair of sandals that match the dress. There are no other items in the box. I guess I am going to be wearing no panties or bra. I have never gone out in public without my underwear before, but I can rise to the challenge.

What is a little discomfort compared to the survival of the planet? I do worry about what this means for my future role though. Sexual slavery is beginning to look like my most likely fate.

I quickly strip out of my own rough clothing, fearful of being walked in on while I change. I pull the dress out of the box and slip it on. The feeling of this smooth cloth compared to my own garments is astounding. Never before did I realize how uncomfortable mine were, leaving small red abrasions on my skin where the material was particularly coarse.

The dress is lovely though. It is a dream to wear—it slides so smoothly up my body and even laces up the side, so I don't need any help dressing. I long for a mirror, but from what I can see this is very flattering on me. The most attractive thing I have ever worn.

It makes my small and thin frame seem dainty instead. Womanly and sweet instead of boyish and unpleasant. I smooth my hands down the front and take one fraction of a moment to enjoy the feel of the fine cloth.

"Are you ready yet, Eleanor? How long could it possibly take you to change, even you cannot be that inept? We are on a very tight schedule," Lady Annabeth calls through the door with a hard voice.

"Yes." I scramble and look around for a place to put my old clothes. With no such luck, I shove them into my tote.

The door opens, and all six of them file back in.

"You know, Eleanor, it is very inconsiderate to have been dressed and not let us know when we told you we are pressed for time," Lady Annabeth chastises me. There seems to be a look of distaste on the males' faces as well.

By the looks they cast in her direction, I think perhaps they are irritated by Annabeth's words but quickly discard that idea. I'm sure I'm the one in the wrong. Again. As my mother says, I have a knack for always saying and doing the wrong thing.

"I apologize but..." I try to defend myself, but her great ladyship interrupts me. I guess it is alright for her to interrupt me; it is only me who is rude if I speak out of turn.

"Yes, I am quite sure you have another excuse for your deplorable manners, but there is simply no time. As I said, it has been requested that you depart immediately. Since you decided to just stand around fully dressed we have no more time for you. The rest of the preparations must be skipped." It takes every ounce of control I have to not tell her that her calling my manners deplorable does not make them so, or that I had barely dressed before she knocked. But I manage to stay quiet, barely. "Please tell me you at least remembered to bring your gift to honor the Gelder?"

"Yes, I—"

She interrupts me again. "Wonderful. Then your new Gelder male will just have to explain whatever it is he wants you to know when you arrive. Now, these Gelder warriors will escort you. Please try to remember what you are and what you represent. We have had no claimed women in twenty years. We need to uphold our obligations, or we risk the treaty. So listen to all of the rules and do your species proud." These last words are the first kind words she has spoken to me.

"I know, that has been told to me every day for my entire life. I will do my best." The warriors give me a peculiar look as I say this. I can't decipher it, so I let it go.

"Wonderful, then you are ready. Good luck and I wish you good tidings and speedy travels." Her words may be polite, but her tone is not. Something tells me if my ship were to perish in the stars she would not lose any sleep over it. I have no idea what I did to cause her hatred toward me, but by the cold glare she is leveling at me there is no question that it is there.

I ignore it and just give a tight smile and nod.

One of the warriors steps forward and extends his hand to take my tote bag. I give him a tense smile and hand it over to him.

"Thank you. My name is Eleanor, Eleanor Sette." He merely inclines his head and then waves me to walk ahead of him. I suppose that means no conversation. As I walk past him, I cannot help but think my eyes see a flash of red. But it must be a trick of the light.

There is another male I did not notice before at the door. As I approach he turns and begins walking with the other five behind me. Again, silently. Maybe there is a rule about talking with slaves. I follow this silent Gelder and all of them slowly take a position around me. I am effectively walking in a circle of Gelder warriors. They must be very anxious about me fleeing.

"I promise I won't try to run away." My assurance is met with stony silence. None of them even look at me.

Well, that is my last attempt at conversation. I keep my eyes straight ahead and follow the mystery Gelder, as I decide to call him.

We walk for another few minutes and then stop at a massive door. It is extremely ornate. The dark metal has very intricate gold work. The gold seems to be in a circular pattern, going in and around itself. It is so fine, it looks a little over the top for a simple door, in my opinion.

The doors slide open, and I see what looks like a dining car from an old train. There are several chairs covered in what appears to be red velvet around the room. The warriors behind me start walking, and I take this to mean I should enter the car. Once inside, the six of them point me toward the chairs and matching couches that line the room.

I choose a wingback chair that faces out to the room, and I sit down.

The warriors all sit on adjoining couches near me. The chairs and furnishings scream wealth. This is a new setting for me. While many of my race are wealthy and would be used to this kind of luxury, I am not one of them.

Area Three class does not include this type of affluence. My family is quite poor. It is by family name only we are able to maintain our position in the third area. By monetary holdings, we are well beneath that. Once I reached six and ten, I helped support my family so my younger siblings would not know hunger as I did.

I hope that my siblings do not suffer for my being claimed. I find comfort that there is nothing I could do about this even if I wanted to. I did not choose this. And I trust Marilee to get my gift to them. She will know to make sure my mother knows nothing about it. It will help them. It is filled with the small amount of savings I had put away, emergency food, and a letter to each of them. I never thought I would be claimed, but still, I was prepared for the small chance I would be.

The warriors all wave a hand over their armrests and a harness appears to lasso them to the seats. The mystery sixth member stares at me. Slowly the other five do as well. I mimic their movements and wave my hand over the armrest to my left as they did. Sure enough, straps appear out of nowhere and cross my chest to form a tight 'X' over my body.

After I am secured into my seat, the entire room begins to dip. My stomach drops as it feels like the whole place is hurling upward. But oddly, I feel as if inside this craft, the movement is dulled. I glance around at the warriors, but they do not seem nervous or surprised. I assume they must have expected this to happen.

Their lack of concern calms me. I know what this must be. It is a shuttle. I am being flown to a greater ship. And the odd sense of movement must be caused by dampeners that are used to reduce the force of such acceleration.

With that issue solved, I move on to my next concern. Our destination. My mind is racing—the ships in the Gelder fleet can travel several times the speed of light. Lady Annabeth said it will take two and a half hours to reach our destination. To pass the time I try to figure out how far from Earth I will be going.

I have never been very studious about the Gelder ship designs or the location of their outposts. While not fully restricted from my class, it is not encouraged that we show interest in such matters. It was not expected that people in my area class would ever need such information. I have no idea where we are going or how far. I recall that their slowest ships are about two times the speed of light and the average speed of their ships is about ten times. I think. But I have heard of some that can reach speeds of fifteen times the speed of light.

I realize that we could be traveling anywhere, but I don't even know what direction we're going in. I have no idea where we are flying to, so why even bother? It is not helping to calm me down or distract me from my worries. I wish they would talk to me.

As much as I try not to, a small sigh escapes me. Being left to my own thoughts just increases my anxiety. I am very nervous. I wonder who this Gelder male who now owns me is. Will he be gentle and kind? Or will he be harsh and cruel?

I suppose only time will tell. I will soon find out, and I must follow everything he says. I will do everything in my power to make sure I keep this treaty alive. I am impulsive and often sarcastic, but I'll have to be sure to keep that under control with my...master? Is that what he will want me to call him?

The Erains have been increasing their attempts on our world; every week we have a new burning ship visible in our skies. Our planet's in a very precarious position. Without the Gelders we would all perish. My sisters and Marilee are counting on me. I refuse to be the reason that happens they suffer. No matter how difficult, I will be a model slave.

Danion

I possess an in-depth knowledge of the inner workings of what humans consider time, but that does not help me understand why it is passing so *deim* slowly. I helped improve travel faster than the speed of light; I perfected it several times over. I know how this can affect the perception of time, yet none of this helps me as I wait for her.

She has been traveling on one of my fastest ships. They are in a league of their own. Nothing else in my entire fleet even touches the speed my beauties can sustain. It might be considered a tad over the top to send one of my elite shuttles to transport her, but I am so impatient. I need her. I need her here with me. And I need her here as soon as possible. We are docked one hundred light-years from Earth, and I have traveled over five hundred more just to meet her here.

It has been over two hours since her ship departed. Not much longer now.

I cannot believe how excited I am. I feel like a youngling. I have watched over her from afar but never have I seen my mate. My protection has come through a third party. Ambassadors on Earth relayed the messages to me. I have been kept updated on her progress in school and work. I know some of her favorite hobbies. It is not enough. Not nearly enough.

I cannot wait to know what she is passionate about. To learn what drives her interest in history to have made her choose it as her livelihood. To know what makes her smile and what makes her cry. I will do everything in my power to make sure she never has cause to shed tears again. I am anxious to experience my mately duties. After centuries upon centuries of being a warrior, I am ready to be a mate. I began to lose hope that I would ever experience a mate. So few of our kind ever do now.

My mind turns to my dying brethren. While we may be the only known true immortal race, our most guarded secret is that we no longer mate with each other. We are not genetically compatible with our own species and we don't know why. We are the reigning power in this galaxy, but it will not be our enemies that destroy us. It'll be nature itself.

We are the leaders in not only war tactics but science and medicine. We protect all life, no matter the cost. It seems somewhat poetic that we defend the very nature of life, and that life itself is what will be our demise.

Our understanding of science causes more primitive races, such as humans, to believe we are magical beings. It is not their fault. They cannot help their age, and as a people, they are very young. Yet even with all of our vast knowledge, our apparent magic, we cannot solve our reproduction problem. We don't even know the cause. We haven't had a new immortal born in centuries. Only mated Gelders can produce children and mates have become an increasingly rare occurrence. Fewer and fewer mates are being found. I have my theories on why this is happening, but that is all they are. Theories. There are no answers to speak of.

"My lord warrior king, you asked to be alerted when the shuttle arrived. It is docking now." My communications liaison's voice echoes through the room. Finally!

"Thank you, Jedde. Once docked, have her escorted to me directly. Also, have Liam meet her at the docks. He should be available to make her comfortable and answer any of her questions." My face feels strange, and I realize I have a large grin on my face. I cannot remember the last time I smiled. "But make sure Liam knows to hurry his progress bringing her here." No need to have Liam delay with an unnecessary tour.

Finally, I can be more than just a warrior to another soul, I can be more than a king whose favor someone wishes. I can be her mate.

Finally, she is here.

Ellie

The shuttle lurches forward slightly as we begin to decelerate. I look out of one of the windows, and all I see is metal in either direction.

As I stare out the window, the shuttle begins to dock onto the spacecraft. This craft is a thousand times larger than anything I ever imagined. I would not have believed it possible to have a spacecraft so large. My stomach gets a sick feeling. I might never leave this floating behemoth again.

This is it. This ship must be the size of some of the cities back on Earth Nueva. I imagine a vessel this large could hold millions of warriors. Anyone of which could be the alien who now owns me.

What is my role as a claimed female? Am I to be a maid? Am I supposed to work for them? My knowledge of human history can't be that useful to them. Am I to be a sex slave? I look around at the males in this shuttle with me.

They are all massive, muscled creatures. They all look vaguely the same, all are over six feet tall and have black hair. Their hair is all different colors in certain lights though, almost like they have highlights. Odd hair colors for warriors to choose though, really. They are the colors of the rainbow. They are faint, but when caught in the right light each one's hair seems to almost radiate a specific color. I take an inventory as the docking continues to keep my mind off of my unknown, and potentially horrific, future.

The male closest to me radiates a deep blue color, and his clothing also seems to have a matching color weaved into it. I can't see where it would be weaved—they are all dressed in some kind of brown material that vaguely resembles leather. I can't even make out the thread marks, but still, the color seems to be a part of the cloth. When the warrior moves, the clothes give off a faint glow of deep blue. All the others are the same. I wonder about the significance of these colors.

The next male is red, and his gaze has been on me almost the entire journey. It is most unnerving, but there seems to be no animosity behind his gaze. Only curiosity mixed with a small amount of reverence is detectable in his gaze. Which makes no sense to me. Why he keeps staring at me, I doubt I will ever know. I am not able to meet his stare for more than a few moments.

I move to look at the warrior on the right of this red male's side. He seems to have a brown haze around him. His body is much more full than the rest; he appears very stout. His expression, while firm, calms me somehow. There is a certain sense of...welcome when he looks at me. I feel my body relax briefly as I look at him.

The next warrior appears golden, and he has kept his eyes closed almost the entire voyage. Feigning sleep perhaps? I am not sure of the cause, but at least I had one male who I felt I didn't need to avoid looking at.

Sitting next to him is a male with purple color sweeping around him as if it is being moved by invisible air currents. This male has a small smile on his face as if he is infinitely amused by something. A drastic difference compared to all the stoic faces onboard.

And finally, the last male is a mixture of them all. As I stare at the mystery sixth male, he changes the color he exudes before my very eyes. This is so strange. He has each color mixed into one.

I stare at these warriors and realize that while all of their eyes are rich in color, they are not the same color as their hair and clothes. They each have a deep, rich brown eye color. They have a warmth to them that I find somewhat calming. Now if only someone would speak to me, I would feel so much better.

As the shuttle makes one last shake and a loud clamping noise, I realize that studying the warriors did what I wanted it to do. Distract me. Suddenly, all the harnesses unlatch on their own accord. The males all stand up, and I follow suit. The doors open and this is it. My fate, whatever it may be, is about to be revealed to me.

I hear a warm voice approaching before I even step out of the craft.

"Welcome! Welcome! Oh, you must be Eleanor! We have been anxiously awaiting your arrival." Yet another male is approaching us with his arms wide open. I look closely, but he does not have a color that he seems to shine. Strange. He is very well groomed, with his black hair styled and brown eyes enhanced with some kind of makeup. Unlike the warriors, he is dressed in a long burgundy tunic.

"My name is Liam Goldsire, and I am the *Sheral*. Think of me as a liaison between our two species. My role here is to help make you comfortable and answer any and all questions about your new life. I want to make you feel right at home here. I am also here to escort you to your Gelder. I am sure he will be pleased once he looks at you," Liam talks with a flare. Very loud and very cheerful. I like him, but I am a little confused about his presence. Why would a slave need to be happy?

Liam is staring at me intently like he is waiting for something from me. Oh, he must want me to say something. I am at a loss. What does a slave say? Fortunately, he is talking in the Star Speech, a universal language that all humans learned once the Gelders fought off the Erains.

"Yes, uh, it is nice to meet you, Mr. Goldsire," I say quietly.

"Liam! Liam, please, now see we will be fast friends. You must tell me any questions you have or how I can help ease your mind. We must talk as we walk, I am afraid, as we need to get you to your male with extreme haste." Liam says this was a small amused chuckle.

"I, of course, understand his impatience, I myself felt it when I was awaiting my mate. Oh, the joys of beginning mate bonds." Liam has a smile on his face as he recalls this mate. He waves his hand to have me begin walking. He gives me a wink as he says this last bit.

I look around tentatively first. None of my previous companions voice any objections, so I suppose I should be on my way.

OK, Elliegirl you can do this. Make your family proud, don't endanger everyone you know, and abide by the treaty. Listen to the rules and everything will be alright..

He indicates I should walk abreast of him, even with him not behind like I was trying to do.

"Now I'm sure you have many questions. My mate herself is of Earth, and she had so many questions." My feet falter when I hear this, but Liam pays no mind. "She, of course, is anxious to meet you, but she is currently on bedrest. When she is able, she will be happy to talk with you further about anything you need to be cleared up." He pauses and waits for me to voice a question, but speech is not something I can achieve right now.

I am still stuck on the bombshell he has just dropped on me. There is another claimed female from Earth, and she might be allowed to speak with me.

"Alright, let me just start by saying we know you are new to our ways. We don't expect anything from you. However, that does not mean you cannot learn them." Liam again pauses. Seeing as I still don't say anything he just nods and continues.

"Now, you have been claimed by our highest-ranking warrior. I am sure you know by now claiming can be thought of as a mating bond. Your mate bond is awaiting you in his chambers." Liam looks at me pointedly. Vaguely I realize that he thinks I know something about this claiming thing. Odd.

"Now I am not at liberty to discuss who specifically your mate is, it will be his decision how he would like to reveal himself to you at first. But, I will assure you, you are in our most capable hands. There is no warrior who possesses more integrity, honor, and strength. But I digress, I must hear a question from you. Let us start off with what is your greatest concern coming to live with us?" Liam waits for my reply.

"Well, I am curious as to what my duties will be or what will be expected of me." I force out the words, my voice coming out quiet and scratchy. I feel this is the best way to voice my concerns.

"Of course, my lady Eleanor, it is perfectly understandable that you want to know this. However, I am not qualified to answer that question. Only your mate will be able to explain what he expects of you, as it is his expectations alone that bear any substance. But please, calm your mind. The sign of a good mate is that he knows how much you can handle and does not ask more of you." Liam says this with a smile.

I am afraid his words have quite the opposite effect though. I am even more concerned now. What does Liam mean by what I can handle? Is this torture? I do not think I have ever been more nervous to meet someone.

It seems we have not had too far to travel to reach the chambers of this mysterious mate of mine. Liam stops at a door, a huge door that appears to be very ornately carved out of hard metal. The design is similar to the golden pattern on the shuttle doors.

"Now, these are your esteemed mate's chambers. You are to enter unaccompanied. Any questions, concerns, or needs just address them to your mate, and he will ensure everything is taken care of. I will see you on the morrow. I give you well tidings and trust I will find you in good health in the morn." With that Liam bows and walks away with a flourish.

The six, as I am beginning to call them in my head, all moved in what seemed to be a coordinated effort to span the hallway from wall to wall next to the doorway. They all look straight ahead and make no eye contact with me.

I suppose there's nothing left to do but go through the door.

This is it. This is my first step to learning my fate.

I push open the door, and the first thing I think is that my mate, whoever he is, must be very wealthy. I am amazed at the rich furnishings inside the room. The entire room appears to be made of gold. The walls, the chairs, the tables, everything is golden. This seems like an unnecessary extravagance to me. A little pretentious, even.

I begin to fear that whoever my mate is, he is more important than I first thought. On a ship this large, who would command such a room? He must be a very high-ranking warrior. No peon would possess chambers such as this.

I brace myself, and I take a step into the room, and then another and another. Once I reach the middle of the room I notice a man to my right. He is standing behind a tall chair, which is why I did not see him when I first entered.

The only word I can think of is *perfection*. He is tall, much taller than the six, which is saying something since these warriors are all well over six feet. The male in front of me must be seven feet tall at least. I feel dwarfed by him, and I am not even next to him yet. He stands with a presence that cannot be argued with, and the room actually seems to pulse with his very being. I feel intimidated by him. As I study him, I can find no faults. Someone that large should at least have one feature that is wrong, something that makes him seem approachable.

He has the same black hair as the six, but the color that radiates around him resembles a blanket rather than just a faint glow. It is always there, not only when he moves. It almost seems to cover him, but at the same time, his colors appear muted and faint.

I feel like something must be wrong with my eyes. I have no idea what these colors I am seeing are, but no one else acts like they see them. Maybe the stress of the day is making me lose all sense. Perhaps I really have lost my mind.

"Greetings, Eleanor." His voice is faint, almost like he is speaking with reverence. "I must tell you I have been very anxious for our first meeting." He looks at me with eyes the color of the lightest gray. It feels like he is seeing into my soul.

How do I respond? I struggle back and forth but decide on courteous with a touch of subservience. As a sign of respect, I lower my eyes to his feet. Maybe I should also start off by promising him that I will serve him well. He would like a slave that serves him well, wouldn't he?

These Gelders may call it a mating bond but I can read between the lines. I am a claimed female, or more accurately a claimed slave. The six warriors escorted me to ensure I did not run away and this mate of mine is no more than my owner. Lady Annabeth said so. Best to begin paying the price to ensure my race continues to survive the Erains' genocidal attacks.

"Yes, I have been anxious about this meeting as well. I will do my best to be a good, obedient, sl...mate for you...that is...uh...assuming you are the Gelder male who claimed me." Oh stars, I messed that up royally.

He smiles at me, and it softens his features. Makes him even more attractive. His cheekbones are high and firm, almost giving him an aloof appearance, but when he smiles they soften. I have a sudden urge to kiss them. And his lips, I wonder if they are as soft as they look. My mind begins to imagine what his mouth would feel like running down my body. What is wrong with me? I have never had thoughts like this before.

"While I am glad to hear that, I am quite confident you will be a perfect mate for me. You're mine. You already are more than I could have asked for," this warrior tells me. I feel quite comforted by his statement. I feel my body slowly relax. I realize that I did say the right thing. Best to keep saying the same things.

"It pleases me that I have met your expectations, I will endeavor to continue to do so...sir." I keep my eyes downcast this time. I do not know what to call him, I hope sir is acceptable.

"Yes, I suppose it is well past time for formal introductions." He moves towards me, his hands seem oddly hesitant like he wants to touch me but pulls back at the last minute. "My name is Danion Belator of Old, but you should call me *animare*. Likewise, I shall call you *aninare*. These are the greetings of mated pairs of the Gelders," he tells me, his words stilted and formal but I scarcely hear that last part.

My mind is blank... It just left my body. I know that Gelder names are unique; there are no duplicates as we have on Earth.

That means my owner is not just any warrior. He is the warrior.

He is the Geldan king.

The greatest and most deadly warrior ever known. I have read of his conquests on the battlefield. He is undefeated. Unchallenged. He has held the throne for so many thousands of years without contest because there is no one in existence who can match his power. It is said that the last person who challenged him was dead before his foot touched the arena, struck down with nothing more than a glance from the great warrior king.

And I just *spoke* to him. I did not bow or appropriately address him. Earth Nueva is going to die because of me. Already I am failing. I've seen the murals that depict the king. Any sign of disrespect and he is quick to reprimand you. In my fear, I forget that he already told me he is pleased with me. All I can think about is making amends.

"Please pardon me, sir." I fall to my knees before him. "I didn't know I was in your presence. Please, please forgive my lack of decorum, it was not meant as an insult, I assure you. It is merely a sign of my ignorance." The silence in the room is absolute. Tense even. For several moments nothing happens.

Then, I feel hands on my shoulders. The king pulls upon me, attempting to get me to my feet. "Please do not bow to me." His hands get firmer when my body refuses to respond to his demands. I hear his words solidify into something hard and angry. "Do not bow. You are above that. You must never feel the need to bow, you are much more than a subject to me. You are my mate, my queen." He pulls again, but my body does not respond. His tone becomes ice, anger coursing through his words. "Stand up."

But I am incapable of that. My entire being is fixated on one word. *Queen*. Did he actually just say "queen"?

Chapter Three

Danion

My mate is still prostrate at my feet. With the exception of forcefully lifting her from the floor, I cannot get her to stand. She does not seem to be moving. I kneel next to her.

I pause and force my impatience and anger to the side. I pray for patience and attempt to soften my tone.

"Please stand up, my Eleanor. It is not necessary for you to bow." As I say this, she slowly raises her head. But she still refuses to stand. I am not known for my patience, but as I stare into her eyes, I notice the fear. She is afraid of me. This realization allows me to regain control of the temper I come by naturally.

We continue to look at one another, and I cannot tear my eyes away from her. She is more beautiful than I ever hoped for. In truth, I have denied myself the privilege of looking upon her. I knew that looking at her was not necessary for me to commit to her, but would make it infinitely more difficult to stay away from her.

I have lived for millennia upon millennia and have never known the grace of a partner. But I have longed for one. Exterior appearance is just frivolous when compared to the mating of souls we will soon share together. Still, I am pleased that I have been graced with such an exquisite creature for a mate.

Stars, she is *fiefling* gorgeous. Absolutely stunning. Within the Gelder race, certain traits are common. The vast majority of us possess dark features—tanned and darker skin, black hair, rigid bone structure, and are exceedingly tall. But this creature before me is a vision.

She has such fine and delicate bone structure, her skin is so light it appears almost white, and while I cannot judge accurately when she remains on the floor, she is almost certainly well more than a foot smaller than I am.

As her raised head stares at me, I notice she has a look of almost complete terror on her face. This does not make sense to me. All I can feel within me is an almost overwhelming sense of protectiveness. What would she need to fear of me?

"Eleanor, why do you seem distressed? I assure you, no harm will come to you," I tell her.

"Of course, my liege. I...mean... My high warrior king... I mean... Oh, I am so sorry, they never told me how to address you. I know your title, of course, my king...but..." Eleanor has tears in her eyes as she slowly stops talking.

At the sight of her tears, I feel my patience disappear. I will not have her on the floor like a commoner merely because I cannot convince her to stand of her own volition. If she will not stand on her own, I will make her stand.

I grip her shoulders and move to stand, pulling her up with me.

"What are you doing? Please, I am sorry! I will do better, please don't hurt me! Don't terminate the agreement! I can do better." Eleanor dissolves into sobs, her silent tears turning into full crying. I can barely contain my distaste. I abhor any sign of weakness.

I suppose she might be upset that I have lifted her off the floor. This cannot be avoided. I refuse to have her laid out on the floor. She declined to listen to both my request and my urging for her to stand up.

"*Aninare*, please, you speak of absurdities. I would never harm you. Now I must insist you calm down, I will not have you crying," I tell my beautiful mate, with precise words holding back much of my anger. I have little experience with delicate creatures. But surely, she will calm down now.

I remind myself that her tears may not be a sign of weakness, she is just in shock. Mates are equal matches for our souls—I would not have a weak mate—and I feel my anger wash away. That is all it must be, shock. She is not quite what I expected, but that is fine.

"Wahhh! I...I...I am tr...try...trying." Her screams take a sharp increase in volume now. My mate has broken down into hysterical sobs. She is making a most hideous sound—what I imagine someone who is both choking and hiccupping would sound like. My previous relief is forgotten. I cannot think with her screams.

"I command you to stop this at once!" In my frustration, I yell at Eleanor. I never intended to yell at my mate, especially on the first day we met. But it cannot be avoided, she must stop this. Her behavior is not fit for my mate or my queen. The Gelder queen cannot lose control of herself over something as slight as not addressing me correctly.

Which she still has not done, as the appropriate address for her to use is her *animare*. I have waited more centuries than I can count to earn the title *animare*. This title is reserved only for mated males. Claimed males. It is the highest honor a warrior can attain, to be considered an *animare*. I have longed to be her protector, her lover, her partner, her *animare*.

At the close of my shout, Eleanor immediately stops all crying.

Finally. Blessed relief.

Now we can begin a more reasonable discussion.

"Thank you, *aninare*." I say softly. I look at her serene face and wonder how she did such an about face from her previous emotional display. Perhaps is was an act all along?

Wait.

She has stopped all movement. No crying, no hiccupping sobs. She merely stares at me, as if awaiting further instructions. She still has tears running down her cheeks that she does not bother to wipe away. It is as if she does not have any control over herself anymore. A meek body ready to do as commanded.

Worry stiffens my spine. I have seen this behavior only a few times before, in beings that are controlled.

This cannot be. I do not possess the ability to control others as some do. It is among one of the rarest talents my people have mastered. Only a handful of Gelders have ever commanded this gift. I have seen it used only three times in my entire existence.

This must be something else. Regardless of what it looks like.

"Eleanor, speak to me."

Nothing. Absolutely nothing.

No response. Even though she doesn't speak I feel some relief. It cannot be a Gelder trance since she is not following my commands. This is good news, I would not like to be discovered controlling my mate. It is one of the least honorable things a mate could do. However, still, she does not speak. Or move.

I shake her. I command her several more times. Nothing works. I cannot rouse her from this trance. After an hour of no success, I decide I must bring in the only male who might know how to reverse this. Regardless of how he is the last male I would want to ask for help with this.

"Jedde, summon Golon to my quarters at once," I call out to my communications officer, using my powers to activate the intercom system.

"Yes, my king, I will find him immediately," the disembodied voice replies.

I also walk to my door. "Lord of *Simul* Kowan, enter now!" I snap at the leader of Eleanor's *praesidium*, the six warriors who will guard her at all costs.

Kowan strides forward and enters the room. I close the door behind him.

"What do you require of me, King?" Kowan's eyes settle on my mate and widen slightly. "Liege, what has befallen our queen? I swear to you she was unharmed in our journey." His voice is slightly panicked.

Kowan is distressed. I know I should relieve him of his worry as he is right, she was well when she was delivered to me. As the leader of her *praesidium*, I understand his concern, but I cannot begin to trifle with aiding him in his worry when I am experiencing real fear. Real fear about what has happened to my mate. I have only just united with her, how is it that I can already have lost her?

"You are to sweep the room and see if you can detect any traces of power or any hint of a weave around the queen." My tone is abrupt, but it cannot be helped. Kowan quickly begins searching the room. As he is a master in all lineages, he can perform this task with ease.

"*Cognata*, you summoned me? I admit I was not expecting you to call for me on your first night with your mate... *Veycha*! What has come over her?" All teasing behavior quickly disappears from Golon as he realizes something is wrong with his new queen.

"Yes, Golon, I summoned you for a real purpose. You are the leading *scientia* officer. Diagnose this. What could be causing her to act this way?" I command him. "Kowan is searching for any foreign weaves."

Golon slowly circles my mate. He slowly reaches out to touch her face. My hand has summoned my *telum*—one of the blades that lie in concealed sheaths down my legs—before I am even aware of doing it. I hold it up to Golon. "Do not touch my mate," I growl.

Golon slowly backs away, looking at me like I am some wild animal. "I mean no trespass, my king, but merely was attempting to see what clues the liquid on her face could provide." I can tell he realizes the severity of the situation, only then does he address me properly. He usually takes much pleasure out of needling me.

"You can ask me about such things, and I will be your hands. Do not touch her." I bite out the words. To think, he wants to lay hands on my mate. "The liquid is her tears. She was...crying right before this trance occurred." Golon's face goes completely blank. No emotion. He looks at me with complete detachment.

"Perhaps you should explain to me the events that occurred right up to her undergoing this trance-like state?" he asks with his voice and face carefully emotionless.

I can tell Golon is censuring me. No emotion in my cousin is always a sign of anger. He is upset with me. He suspects that I have made my mate cry. The fact that he is correct does nothing to calm me. I can feel anger begin to build up within me. He has no right to interfere in my relationship with my mate. While I am a fair king, I am a warrior king, and I did not get this way without a backbone made of ruthlessness and no small amount of power.

"You can remove such lecherous thoughts from your mind, my infer. I performed no actions that should have caused her tears. Merely greeted her and informed her I was well pleased with her as my mate." I defend myself with a bite in my voice. My eyes spark a fire, searing into him.

"Apologies, my king, I did not mean to imply you treated her with anything less than the respect a mate deserves." I know my cousin well enough to know that is precisely what he meant.

His words are now explicitly aimed at ensuring I know he feels I have not met my mately duties. I feel the anger rising within me become an inferno. This could be deadly if I cannot get a handle on my emotions. I can feel my control of *ignis* rise and break free of my grasp, flames are seconds from erupting from my hands. If I cannot contain this, I could kill not only Golon but my mate as well. But the power is too strong. It feels as if my energy is not my own.

There is no way that I can pull this back and prevent it from reaching Golon. The power is feeding my emotions and straining to connect with him. I force my anger to change direction to myself, not my cousin for his safety. I am the one who has failed my mate. Had I not, she would not be in this predicament.

"But my sire, I must know what caused her tears and how she became unresponsive," Golon insists. It seems he did not realize how close he just came to his own death.

"Yes, Golon," I say through clenched teeth. I avert my gaze; it is taking every ounce of control I have to contain my rioting powers. "Once I had let her know I was pleased I introduced myself. She recognized my name and went into full hysteria when she realized she was addressing a king. She seemed to feel that she performed some great offense to me by not knowing how to address me. I reassured her that she is not a subject and to not worry. This was unsuccessful. She continued to sob at my feet." I say these last words with a sigh. It is well known that I dislike signs of weakness. I doubt one can be any weaker than crying at someone's feet. I try to remind myself that she has gone through a huge shock.

"I see." The words are clipped, full of distaste. "My liege, you must try to see things from her perspective." Apparently, I did not mask my disappointment in her show of weakness well. "She is a mere two Earthen decades old. They are taught of the great warrior king of the Gelder race as a legend. No details on how to hold oneself when in your presence. She probably had no idea how to address you and worried she offended you. She is quite young." I am growing tired of hearing censure from my cousin. Nothing is quite as frustrating as arguing with someone who has logic on their side.

"Yes, Golon," I sigh, "I understand she is young. Remove that look of judgment. I do not find displeasure in my mate, I am quite pleased with her. How could I not? Just look at her. I merely was reciting her actions. I understand that I gave her quite a shock. Would you care to continue or are you not done reprimanding me yet?" I glare at my overstepping cousin.

Left unsaid in my words is a reminder of who is king in this room and who is subject. Between us, Golon would win in a contest of scholarly pursuits, but as a warrior? There is no one that can compete against me. This is how I have held my position of power for all these millennia.

"Of course, my great warrior king, I mean you no insult from this lowly peasant soldier. Please, do continue," Golon sneers condescendingly. He has never been good at knowing his place.

"Golon!" I snap. His behavior is chipping away my already haphazard control. Adding to my fear that I have harmed my mate and I am mere seconds away from releasing a fatal blow to my cousin. "That is quite enough. I am concerned for my mate and have no time for your unsolicited censure!" I can feel my tenuous control breaking—power is slipping into my words.

Golon stiffens and looks contrite and a tad worried. He finally seems to grasp the precarious position he is in. "You are quite right, *cognata*, this is no time for familial banter. Continue so that we may aid your mate."

"Yes, next I could not convince her to remove herself from the floor, so I carried her over to the chair you see and deposited her there. When I picked her up, she began to wail and thrash, pleading with me not to harm her. I once again assured her that she need not fear me, but she continued to cry, and she was getting increasingly louder and frantic.

She appeared to be struggling for breath so I…I…I commanded her to stop. And…she did. Immediately…" I taper off.

I feel a strange sensation as I recall my behavior. It is a feeling I have never felt before and it takes me a moment to identify—shame. Speaking it aloud I hear what I did and realize it is vastly different from what I should have done. For years I have talked about my desire to care for my mate, but when I am given the opportunity to do so, I do the exact opposite. My mate is a fragile, sweet creature. She needs a gentle hand. I stood before my mate while she was upset and I did nothing to comfort her, I just yelled at her. I need a *scimitar* to the heart for my behavior.

"I see." Golon looks over to where Kowan is feeling the room for auras. "Kowan, you may stop. There is no outward force acting upon our queen. Our king caused this trance. You have used *abiciant* upon her and commanded her to stop. So she has." Golon's voice drops like a stone in the room. "She has stopped everything."

Kowan walks over to join us, his face carefully masked in a veil of indifference. Both males look at me like I am some *dreg* beneath their boots, and I feel like it as well. This is not a feeling I have ever experienced before. Or at least not that I remember. I have always been exceedingly confident in my actions. But I feel that I did not do right by my mate, and I despise it. I can't accept what he says, it's impossible. I couldn't have done this.

"How is that possible? I do not possess the gift of *abiciant*, and I did not call forth power to use on her in any case. Also, she is my mate. The *abiciant* weave should not work on my mate even if I did cast it. There, three contradictions to your explanations. So I ask again, my leading scientia, what is causing my mate's distress?" I ask with a bite in my words. Because I know that I cannot defeat Golon in this medium, he is the leading expert in all the power lineages.

While my argument is strong, I also know that it is just made in desperation. Golon is never wrong. I know that my objections will quickly be discarded. No one is better versed in the lineages than Golon.

"You believe you have given me three contradictions, but each is quickly thrown away. Your claim that you do not possess such a gift is a falsehood, you did not possess such a gift. All gifts that we can wield were at one point not available to us. Even you, our most ancient one, are still gaining power.

"Second, you did not intentionally draw forth the power. But seeing as you did not know you could do such a thing, it is not absurd to assume that you did not know you drew it forth. Your power is raging against the confines you hold it in, You would not be aware of it as you have never wielded it.

"And for your last contradiction, gifts do not work on fully bound mates. You have just met yours, and she has yet to accept the bond, let alone be happy and secure enough in the mate bond to accept you," Golon states quite calmly, but with a distinct sense of triumph. Sometimes I really wish I did not have a cousin.

"If what you say is true, then why did it not work when I commanded her to speak again? I too first thought maybe it could be as you say but it did not work. What say you?" I challenge Golon. In my gut I know he has an answer, I just want him to be wrong. To admit that I caused any distress to my mate is enough to send a knife through my heart.

But it is not Golon who answers. "My king, I might suggest that if you did not know you were using the *abiciant* to silence her tears, how could you knowingly call forth the power? In my experience, you cannot wield a gift if you reject its existence." Kowan has stepped closer to my mate, placing himself between us.

While I understand he must protect her, the implication that she needs protection from me is ludicrous. A rage blacker than anything I have ever experienced rolls through me. The anger I felt toward Golon is minuscule compared to what Kowan has sparked by coming between myself and my mate.

"I would recommend you step away from my mate, *infer*, or I will move you myself," I growl at Kowan. "In pieces."

I can feel my powers radiating from me in waves. However this time I do nothing to stem their flow. This is peculiar though—my weaves, I can barely contain them. They are more potent than before. They seem to be bursting from my control. I quickly add more concentration to my containment threads. I want to kill Kowan, not harm Eleanor.

"Sire, if I may be so bold. Your aura is seeping out of you. You are normally more contained. Is anything the matter?" Kowan inquires. But he also steps aside. Wise warrior. With the male no longer close to my mate I can begin trying to force my power and anger down. It is not easy, there is so much power to control.

"He is right, *cognata*, you are filling this room with your threads. It is as if your power has doubled in the mere hours it has been since we talked earlier this morn." Golon adds his thoughts, his words pensive.

"Aye Golon, Kowan, you are correct. I am needing to exert much more control to contain my lineages than I normally do. What could cause this?" I ask of Golon. I have never experienced such a sudden increase in power. Not even during my coming of age did I produce such a surge of energy.

Golon seems to be in deep thought for several minutes. He closes his eyes, and I can tell he is performing his *medate* so that he can access all of his knowledge and determine a solution.

This skill is what allows him to have climbed so high among the scientia officers. He can recall anything he has ever read or heard. When you have over two thousand years of reading to contend with, that is quite a feat.

He created this lineage, the *medate*—he is one of the elite Gelders who is so well immersed in the very physics of our power that he could create his own power line. To this day he is the only one who can wield it. The level of concentration needed is beyond the control of anyone he has tried to mentor.

"Well, I believe the answer is right in front of us in the form of your tranced mate," Golon finally says.

"Explain this, Golon, how can my mate be the cause of this? She is human," I demand.

"Well, in our deepest histories, I have read recollections of the great mate bonds bringing forth immense power to their mates. It is thought they might have been the spark that saw us through the transition. Either on one side or on both sides. Some tell of new great powers being called forth, and others speak of their control of their lineages drastically increasing. I think this explains what we see here. Upon merely meeting your mate, you have not just gained the gift of *abiciant*, you have also gained more strength in your existing lineages." Golon looks quite pleased with this. I want to know why.

"Golon, you are withholding something from me. I require you to bring words to the thoughts you think."

"It is nothing dire, dear cousin, merely I am thinking our queen is powerful indeed if upon the first few minutes of her arrival she has advanced you in power by at least half a millennia. She may indeed be what we have so desperately waited for. Our savior." He is studying my mate with awe. And for once, I feel no jealousy. No rage at this other male gazing at her.

I let his words sink in. The powers that she has unleashed within me cannot be argued with. She has indeed made me even more powerful.

She has given birth to a new form of power for me to wield.

And I thought her weak. Shame fills me as I recall how I reacted, when her behavior should have been expected. I should have treated her like the gift she is, not angry that she did not act as happy as I was to meet her.

She is powerful, just perhaps in a different way than I am. Maybe her power will lie in unlocking mine, but I suspect that my mate has only begun to surprise me.

I glance at Kowan and Golon, and I see the reverence in their eyes. I completely understand the softness in their eyes. As I turn to look at Eleanor, I am sure my eyes match theirs.

I too am in awe.

Ellie

If I was not terrified before I sure am now. The king merely spoke a few words, and now it is as if I am locked in full-body paralysis. I can't do anything. I can merely sit where he placed me and stare. I am fully aware of what is going on around me but have no way to interact with my surroundings.

I would like to think I am not a stupid woman. I can tell this was not the king's intention. He seems legitimately concerned that I am like this. He is telling me to speak. I would love to, but still, I am held mute as if some foreign entity is holding my vocal cords hostage.

Now he is shaking me, but still nothing on my part. He seems angry, frustrated that I do not move for him as he asks.

Well hey, I would move if I could, asshole.

This thought instinctively causes fear for me. He will know that I am thinking unkind thoughts at him—my mother could always read it on my face and was sure to be quick in reprimanding me. Then I let my mind relax. One benefit of not being able to talk or move my body is that it allows me be myself without worrying my thoughts will somehow be shown on my face.

This has its benefits. I can think what I want of him with no reason to fear a consequence. For once, I can be myself and stop fighting my instincts at every turn.

Asshole.

It feels good to think that because he really is one. Yelling at me as if this was my fault.

It appears that he is now calling for help. Hmm...I would not think a king would need help.

Not so high and mighty apparently, asshole, I think uncharitably toward him. In his defense, he is trying to help me, but he also caused this.

So he is an asshole, but maybe only like a part asshole. If I could, I would laugh at my thoughts. He has asked for some Golon character to come here, and now he is at the door. I wonder who he is calling in. Oh, the rainbow one from my travel here is now in the room.

The king calls him Kowan. I feel a little at peace now that I have some names to put to these males. I have Liam the friendly one. Kowan is the mysterious rainbow one. And Danion. The king and my apparent owner also has a rainbow haze around him but much brighter now. I wish I could shield my eyes or at least close them.

As I observe the king speaking to Kowan, I am beginning to suspect there might be some credibility to this queen thing Danion spoke of.

By the way they are acting I do not appear to be just some lowly sex slave or a piece of meat to them. They both seem genuinely upset about my current state. Of course, maybe it is some sort of warrior code of honor, like the knights of old. Or that I am frozen before I could perform my duties. But it feels like more than that.

I can see the genuine concern on their faces, over me. They are concerned about my well-being. If I could move, my mouth would drop in surprise. In all my life I can only think of five people who have ever been concerned about my well-being—Marilee and my four sisters. Apparently, I now have a king and a warrior to add to the list.

As much as I fight it, a warm sensation rises within me. Someone cares about me.

Apparently, this Kowan is trying to deduce if there is some kind of aura thing causing me to be in this trance-like state. How odd. I never thought of that. I was sure my owner—or King Danion I suppose—brought this upon me. When I focus on the king, I see a small, thin, almost transparent thread stretching between us.

As I watch Kowan walk the room while waving his hands, or as much as I can see of him when I cannot move my head or eyes, a new male enters the room. This must be the Golon he called for. He seems friendly... Maybe not. Now he looks distressed. Distressed about me. Now I am beginning to honestly worry. How bad is this if three Gelder warriors are so nervous?

Why are they so worried? I am just a human he claimed to be his slave. Aren't I?

Unless I am not just a slave. I think over each and every one of the conversations I have had with the Gelders so far. Admittedly there have only been a few, as well as this one, that I have now overheard. None of these males seem to think of me as inconsequential. I hear him say queen, but it cannot be true. Maybe queen means something different?

Maybe it is merely an issue of semantics. Perhaps a slave to the Gelders has a greater significance. Maybe I fulfill some sort of role that only slaves do. Just because *slave* means one thing in Earth culture does not necessarily mean it has the same definition in Gelder culture. The king has called me many things, and as I listen in on his conversation with this Golon I hear myself called mate more than anything. And Liam had a strange word, what was it? Mate bond.

Mate. I know the implication of the word in my world. *Sex*. It is more a verb, to mate with another. I can tell by the way they use this word that there is some crucial meaning I am missing. Maybe they are very selective in who they mate with. There is a chance that this king has some sort of perversion that is so depraved he does not wish to subject one of his own people to it.

I observe my owner...or mate I suppose. While I might be beginning to believe that I am more than just a faceless slave to him it changes nothing for me. I still must make sure that I please him.

I remember my mother berating me nearly every day of my life until I finally moved out right before I turned of age that I would one day bring even more shame to the family. In my mind, I also see all the advertisements back home urging us females to obey the laws set forth by the Gelder, *this* Gelder, so that we do not lose our protection. I won't be the reason Marilee and my sisters die. If he wants a mate, I will figure out what that is and be the best damn mate he has ever had.

I already bring shame to the family by merely existing. In this modern world, you would believe that such archaic principles, such as punishing the son for the father's crime, would have died out. Or daughter for the father's crime as it were. But alas, I believe it is worse than it has ever been. I am a shameful reminder that my mother not only failed to please my father enough to keep him, but that he was so displeased with me that he abandoned me as well.

The rulers of Earth Nueva are very strict on how we must behave, as our behavior is what the treaty is hinged on. My mother's actions and my own are an indication that we are defective, that we will not be able to hold up the treaty. I am sure they are sweating bullets back home, but I will prove them wrong. I will prove them all wrong.

I have read of times where judging one's neighbor for actions that the parent committed was frowned upon. This is a thing of the past. Ever since the Purge War, my fellow man has become even more suspicious of each other. We are a planet barely surviving. We see nearly daily proof in our skies of the Erains trying to wipe us out, with only the Gelder shields to save us from extinction. Panic was quick to set in; it is our constant companion.

On any given day on Earth Nueva, you can look up and see fires in the sky. These are the Erain ships that are being destroyed by the Gelder defenses that surround our planet. It is a constant reminder that while we thrive on our surface, a slight whim from this male in front of me could mean the end of us.

Something from the conversation going on brings me from my own thoughts. Apparently, the king has used some sort of magic upon me. Something that they are calling "*abiciant*." I do not know what this is, but it seems the king does not believe he has cast any such magic. The powers of the Gelders are unrivaled by any race. The things I have heard them do, it is as if they control the very universe around us.

"Gifts do not work on fully bound mates. You have just met yours, and she has yet to accept the bond, let alone be happy and secure enough in the mate bond to accept you," I am drawn to what Golon is saying. Apparently magic should not work on mates? But only if we are happy? This makes little sense to me, and I feel even more confused. I am beginning to suspect this will not be an unfamiliar feeling to me in the coming days. Everyone seems to think that I know more than I do about this mating thing. Why they would care about if I am happy is beyond me.

This does give more evidence that I am more than just a body. Interesting. If I can ever gain the ability to control myself again, I will have to gather the courage to ask my new...mate...what this means. What my role will be.

I have distracted myself as long as I can, terror is bubbling up inside of me regarding my situation. Even more so now that they do not seem to know how to reverse it. If they caused this, shouldn't they know how to fix it? Maybe I will be like this forever. They will leave me to sit here in eternal stillness. They will assume I am not aware and just leave me.

I can feel my mind wanting to hyperventilate, but my body will not obey the command. This is the strangest sensation. My mind is filled with panic, yet my body remains calm. I feel breathless even though my breathing is smooth and rhythmic.

In an effort to calm myself down, I try to once again focus on what the Gelders are discussing.

"It is nothing dire, dear cousin, merely I am thinking our queen is powerful indeed if upon the first few minutes of her arrival she has advanced you in power by at least half a millennia. She may indeed be what we have so desperately waited for. Our savior."

I must have misheard. Or misunderstood. I am no queen and certainly no savior. How could I possibly have been the cause of the king gaining power? Maybe he can siphon life energy, maybe that is why he has claimed someone expendable like me.

"You are saying that this child, my mate, has excessive powers. Where are they? I do not sense any power within her." The king questions very harshly. I don't know why, since he only speaks the truth, but his words make me angry. A child. Thought I was a queen, but now I am a child. Again, asshole.

Being able to think freely for once is so liberating. It helps dispel some of the panic within my mind. Giving me something to focus on.

The one they call Golon responds, "Yes, *cognata*, mates of old were commonly known to be either matches in both strength and power, or they were capable of bringing forth great power in their mates. We have not seen such a match in several thousand years, so I understand if you are skeptical. But it appears that we finally have a true mate. A true, even match of souls. Your *aninare*."

Golon says this last word almost reverently. He is looking at the king with such blatant envy, and while he masks his features quickly, I am surprised the king allows this, based on the rage you can see this look has ignited.

I may not know much about what it means to be claimed by a Gelder male, but I do know that they are possessive, even territorial over what they consider theirs. I worry over the reaction the king will have after he notices this look on Golon, and my foreboding is proved justified.

"Golon, need I remind you of our laws?" The king's tone is harsh, and even in my frozen state, I can feel the power he is barely containing within himself. "It is a crime of the highest order to desire another's mate. I would caution you, *infer*, that you do not do so again." As he speaks, his voice becomes calm and quiet with every passing word. It is even more terrifying than his loud voice.

"Of course, King, it is not your mate I desire." The king scoffs at this. "No! Truly, I am merely envious of what she represents. You have been gifted with a true *aninare*. This has not occurred in so many years, I began to feel that we evolved away from such a gift. But you prove we have not."

The king stares at Golon. I can tell he is trying to combat his anger. I begin to sense his overflowing power gradually recede.

"Fine, I accept your explanation, for now. But heed my warning, dear cousin"—the way he says *cousin* almost sounds like an insult to Golon—"continue down this path and, family or not, I will end you. Now earn your keep in my rank. What is our next step with awakening my mate?"

"It is simple, my lord, now that you know what this was caused by. You summon your power and enter into a *merate* allowing you to evaluate all of your powers at once. Once you identify your control of *abiciant*, you must learn to harness it, call it forth, and then release her from your command. It is the only way."

Golon speaks of this so calmly. His confidence helps me relax. If he is so confident, he must be sure it will free me.

"A *merate*? You know as well as I that such a deep meditation will require time. Vast amounts of time. They can last for days or weeks. She cannot last days without sustenance of some kind." Oh no. My relief was short lived. I might slowly starve to death while watching them try to free me.

"Many who have been cast under an *abiciant* weave are often sustained by the compulsion," Kowan points out. My mysterious number six.

"Yes, but do you know if that was itself threaded into the compulsion weave? I do not possess this knowledge as I have never been under a weave such as this. I am not willing to take the chance that you may be wrong. Golon, how do we fix this issue in less time?" the king demands.

"There is no other way. You best enter the meditation quickly and then be sure to focus only on the root of the power you want to gain control of. This is the only way. Kowan and I will remain vigilant and attempt to hydrate and sustain her if you remain in the trance too long."

The king seems frustrated. Well, la dee daw, I say. I am the one who may be stuck like this for days. It is too terrifying to imagine. Although it is mildly comforting to know he is worried about me.

"Fine." The one word is succinct and packed with meaning. His displeasure at entering into a *merate* is made palpable by his stiff tone.

The ruling king of the greatest warriors known in the galaxy sits on the floor directly in front of me. And sits. And sits. I guess he is doing the meditation thing now. Both Kowan and Golon take up positions on either side of me and the chair I was placed on.

There are no words exchanged between them. I guess all I can do is wait. As I wait, I study my new mate. I suppose if I must be enslaved as a mate to an alien, he is not a bad one to be enslaved to.

He is very masculine. And very human looking. Humans have interacted with a few other alien races, and many have fur, horns, or even worse, slime all over their bodies. Gelders are not even much different from us in terms of size. From what I can see he is nothing more than a gorgeous virile male. With his tall and wide frame, his shoulders are broad and taper down to a lean waist. He seems perfectly proportioned.

His dark hair is cut short, close to his head on the sides and a little longer on top. It would be just enough to grab a handful of. His gray eyes are closed, and I mourn their loss; I could stare at those eyes until the day I died. I imagine staring at those eyes while he is above me. His arms wrapped around me, cocooning me from the world. Maybe even in bed...

Oh no. I realize there is one part of Gelder anatomy I have no comprehension of. How do they have sex? Do they have a normal penis or is it disfigured? Or huge? Or tiny?

My mind runs wild. Plagued with a million scenarios. As the king sits in front of me, I cannot quiet my mind. I tell myself that I do not even know that he intends to mate with me in that sense. With no small amount of willpower I focus again on this male in front of me. If his face is the last thing I will ever see before I die, I decide there are worse ways to go.

Chapter Four

Ellie

"Wake up."

I am jerked awake by the loud command. Standing in front of me is the king himself with a pleased look on his face.

"Welcome back, my sweet *aninare*." It is then I realize I am looking up at him. I turn my head to the left to look at Kowan, and my head moves! "I am deeply apologetic for any discomfort I caused you. I will spend the rest of eternity making amends." He keeps talking, but I stopped listening as soon as I realized I could move again.

"I can move!" I jump to my feet and move all my limbs. "Oh! Wonderful! You have no appreciation for movement until it is taken from you." I am babbling, but I cannot contain myself. I am so happy to be freed from my prison within my own body. In my elation, I forget everything and listen to my instincts. I jump up and throw my arms around the king.

"Oh, thank you, Your Highness!" As I wrap my arms around him, his body goes stiff. But then, after a moment, I feel his arms come around me, and he tucks my head under his chin. I do not think I have ever felt so secure and safe. I feel nothing but warmth and strength all around me. I close my eyes and get lost in the refuge of Danion. Something deep inside of me seems to be reaching for him as if a part of me recognizes him.

"Are we in the way? Maybe we should give you two some privacy?" A sardonic voice interrupts my cocoon of safety.

Now that I am aware of what I am doing, hugging a king, I pull back. But Danion Belator of Old refuses to let me go. The most feared warrior in the galaxy holds on to me with arms that tighten like iron vises around my body. He prevents me from putting even an inch of space between us.

"Yes, Golon, you should go." His voice is as hard as diamonds. He is furious. I should never have hugged him. I pull back again, and his arms tighten even further. It begins to hurt.

"Please. Please, I did not mean any harm, please let go," I plead with him.

"Harm? Of course you did not harm me. If you wish to put your arms around me, you are allowed. In gratitude or for any reason." His arms relax a fraction which stops the embrace from being bruising like before.

"If it is gratitude, then do we not deserve equal treatment? Kowan and I not only helped to free you, but we also stood watch over you. I would enjoy a hug. What about you, Kowan?" Golon, who I now know to be the king's cousin, asks with a smirk and throws his arms out when I turn my head to stare at him.

"Don't bring me down with you, Golon. I like my head and organs right where they are," Kowan responds.

The king's arms tighten again, and I can't help the whimper that comes out. This makes his arms constrict even further.

"You find this amusing, mate? You would enjoy the arms of my warriors?" With each word, his arms grow tighter. I know I will have dark marks around my body in a few hours.

"No, it's not that—" I am cut off from my explanation.

"Then why do you fight me now?" His arms tighten even further. Now it is not bruising I fear but broken bones. "Why struggle in my embrace if you do not crave another's?" His words are as hard as his arms. I can barely get air in, let alone words out.

"Please, you're hurting me," I manage to gasp out. His arms immediately loosen. I raise my face to look at him, and he has turned pale—his entire face has lost color.

"Apologies, Eleanor, I did not mean to harm you. This bond is damaging my control greatly." The king bows to me. To me. Having a king bow to me is not something I ever anticipated. "You humble me, and I disrespect both my ancestors and the name of my house. Deepest apologies I give to you, again. I deserve a thousand lashings after all the suffering I have caused you."

"Thank you, Your Highness, but it is me who is sorry for taking liberties on your person." I am so embarrassed. Mainly since there were witnesses to my spontaneous embrace and subsequent punishment.

"You are free to touch me, I just forgot how strong my hold is and how fragile humans are. I ask your forgiveness." He seems genuinely upset he hurt me. That did not stop him from bruising me though.

"Of course, my liege." He is a king and the male standing in between my people and extinction, so I am not going to hold a grudge over something as foolish as a few bruises. I believe it was not done on purpose.

"For the last time, you are not to call me Your Highness or my liege. Please call me *animare* or at the very least, call me Danion, or Dane. All my intimates do, and we will be much too intimate for such formality." With those last words, his voice has dropped into a sultry, seductive tone. I recall my curiosity about his anatomy.

"But..." I try to protest.

"No, I require you call me such, or I will be forced to take action," he says with a look I can't decipher.

Action? I freeze and immediately stop my protests. I must do what he requires of me, and when I think about it calling him by his name is not such a hardship. But now I am so afraid of what he will do to me I cannot force my throat to form words.

"Well done, Dane, you are terrifying the poor girl." Golon is glaring at Danion while he, in turn, is glaring back at him. "First you paralyze her, then bruise her, and now jokes veiled in threats? I would think you could do better." The air has a definite crackle in it. I do not know why Golon seems bound and determined to rile Danion, but he is very good at it.

"Might I make a suggestion?" Kowan interrupts the mounting tension.

"You are free to speak," Danion answers with a distinctive bite in his tone. His hands are closed tightly into fists, and his body is rigid. He looks like a man on the edge.

"From my observations, our young queen is confused about her role to us. Based on the beliefs of her people and what was told to her in her preparation performed on Earth, she thinks she is your slave, my lord. Maybe if I and the rest of her *praesidium* introduced ourselves, it will make her more at ease." Kowan speaks with very little emotion. It is as if you gave a wall the ability to talk.

"Wonderful idea, Kowan, and maybe after that our king could escort her to dinner and maybe stop glaring at her every two seconds, hmm? Think you could do that, oh great one?" I cannot believe the sarcasm and attitude in which he speaks to his king. His behavior baffles me.

"Just because you are my cousin do not think you are above being thrown in a cell, Golon. You push boundaries you dare not cross." Danion is almost boiling with bad temper completely directed at his cousin. Then his gaze turns to me. "Is he right? Do you think you are to be my slave?" The distaste he has for the words is evident, his lip curling up in disgust.

His question throws me off. "Um...I think..." I stammer, but I cannot verbalize a coherent response.

Danion sighs. "It appears you do raise a point. Kowan, call forth her *praesidium* to make themselves known to her."

Kowan bows severely and disappears out the door. Danion takes my arm and escorts me to the far side of the room away from his cousin.

"Eleanor, I have no concern about what their thoughts and opinions of me are and how they view our bond, but their comments do raise the concern that you are fearful of me. Is this true?" His eyes are boring into mine. So earnest and so strong. I realize his arms are not the only thing that can make me feel safe. I feel cocooned in just his gaze. Because of the warmth in those eyes, I am able to answer him truthfully.

"Yes." I move my eyes down to his chest. I am worried about how he will take this piece of news, although it will tell me how he views me. If he truly wants nothing but a slave, as I suspect is not the case, he will either not care or be happy that I fear him. But if being his mate is something more, he should want me to be unafraid of him.

"You truly fear me?" His voice is the voice of a man who is in immense pain. The pain I hear pulls my eyes up to his. "How can you fear me? Eleanor, I... No, Eleanor, please do not fear me. No one has less cause to fear me than you. I would give my life to keep you safe."

"Why? Why would you sacrifice your life for me? You don't even know me." His words shock me. They speak of a devotion that makes no sense to me.

"Because you are my mate, Eleanor. Surely you know what this means?" he asks me incredulously.

"No, not really. No one on Earth Nueva really knows why you claim us. We are taught about subservience and instructed on how to obey you if we are claimed. So I am not completely unprepared to serve you," I reassure him.

"Subservience? Obey me? Why do you tell me this?" His voice is dropping, his words are ice cold.

"I just want you to know I will work to please you."

"Please me. By obeying me?" He makes a derisive snort. "I can see that Golon and Kowan were right. You are not aware of what being my *aninare* means. Why you do not know, I will find out, and for the sake of all the stars, I hope there is an acceptable reason for this. After you meet your *praesidium*, you and I will spend time alone, and I can explain to you why you should never fear me."

His eyes are looking intensely at me, waiting for an answer.

"Oh...OK," I stutter out.

"'OK.' I suppose that is as much enthusiasm as I can expect, under the circumstances." He gives a self-deprecating smile. "Alright, let's introduce you to your *praesidium*."

He offers me his arm, like a knight of old. I place my arm in the crook of his elbow, and we walk back to the other side of the room where all of the six are waiting patiently.

Kowan steps forward and gives me a deep bow. "My queen, it is my deepest pleasure to introduce myself to you. My name is Kowan Viribus, and I am your master of *simul* in your *praesidium*. This gives me the pleasure of being the leader of your *praesidium*, and with your permission, I will introduce the rest of us." He stares at me patiently, waiting for my response.

"I'm sorry, I would love to meet all of you"—I wave my hand to encompass all of the six—"but I am afraid I am not sure what a pray-seed-ium is?"

The room is silent, everyone is just staring at me as if I am an enigma. Finally, Danion speaks.

"Eleanor, you do not know of this either? How can this be? Are not the Earth beings taught of the ways of the Gelder? Do you know nothing of our culture and our expectations if you are claimed?" The look he gives me is one of complete confusion.

"Well...we are taught some things. For instance, we are taught about your ships and the location of some of the major planets and moons where life thrives, and we are told stories of some of your strongest warriors. You, for instance. Nothing is told to us about culture or what to expect if we are claimed though." I pause to think over the very little we know of the claiming process. "I know only that we leave immediately upon being claimed, and that we are only allowed two items with us... Oh! I never gave you the gift!" I am mortified. How could I forget to give him the gift I brought especially for him?

"What is this gift you speak of?" The king is confused again.

"Well, we are allowed to bring one item of our choosing to keep with us as a token of our old life." I talk while I head over to where my bag was placed to pull out the gift I brought for him. "And then one item that we are to give to the Gelders as a gift of thanks for keeping us safe all these years. I hope now is not too late for me to give it to you?" I ask him.

"There is no such requirement, but I admit to curiosity. Please feel free to bring it forth," the king says with a nod.

I pick up my tote and begin digging through the sack. The clothes that I stuffed in the bag fall out. I look at the old, worn, ratty cloth on the floor in front of me and flush deep red with embarrassment. It makes a stark contradiction to the extravagance all around me.

"I am so sorry," I stammer out, beginning to bend down. But before I get there, Danion has already knelt and grabbed the cloth.

"Is this a cleaning cloth? I assure you, Eleanor, I will not be requiring you to clean for me." He mentions this with a chuckle.

"Oh..." My face burns with mortification. I am trying to think of how I can respond. How could I admit that he is holding my clothes and not a cleaning rag? The embarrassment is infinitely worse now. I will try to play off the clothes as a rag and try to bury them back in ...

"Sire, I believe those are the clothes she was wearing before being dressed in the clothes provided for her travels." My hopes of redemption are dashed by Kowan's words. Danion's face, open and smiling a moment before, crashes down into immense, biting fury.

"These were your garments? These are the clothes that my queen was dressed in? How?" His voice has steadily risen in volume culminating in a roar that shakes the walls.

"They are all I could afford. I am sorry that I brought them with me." I try to defend myself and calm his ire. What has made him so angry is lost on me, but he is terrifying in his anger.

"Shut up!" Danion snaps, and then continues in a slightly calmer tone. "Just stop talking. Please. I cannot handle any more without losing my tenuous control. The bond madness is difficult enough as it is, and this very well may break it. Just. Show. Me. The. Gift." His voice does not allow me to disobey. "Please."

I bring forth the gift wrapped in a simple cloth. I know gifts used to be covered in colorful paper, but paper has long been a rare commodity as the Gelders monitor all of our resources, and they confiscate a large amount of our wood.

I become very nervous, I do hope that he likes this gift. To me, it is quite unique, but for a king whose chambers are covered in real gold, it is most likely to be seen as a small worthless trinket.

"Here, this is what I brought for you." I hold out the cloth-wrapped gift. "It is not much, I hope it is acceptable. They do not give us any guidelines on what you would expect so I did my best." With a flush of embarrassment high on my cheeks, I stop my rambling.

Utterly silent, Danion takes the gift from me. Our fingers graze each other, and I feel a shock. Not electricity but something more profound. It is as if my soul is reaching out to him and his answered. I quickly withdraw my fingers from his. I rub them against the fine material of my new dress, a vain attempt to wipe away the sensation his fingers left me with.

His fingers deftly open the cloth to find a small figurine nestled inside. It is an image of a great cat—they are long extinct on Earth, but they were supposed to be fierce creatures in their day.

"It is a likeness of a great warrior of our animal kingdom. They were called tigers. They have all died off now. At the start of the Great Purge all the work that was being done to save them was forgotten, and by the time that people thought about them their population was beyond saving." I get a little teary eyed thinking about an entire species merely fading away. The symbolism is too much for me.

"I made you this as a representation of what would have happened to us, humans I mean, had you not intervened. It is a token of appreciation for all that you and your people have done for us. I carved it out of a river rock that I collected from a riverbank I hike to every week. It is my favorite spot of reflection."

I am rambling on about this gift, but he is still not talking to me. I do not know what this means, so I do what I always do when I do not know how to handle a situation. I keep talking.

"Yes, it is not expensive or particularly good so feel free to not keep it. I am sorry if this is not acceptable..."

"No, this is quite...adequate. I merely was silent because I did not expect a gift from you." His words are carefully blank. I can't read him.

"But...we are required to bring you a gift. Why would you think I would not bring one?"

"This gift requirement, it is not one set forth by the Gelder. It must be a human custom they enforce." He has not taken his eyes off of his little tiger this whole time. Maybe he truly does appreciate my gift.

"This was most thoughtful, my queen. A truly rare gem is what has been bestowed to our king this day." Golon speaks up from his seat on the couches to my right.

"Oh, it is not a gem, merely a river rock I collected. I am sorry I did not get a gemstone." I answer, it is a pretty rock. Made smooth by the water and possesses a deep amber color. When I saw it I instantly fell in love with the stone.

"It is not the tiger I speak of," Golon says with a smile. I am not sure what he means by this cryptic message. Golon seems to be the type who enjoys jokes, particularly when they are at the expense of the king.

"Golon, you speak the truth. I am a warrior who has been gifted the most rare of gifts this day." Danion speaks up. He appears calm once more, his earlier anger seemingly forgotten. "Now, my dear Eleanor, I am most pleased with your gift. A gift created by one's own hands is superior to all other gifts to the Gelder." Danion looks at me with something that can only be described as complete wonder. "I do not possess the words to describe to you how pleased I am with both my gift and you, my mate."

As I stare at my new mate, I get lost in his eyes. The worries I have about what it means to be a mate and what the future holds for both myself and my people all just fade away. I feel like the entire world is right here in this room. Right between the two of us. It reminds me of when I was in his arms, never before have I experienced a feeling such as this. Of such complete safety and happiness. Of such longing.

"I hate to interrupt this touching moment, truly I do, but should we stay and introduce the members of her *praesidium* to our lovely queen or should we just leave?" We are interrupted by a sardonic voice.

"Golon, it's as if you want me to kill you." Danion glares over at Golon. "But I believe it would be prudent to continue the education of my *aninare*, so you will live to annoy me another day."

Danion takes my arm and moves us in front of the six. "Now, you expressed that you were not familiar with what a *praesidium* is. Simply put, all nonwarrior class members of the royal houses are assigned an elite guard. They are the most skilled in their respective lineages."

I have no idea what he means by lineages. What are the lineages?

"If I may interrupt, sire, I believe our queen is confused about what you mean by lineages," Kowan says.

The king seems surprised. "Truly? Are you not familiar with lineages and the roles they play in Gelder hierarchy?"

How I wish I could tell him I know what he means. If only I were not so ignorant of his ways. I wish that he did not seem to think that I should know what he is talking about.

"I am sorry, but no, I do not know what a lineage is. I have never heard of anything like Gelder lineages," I whisper.

The entire room is silent, but then Danion smiles. "It is not of consequence, my Eleanor. I can teach you all you need to know. *Lineage* speaks of what kind of threads of the cosmos, or simply put what type of power, we can weave. Are you aware that our warriors can wield powers similar to what you think of as elements?"

"You mean it is true? You are magical? I thought that was a myth." I heard of such a myth a long time ago but never believed it. I notice that Danion is smiling at me like you smile when a child does something amusing. "What? Why are you looking at me like that?"

"It is something I have always found amusing about humans. All mortals, really. Whenever you see something that you cannot explain, you always turn to magic as an explanation. The world is more than what you have observed, young one." He holds his hand out in front of me and conjures a ball of fire, and before my eyes, the ball of fire changes shape and begins to resemble my tiger figurine. Then the tiger starts to move. I am enthralled, just watching this little tiger made of flame. How is this not magic?

"So you can wield fire, but it is not magic? How am I to believe that?" I ask him.

"My sweet Eleanor, what you call magic we call science. It is simple biology. Everything you see around you is made up of elements." I nod at this, this I know from my high school chemistry classes. "And due to the very essence of being a Gelder, it means that we see the world in a different way. We can manipulate these elements without the aid of technology. Is that magic? We say it is nothing more than biology."

I take in what he says. I suppose that makes sense. Knowledge is power, and when you have vast amounts of knowledge, much greater than any other race, it can appear like magic. We have animals on Earth that can camouflage themselves to match their surroundings. Cephalopods can even change the texture of their skin to match the environment that they are in. This is not magic, it is just biology. We accept it easily enough. But to some, it would appear magical.

"So you all have this ability? All Gelders can control the elements? And this is just a genetic thing?"

"In a way, depending on what lineage we come from. Some are stronger than others, and some only control one element. Only a small percentage of us can control any of the six major lineages. The majority of our people possess no control over the major lineages, usually, they just have a small control over the minor lineages. Strands of power that branched off from the major lines long ago. Standing before you represents the best of each of the main lineages. I will let Kowan introduce his men and explain briefly what each lineage is." As Danion finishes his explanation, he wraps one arm around me, and we stand together.

I feel that I should move away, that I do not know him well enough for such familiarity. But I cannot fight the feelings that I brought with me onto this ship—that I am to be a slave and obey everything that he says. I know that they say I am to be queen, but my mind cannot wrap around what this means.

Never in my wildest imagination did I ever think I would meet their king, let alone be their queen. I clearly am not a slave as I first feared, but I still worry that if I do not make the king happy, my people will suffer.

So I stay in his embrace. It is not that the embrace is not pleasant, but it does bring forth odd feelings within me.

"Yes, my queen, I would be delighted to explain our power to you. As I said, I am the master of the *simul* lineage in your *praesidium*. This can be thought of as wielding all of the major lineages. So for every master you are about to meet, I too can call forth their power. This ability is what marks me as the leader of your guard. We will begin the introductions with our master of *aniun*, Mailn Mulus."

As he speaks, the one who has a blue color to him steps forward. He makes a deep bow. "It is a pleasure beyond words to be serving as your protector, my queen."

"It is very nice to meet you, Mr. Mulus," I say with as much formality as I can muster up.

"Malin is fine, my queen," Malin says before he raises his head.

"Likewise, I would feel much better if you called me Ellie, for all of you actually. I feel a little unnerved by being referred to as queen if I am honest with you." I speak up. I would feel much better if I could at least pretend I was still Ellie.

"If our king has no objection, we would be more than pleased to call Your Highness whatever would make you most comfortable," Kowan speaks again and then raises an inquisitive brow toward Danion.

"I would like you to be most comfortable, Eleanor." I can tell by the way he stresses my full name that he is warning the others that they should call me by my full name, not the nickname I gave. "If this will help you there is no need for them to address you formally in privacy. But do understand that in any public setting these warriors would do you a dishonor if they were to address you with anything less but the highest formality." Danion glares at the warriors before me.

"Of course, sire. Eleanor, if you would permit me, I will continue explaining the lineage that Malin masters and the rest of the introductions?" Kowan seems unaffected by the king's cold response. However I notice how he is careful to use my full name.

"Yes, thank you, Kowan, I would like that." I feel as if I am persistently interrupting the introductions that they are trying to do with my ignorance of their ways.

"As I said, Malin weaves *aniun* which can be thought of as the elements of water. While not fully accurate, you can think of him as being able to control water. Does this make sense to you?"

While I know that Kowan is making this very simple for me, I would like a little more detail. If their control of the elements is not based in magic, I wonder where it comes from. But I have been taking them off track so much I still have only met one of them. I will ask him later once I have had some time to adjust.

"Yes, Kowan, I am sure the more I am around you I will learn even more. I would love to meet the rest of my prae...um, praesi..." I trail off as I do not remember what they actually called my guard.

"*Praesidium*, and of course. I can assure you we are all eager to formally meet you as well." Kowan gives me a kind smile and then waves his hand again. "Next may I introduce to you your master of *ignis*, Arsenio Tempestas. *Ignis* can be thought of as the elements of fire. These are the threads our king used earlier." While Kowan is talking, the male with red color steps forward. He has a cocky smile on his lips. He too falls into a bow to me, but not as low as Malin's.

"Eleanor, I am grateful to meet you formally at last. It was pleasant to guard you silently on your travel here, but I look forward to getting to know you better." I find him very open in his speech. Almost flirtatious in nature and I do not know how to respond to him.

The room tightens in on me, at least that is the best way to describe what is going on. It is almost as if something is making the air smaller. I glance over at Danion to see if he too is feeling this and I notice that the colors that fly around him are exploding out of him violently.

"Arsenio, you will get only this one warning," Danion speaks very slowly with a deep growl, as if the words are difficult for him to form. The grin that Arsenio had on his face vanishes.

"Yes, sire, I do not know what came over me. Apologies, Eleanor, please forget my inexcusable behavior earlier. It will be an honor to protect you." Unlike Malin, he does not wait to rise up and step back with the other five.

"Nice to meet you, Arsenio." This is all I can manage before Kowan continues with the introductions. I feel that he wants to move past this quickly. My new mate is displeased with other males being overly friendly with me. I suppose this is not surprising based off his behavior from before. I have never met a man who seems to be more of an alpha male as Danion.

"Next we have Amell Solidium, the master of *terra*. You can always count on Amell, for his lineage is that of the ground elements. Think of rocks and minerals. He is also one of the oldest and most trusted advisors to your mate." As Kowan speaks, the male who has bright earthy-brown colors around him steps forward and drops all the way down on one knee.

"My queen, I recognize that you wish to be called Eleanor and I will henceforth refer to you as such, but for a first meeting anything but complete reverence is an insult." This last sentence he directs toward Arsenio. I am getting the sense that Arsenio is not highly liked by this group. "If there is ever a cause, you may look to me for guidance or protection. From any and all things, nothing is too small for my queen."

"Thank you, Amell, I am very thankful for your welcome. I assure you if I ever need help I will come to you first." I give a small smile to Amell. He is the first person since I read my name on that stage that I have felt truly comfortable with. I think I might have found my first, possibly only, friend here.

"Second." I look up at the abrupt word that Danion has said. It sounded more like he had bitten the word out it was said with such violence. I look at Danion with a question in my eyes.

"You will come to Amell second. I am more than capable of helping you in all matters, and as your mate, you should come to me first. Amell should be a mere afterthought if I am unavailable to you," Danion says with a leashed anger in his voice. "Which will never be the case." He says the last bit with a challenge in it. Whether the challenge is directed at Amell or me, I don't know, maybe both of us.

"Oh. Yes, I will not go to Amell without first consulting with you." I look over at Danion but keep my eyes focused on his chest. The anger that is pouring off of him makes it impossible for me to raise my eyes any further.

I am appropriately chastised, and I worry if I look him in the eyes and see his fury firsthand that I will burst into tears. My emotions are all over the place, I am barely holding myself together. I have no desire to provoke his temper too far that it breaks and he traps me within my body once again.

I am swiftly learning that Danion is quite possessive, and quick to anger.

"Kowan, continue. The sooner these meaningless introductions are over with, the better." The bite in Danion's voice is even harder now. Oh great, I made it worse. I do not know what I did. Obviously it was the wrong thing in this male's eyes.

"Of course, Danion, we will continue once I have a chance to conclude with our queen," Amell speaks before Kowan is able to. "My queen, Eleanor, I swear my life to the protection of yours. I have waited more years than I can count for a post as noble as this, and you have exceeded all my expectations. It is truly a blessing to my soul to meet and serve yours." Amell slowly rises and smiles at me. I cannot help but smile in return.

"Kowan. Now." Danion utters these two words with such anger I am surprised that sparks do not fly into the room. I quickly divert my eyes to the floor in front of me.

"Yes, of course. It is my pleasure to next introduce Etan Honoris, the master of *caeli*. He controls the elements in the very air itself. You will be most well-guarded with Etan serving as your *caeli* protector." Now the male who is surrounded in a slight purple glow steps forward. His hair which was pulled back before is now loose around his head, falling to kiss his shoulders. He has a bounce to his step and has the happiest grin I have ever seen.

He bows deeply, his long hair falling forward to kiss the floor. "Oh, my queen Eleanor. I am so filled with joy to be serving you and look forward to learning more about you." However, he seems to have taken Danion's warning to heart and quickly steps back without saying anything else.

"Yes, I am pleased to have you in my guard as well, Etan. I look forward to getting to know you better." I can barely get the words out before Kowan has introduced the last and only remaining member.

"Finally, may I introduce Griffith Vitae, your esteemed master of *vim*, and this is one of the most difficult lineages to master. It is a very complex idea to grasp as well but based off of Earth language and meaning, I would call this the elements of life. Imagine that all living things have energy—this is what a master of *vim* can harness."

The golden one who kept his eyes closed for the entire journey steps forward. He gives a bow. "Pleased to make your formal acquaintance, my queen. It brings joy to me to know you will henceforth rely upon my strength for protection." And with another nod of his head, Griffith steps back.

"Thank you, Griffith." I am at a loss of what to say to all of these warriors. What am I expected to do next? I have never had etiquette lessons. I am merely a human and a pretty small one at that. I never imagined I was to be a queen and within a few hours, I suddenly am one, complete with expectations and duties to fulfill.

I feel as if I am back in school and I am in a play that no one told me I was cast for. Suddenly on stage, and having no idea what my lines are. But I can tell by the stares in the room everyone is waiting for me to say something.

"I am very pleased to have met you all, and I look forward to you all...protecting me in the future." Oh, I botched that up, I know I did. I am sure I will see snickers in my prae...oh, whatever they call themselves...eyes. It's the best I can do though, no one ever expected me to need to know how to act in a situation like this.

But when I look up, no one is laughing. As a whole, they give me a nod of their heads, as if in acknowledgment of some bigger meaning. If I can get out of this room without utterly destroying the treaty between our worlds, it will be a miracle. At this moment there is nothing I want more than to have a few moments to myself.

It seems Danion has other ideas though. "Yes, now that everyone has had a chance to be introduced to my mate, I will be escorting her to dine with me. Alone. Now you all can go find other arrangements for the evening meal. You are no longer needed." Danion dismisses everyone with a curt jerk of his head.

Be alone with Danion? Now? I am so exhausted, and while I have not eaten for over a day, I cannot imagine eating right now. I am tied up in knots from everything that I experienced. There is nothing that I want more than just a little time to myself to try to organize the flurry of emotions and thoughts I have inside me.

But for my people, I will muddle through. I am still too unsure of him to risk disobeying him. I am hungry. I will just have to try to dine quickly and then excuse myself.

"OK." I agree to dinner. I imagine that this will make him happy. But when I turn my gaze to him, finally gathering the courage to look him in the eye, I am met with a stone-cold gaze filled with anger. Fierce, blistering anger. It positively jumps between us. I quickly lower my gaze again.

"Perhaps, Danion, Eleanor might like to first see her chambers and then take a few hours to relax. If you recall she arrived here late yestereve, and it is now late today. She might wish to change and freshen up. Collect her thoughts." Amell has spoken up.

It appears that there is one male in this room who can read me well. That was my exact thought, just a little time to come to terms with everything that I have learned today. However, Amell's suggestions seem to enrage Danion even further.

"You are becoming quite presumptuous in your old age, Amell. Do you wish to challenge me for my mate?" Danion words literally vibrate with power.

I can feel his very words within my bones. My heartbeat seems to pulse to the tempo of his words. This blatant exhibition of his power is why he is king and has held this seat for thousands of years. Never before have I ever experienced something so raw in power. His energy has flooded the room, and the air itself seems to be charged.

"Danion, of course I do not wish to challenge you for her. You are being foolish, letting the bond madness rule you. You are better than that, Dane, and we both know it." My jaw drops at Amell's words. Does he want to die? Can he not feel and see what I do? Danion is seconds away from silencing him in a very permanent way.

This does not seem to deter Amell though, because he continues on as if he has not a single care in the world. "We both serve your mate, and I will not overlook her needs merely because you are too blind to see them. Nor will I apologize for that." I suck in a quick breath at Amell's response. That cannot go over well. He just insulted his king, his very, very furious king.

"Are you implying that you are more qualified to take care of my mate than I am?" Danion now sounds outraged as well as angry. Almost as if he cannot believe the words Amell just uttered. Well, that makes two of us.

"In this instance yes, since you appear unwilling or incapable of noticing that she is in need of rest and solitude over food at this precise moment." Amell refuses to back down.

It seems Amell has a death wish of some kind. The rage that Danion is holding inside is growing so violent that I am becoming fearful for Amell's life. He seems to have little regard for it since he insists on needling Danion. He must know what he is instigating with his words.

Danion does not say anything, he does not need to. I can feel his presence fill up the empty space, and I am nearly blinded by the rainbow of his aura swelling up to consume the room. It is thick ropes through the room now, no longer the transparent threads it was before.

"Danion, think! Stop reacting and think! Flooding this room with your power will accomplish nothing, but could be deadly to your mate. You need to calm yourself!" This comes from Golon. For a brief moment, the colors pulse brighter, and then gradually fade until they are a mere haze around Danion once again.

"Golon, do you agree with Amell?" Danion asks of Golon, but those gray eyes are locked onto me, staring at me so intently it is as if he thinks he could burrow into my mind.

"It does not matter what I think. Perhaps you should ask your mate her opinion and make a decision based off of that," Golon replies.

I can feel the weight of Danion staring at me, but I avert my eyes. First looking at the walls, then studying the furniture in the room, and finally resting on a spot on the ornate rug at my feet. Anything to avoid the angry warrior before me.

"Mate. Mate. Mate! Look at me." His tone is as cold as ice. I am terrified to look up. I know it will only enrage him further, but I am physically unable to raise my head and look up at him. Not with the weight of that rage-filled stare beating down on me.

I want to obey him, I really do. I can feel a part of myself, deep inside urging me to stand my ground and to meet his stare. But that small flicker of independence is masked by a torrent of self-doubt and fear.

I can hear him move and soon I see his feet in my field of vision. I feel his hand under my chin, it is like a burning ember on my skin. I gasp and jerk my head away, trying to escape the pain.

"Can you not bear my touch now, mate?" My flinch away from him is the last straw, his fury explodes out of him. So powerful that I can literally feel the anger crashing against my skin in waves. His voice is pulsing with power. I can feel it beating against my skin. His rage can actually be felt in the air like a living thing.

I know I need to try to calm him, but I do not know how. Everything that I have done since meeting him has done nothing except fuel his wrath. I know I am somehow the source of his anger, but I have no idea what I have done wrong. I am so frozen with fear that I am too frightened to help even myself, let alone him, calm down.

"Or speak? Is this now your decision? You wish to reject me as your mate before we even begin." His voice is scaring me, transforming from loud anger to a quiet and lethal calm.

My stepfather was the same. He was the most dangerous when he got quiet—that is when the real pain would always come. Mustering all my strength, I manage to open my mouth and form words. I have to try; it seems even the other warriors in the room with us are hesitant to intercede this time.

"No, it was not that," I whisper, the words small and brittle sounding.

"Then what was it?" Danion demands.

"Your hand it...it burned me." I force my eyes to rise and meet his but quickly drop them again, unable to hold his gaze. I am so out of my depth here. I wish that I could do what he wants of me.

"What do you mean? How did my hand burn you?" Danion demands an answer, but for that, I have none to give him. His voice and his anger seem to be calming slightly. His rage is not beating against my skin any longer. All I can manage is a small shrug in response to him.

"Danion! You are terrifying her. I will not stand for this. She may be your mate, but she is our queen and the holder of our *praesidium* oath. Look at her chin, you will see the mark. You did burn her." I hear the disgust in Arsenio's voice. "You are calling forth *ignis*, and it is too hot for her tender skin." Now I hear sympathy in his voice.

Danion slowly raises his hand to my chin again, only on the other side this time. He raises it up high and examines the mark that is there.

"*Deim*!" I hear the deep rumble in his voice, and I can tell he is appalled by his actions. But his behavior has been so hot and cold since I arrived, I find little comfort in that fact, "I am sorry, my mate. Here, I will take away the pain." He guides me to a chair and sits me down. Malin walks over and hands Danion a small jar made of a dark gray metal. With a wave of his hand, the top of the pot seems to fold in on itself, and he takes some type of ointment out.

"Now, mate, this will take away the pain as well as remove the mark. Your skin will be flawless once again." He gently rubs the ointment onto my skin, and he is right. Immediately the pain is gone.

The anger seems to have disappeared from him. I have no idea how I am to keep him happy when his mood swings so rapidly. One moment he is filled with rage, the next concern. It is enough to give me a migraine though.

"Thank you, Danion, it feels much better now." I try to muster a small smile for him, but it feels forced. By the look in his eyes, he knows that it is forced. My shoulders droop despondently once more.

"Now that the pain is gone"—again there is a bite to his words—"is it true? Do you wish to retire to your chambers for a while? To not dine with me this hour?"

"Whatever would make you happy, I will do." I hope that this is enough to satisfy him. As I look into his eyes, I see this is not the answer he wanted. Instead of the anger

I expected though I see... disappointment in his eyes. For some strange reason, it seems worse somehow, this disappointment that is so evident in his gaze.

"Dinner, I would like to eat with you." I change my answer, hoping that this is what he wants. I get a blank stare from him. "Or retire to my chambers. I can stay there if that would be better?" Still nothing from him.

I cannot decipher what he wants from me. All I truly want at this moment is to have him happy once more so that I can breathe for one freaking second. Ever since I read my name as a claimed female, I have been on edge. My nerves are fried. I just want some breathing space. His constant disapproval is causing me so much stress, I feel like I am seconds away from collapsing.

"Mate, you are merely saying what you think I want to hear. This is displeasing. I want you to answer me this time, honestly. I will know if you lie again." There is an underlying threat in his words. I am so tired I fail to keep the sarcastic bite out of my reply. If he wants to know what I want, fine, I will tell him.

"Honestly, I am just beyond drained from everything that has happened and would enjoy being able to relax in solitude for just a little while, not even the whole evening. Just a small reprieve would be great. Just enough to give me some time to come to terms with everything that I have learned here today." I take the risk and answer him.

He has not released my chin, so I am still staring straight into his eyes. This close it is impossible not to see the disappointment in his eyes. It pains me to know that I have caused him this sadness. Seeing this prompts me to say, "But only for a bit. I would still like to dine with you later, if you would not mind maybe waiting just a little while?" I can tell by his eyes that this was the right thing to say. Finally.

"Yes, Eleanor, I can wait for you. What are a few hours when I have already waited this long? I will have Kowan escort you to your chambers to rest." With that, he takes my arm and helps me rise. He accompanies me to Kowan, who holds out his arm for me to take while I walk. As I am about to take his arm, Danion warns, "Kowan, tread carefully." I am not sure what that means. "Mate, I will call upon you to dine in two hours' time."

"Thank you, Danion. I look forward to dining with you." As fearful as I am of him I hope to even be able to stomach a little of the food. As Kowan escorts me from the room, I look back and see Danion staring at me. The last thing I see as the doors close are his beautiful gray eyes.

Chapter Five

Danion

As I watch my mate disappear as the door closes, I lose the battle with my bond madness. With a growl, I release the power that is threatening to erupt out of me uncontrolled and give it focus. Amell and Arsenio. The two males who stretched my control so thin while speaking to my mate. In the more civilized part of my brain I knew my behavior was barbaric. But it was not the time for my evolved self to be in control. No, it was time for the warrior to have control and I was running on instinct alone. And in doing so, I rejoiced in the grimaces they both now sport, as my rage-powered energy pummels into them.

"I will make myself abundantly clear, I am your king!" I lash out at them; with every wound my power inflicts I feel the mate bondness peel back layer by layer. Lessening it's hold on me. Granting me control of my thoughts once more. "You will keep your eyes and your thoughts off of my mate or I will separate your heads from your bodies and introduce you to death in a way nature never will. Am I clear?" My energy-laced words pound my aura into them with no reprieve. They need to know they will never have what is mine.

I focus on wrapping my power around their necks harder and harder until the pressure causes blood to seep out. For several, tense moments I hold them here. Their deaths would be easy. Simple. The mate madness, something I never truly understood, is like a breathing thing within me. Whispering me to remove any competition for my mate. Luckily, I have managed to regain enough control that I can ignore my more primitive instincts.

With my eyes locked on them both, I free them from my hold. Once I release them, I feel marginally better.

Amell is the first to speak. "Well, you sure showed us, Your Lord Elite Highness. Now may you allow me to speak freely or do you feel the need to continue showcasing your superiority?" His words are slightly gravelly, strained from the constriction of his throat.

His words, so flippant, but still true combined with the blood seeping from his neck grounds me. I see his wound is already closing and realize I need to get a handle my emotions. I came very close to killing my oldest friend. The mate bond is known to tear at a warrior's sanity, but I never expected it to be like this. I thought I could control it, but it has only been a day, and I am already attacking my warriors with very little provocation.

Seeing the damage I inflicted on Amell, a warrior I have known for well over two thousand years, brings me to my senses. I must be more careful, or next time I might do real damage.

Amell is right. It is beneath me to flaunt my powers to my own men. I am the only one of my people who can harness my very aura and use it as a weapon without needing to pull from nature. This is known to all as I have never lost a battle, thanks in no small part to this ability.

Using this gift to make a point is childish. It is too potent of a power and is one of the reasons I am so rarely challenged for my throne. However, raging jealousy and envy at how Amell can so easily cause my quiet mate to smile while I get nothing but terrified glances is still tearing me apart. It's burning me alive from the inside out. I cannot apologize when it is all I can do to prevent myself from entering into a full rage, where I will have absolutely no control of my power.

"Speak then." My words are short and abrupt.

"You cannot continue the way you are with the girl." Amell has the audacity to reprimand me. As if he is unaware of how close I am to ending him. I forcibly pull back my powers. Calling for strength to keep me here and somewhat sane.

"Again, you wish to lecture me on how I handle my own mate." I can feel the fury inside of me boiling over again. Never before have I been so out of control. All I can say for my actions is that since meeting my mate, I feel like everything I knew about the world is wrong. As if I was looking at the world through only one eye and now I have full vision.

This time it is Arsenio who speaks. "When you burn our pledge holder, yes, we most definitely will. We will most definitely criticize how you handle her." Arsenio speaks with revulsion on his face.

That takes the wind out of my rage. Leaving embers but drawing back the flames. He is right, I burned my queen. My mate. "But how did I burn her? I was not aware of any great amount of *ignis* running through me. I wasn't actively weaving any. My hands should not have harmed her." It is a feeble excuse but I do not wish to voice my shame at bringing physical pain to my precious mate.

"Perhaps the boost you have gotten from her increased your power more than we first suspected and you called much more *ignis* than you thought." This comes from Golon. It is a possibility. "But I suspect what it was is that the way your power manifests itself is different now. It is becoming more a part of you. A union such as this has never been recorded so therefore will bring about many unforeseen complications." Golon's words are quiet, it is obvious he is attempting to dissect all he has heard and seen here today.

A derisive scoff turns our heads to the fire master in our mist. "Impossible, I am a true master of *ignis* and I felt the strength of your weave." He sneers his words, his distaste for all of us in this room more than apparent. "It was nowhere near powerful enough to be an accidental surge. It was a controlled and steady burn. You were angry that she preferred us to you and you branded her for it. You are a disgrace to the Belator name," Arsenio throws back at me.

My voice goes deathly low. "I would tread carefully, Arsenio, you are only in this position to lecture me because I forgave your transgressions in the Great War. I can easily retract my assignment and sentence you back to waste away in the hell I pulled you out of." I back my reprimand with power. "I have no desire to listen to a male who disgraced himself in battle. I will not stand for it, do I make myself clear?"

"Oh, yes, of course." He dares to even roll his eyes. I begin to suspect he truly must have a death wish. "I have just one thing to add." The curl of his lip is anything but apologetic.

"What might that be? I would choose your words carefully, Arsenio." My glare burns hotly into him. "Or they very well may be your last," I growl.

"You do not deserve the gift you have been given. She is a prize beyond measure, one that you have done nothing to deserve. You should be thanking the stars that they blessed you with a mate, and yet I have seen you do nothing to treasure her." With that Arsenio leaves my chambers before I am able to lobby a response.

His words have struck me more than any blow he could have ever landed. Because I fear that they are the truth. I have not treated Eleanor as she should be treated. For the bulk of our brief encounter I locked her in a trance, and although it was unintentional it does not change the fact that I brought it upon her. Then when I finally freed her, I acted like a complete barbarian.

The way she smiled so readily with them, blushed so prettily to Arsenio's flirtations, and bonded so eagerly with Amell, drove me mad. Her actions were so different from how she was with me. Me, her proper mate.

"Amell, you stay, everyone else leave us," I hear Golon say to the rest of my top warriors.

I move over to the window and look out into vast space. Arsenio, while an honorless, reckless imbecile, is right. I have been granted a great gift. I know I was expecting someone with a little more...fire. I fear that I took out my initial disappoint on her.

It is not that I am displeased with her. Her beauty is unparalleled, and her demure countenance is all the better for my protective tendencies. She is my exact match, no other could move me like she can. And the power boost she has awoken in me is further proof of how compatible we are. I suppose I just expected her to be less wary of me.

I resolve to show her no more anger. She is a precious gift, and I will make sure I treat her as such. She will be with me for all eternity, and I want her to smile for me, not Amell. Not Aresenio. Not Malin. Me. I want to look up years from now and see her smiling face looking at me, only me, knowing I caused her happiness. No one else.

"I know that look, Dane. And I know what is bothering you." Golon walks over to join me. He is followed shortly afterward by Amell. "You are upset that she did not come readily to you. You feel that she responded better to Arsenio and Amell."

I do not respond, refusing to shift my gaze from the window I peer out of. Hoping he would go away. I should have known better.

"You should not concern yourself with her reaction to them." Golon words are casual, he moves to sit in the set of gold and cream chairs to my left.

"And what makes you an authority on my feelings toward what my mate does? You possess no bond, you cannot believe the struggle that battles within between the primal instincts and our more rational minds." I look at Golon with an icy stare.

He is trying to make me feel better, but I neither appreciate his effort nor do I wish to hear it. Deep down I fear that my Eleanor prefers the company of other males more than my own and I can't stand it. My skin literally crawls with the desire to enter our chambers, strip her down, and exert my dominance over and over until she cannot bear to even look at another male, let alone smile at them.

"She does not smile at them because she prefers them to you. She smiles because she feels no threat from them. They stir no inner feelings within her. Truly, you should be more worried if she reacted to you with an easy smile." Golon smirks at me. "She is uneasy only because she feels more for you than she feels for the rest of us."

I mull over his words, looking for any sign of falsehood and I cannot sense any. Maybe he speaks the truth; she is so young compared to me and did not know what to expect when she was brought here.

"Amell, your thoughts? I have trusted your knowledge and views for over two thousand years. I would like to know your opinion, since you seem to be one of the males she seems so keen on." I try to keep the bite out of my voice but fail miserably.

"Dane, I agree with Golon on this matter. You affect her more than you realize. Especially your touch—I can sense it when you are close to her." Amell's gaze is direct and unforgiving. "But I do feel that you should be made aware of how the humans seem to view our claiming ceremonies. I believe the majority of her reticence toward you comes from the false propaganda she has been fed." His voice has a tone of censure.

"What is it?" I am curious; I have never given much thought on how the mortal races we protect view us or our treaties. Their opinions matter naught. To protect the mortal races is more than just our solemn oath, I believe it is the key to our very survival.

"When we were on the planet Earth awaiting our queen to be claimed, the mortals seemed to look upon the claiming ceremony as some sort of ritual sacrifice. I overheard many females mention that once a female is claimed no one will ever hear from them again. Once our Eleanor was claimed the shock and terror in the room was evident, and the fact that we have not claimed anyone from Earth in twenty years seemed to truly make the entire room concerned." Amell pauses. He is holding something back.

"Amell, continue. I can tell that you have more that you wish to tell me. Your look is worried. Explain." My voice is tight with controlled anger.

This could explain why my mate was so distressed upon her arrival. Thinking she was to be slaughtered at my throne. The entire journey here worried I would kill her or harm her. The thought disgusts me. How could this be? Earth Nueva knows of the reasons behind us claiming women. Well, not the exact reason, but a reason all the same and it is definitely not for a sacrifice.

"When she was being prepared, one of the handlers intentionally made it sound as if she was to be transported to an...owner." Amell's lip curls in disgust. "None of us interrupted and corrected her, as honor dictates no unmated male speaks to a claimed female before her mate does, but I strongly feel she came here with the understanding that she was to be your slave. This may be why she was so overcome when she failed to address you correctly."

I merely stare at Amell. "She believed herself a slave to me? Handlers know full well that our claimed women are treasured among our people." My anger is growing by the second. This makes no sense. "My queen was intentionally misled by a mere mortal girl! Why?" My words erupt from me, echoing off the walls around me.

The whole purpose of the handlers is to prevent misconceptions such as this, to prepare females about being a mate and to make sure they can say goodbye to any family or loved ones they have. "How did she fall for this? Surely she should know that our claimed women are precious."

"Well, while I was only on the planet for a short amount of time, I believe there is some false propaganda being used by the controlling powers there," Amell states blandly.

"Explain." One word, bitten out with barely leashed violence.

"As a means to keep the women of the planet in line and to obey certain rules, it seems that they have used the claiming as a fear tactic." He speaks baldly now.

"How can we be used to instill fear? What? Are they told that we will come to slaughter them all if they do not follow the rules? We have more important things to do than monitor the behavior of some humans. That is absurd."

But as I say the words, my mind, sorts through the facts and I decipher how they are using this propaganda. They are shrewd and very deceitful, these humans, I will give them that. More than I believed possible. I guess the desire for power was too much for the greedy beings. Sometimes I genuinely despise the mortal races. So full of faults and lacking in honor.

"They use the treaty, do they not? If they are not perfect females, if we claim a woman who proves to be 'unworthy,' they, therefore, break the treaty and are left for dead? Putting the weight of their entire planet on these young souls' shoulders." I spit the last bit out in disgust.

This reminds me why I have always disliked dealing with these very young peoples. Give them another millennium and they will be much wiser in the way of the universe and stop this useless bickering and power grabbing. They will come to realize how inferior they actually are when compared to the cosmos. We all are, even the Gelders are useless against the Powers themselves. My thoughts are interrupted by Amell.

"It is not just the controlling powers of Earth who do this. Once we arrived for the claiming ceremony, Kowan and I took it upon ourselves to observe her family and get a feel for her home life and what she is accustomed to. We have been deceived about her circumstances. What we observed caused great concern, so Kowan performed the weave of past sight and what we saw was an insult to the treaty. More than enough to violate the treaty if this was really a concern for the ambassadors of Earth," Amell says.

"We sent more than enough to provide for her a very comfortable life while she waited for you, but she must never have been given the supplies. She comes from poverty, absolute poverty in fact. Her mother and stepfather are vile people. She was used as little more than a slave there in the hovel she grew up in. The mother spoke to our queen as if she were little more than garbage beneath her feet, threatened Eleanor that she would disgrace Earth if she were ever claimed, along with countless other insults too numerous to name. She did not even live at home anymore, but was living in a small, dangerous apartment in one of the worst areas possible." Even steadfast Amell cannot mask his anger at the insult done to our queen.

Amell's words slam into me. Every additional word pummels me as if I was taking on a debris field in open space. None of this should have happened. I took steps to protect her from the moment I knew of her existence. She was to have a life of luxury. Her people swore she would receive it.

"How did she come from poverty? I gave her people a fortune to bestow upon her to ensure she was provided for until she came of age. I have been given weekly reports on her for her entire life. The Earthlings have LIED TO ME!" Power erupts out of me. My control breaking. Golon leaps aside as the chair he was perched on is violently thrown along with everything else near me.

I have never felt such rage, not even the anger I felt toward Arsenio rivals this. Due to their deception, they have caused my mate to live a life a hardship and pain. My mate. I swore to protect her from the moment I knew she existed.

"Someone must pay for this." Golon looks at me when I utter these words. "Someone will die for this."

"Yes, but try to calm yourself. I will get to the bottom of what happened. You have more important tasks at hand that you cannot perform if you let anger guide you."

"What is more important than taking vengeance on the people who wronged my mate?" I stare at him incredulously. He must be demented to believe I will not right this wrong.

"Ensuring her peace of mind here, bringing her joy, showing her love now. She needs you. You are the only one who can help her." His words shock me out of the rage that is descending upon me.

I realize he is correct. While I despise letting this insult pass, my mate's current needs are more important. I need to start reversing the damage that has been done to my mate before anything else. Nothing is more important. Not even vengeance.

"Fine, but I expect you to come to me soon with an explanation, and for Earth's sake I hope they have a *deim* good reason for the crime they have committed."

With that, I dismiss them from my public chambers. I have a little less than an hour before I get to be in the presence of my sweet Eleanor, and I need to refresh my appearance as well as attempt to force a calmness I do not feel into my body.

Ellie

Kowan doesn't walk me far, just down the corridor a little way. The door to this room is just as ornately carved as the last, with gold seemingly intertwined within the metal. As I watch Kowan press his hand into a panel to the left of the door that I did not even see was there at first, I reach out and smooth just the tips of my fingers over the metal.

It feels warm to the touch, and I can feel the faintest vibration coming from the metal itself. It as if the door itself is alive, as if it is trying to tell me something. Curious, I lean my head closer to get a better view. I tilt my head to see if I can hear anything.

"We are here, Eleanor." I jump back at Kowan's voice so near my ear. My heart pounding, I pretend I was not just trying to listen to a door. "Whenever you wish to enter you need only place your hand where I did, here." He motions to the panel with his left hand while his right reaches over to direct me to look at what he is doing. "Your biometrics have already been added to the security system. Just hold your hand and it will open the door for you." With that the door opens, and I enter a suite no less grand than the king's chambers I just left. I take a tentative step inside and look around the beauty surrounding me.

The rooms are still adorned with gold, but it is more muted than the King's chambers. Not less, per se, but the gold seems more subtle in this room. There are small gems as well used in this room—I think they may be pink diamonds. They grace the walls in a network of extremely fine designs that make the light reflect off of them and filter into the room. The effect is dazzling, almost as if the air itself is shimmering.

Kowan leads me farther into the room, and the size is staggering. The room seems to be fit to accommodate dozens of people, not just me. With a motion of his hand, Kowan guides me past a small sitting area. This area is equipped with one couch that has two chairs sitting in front of it, and a small table between them.

The furniture is so beautiful—it is a deep ivory color with small golden buttons running along the seams. As we pass them on our way to the far corner of the room where another door is located, I run my hand along the couch. I slow down, just a little, so I can enjoy the soft, silky smooth cloth on my hand. They are so plush I imagine sitting on them would be akin to lounging on a cloud.

I file a mental note to sit on these as soon as I possibly can. Once we have reached the far door, Kowan opens it and motions for me to enter before him.

"This is your bedroom and attached you will see a spa for your own personal use only. There are automated options for you to use that provide various treatments. Anything you wish is but a mere word away as we have added a voice command in the universal language since we did not know how familiar you were with our written language." I give him a tentative smile to show my thanks. He is being quite kind but I am a little confused.

"What do you mean treatments?"

He looks at me with surprise. "Why various types of massage, or adding paint to one's skin or nails, different types of skin care. Beauty activities." He says this as if I should know what he is talking about.

"Oh," I say lamely.

Now I feel foolish. I have heard of these things on occasion but never considered them as an option for myself. Before this whole business of being claimed I always thought that the best I could aspire to would be to escape the desperate conditions of the poverty that I grew up surrounded by. People in Area Three would never have the time or money for something so frivolous.

Sitting on the couch in the other room is the most luxurious thing I can imagine, let alone what he is describing. Which is apparently now available for my own personal use. I cannot even begin to process all of this. Everything is changing so drastically, and I have no anchor.

I look around the room in wonder. This is so much more above poverty I cannot grasp it. The furnishings in this room are even grander than the outer sitting area. Luxurious items that provide no practical use. They are meant to provide nothing but comfort. This is a life of leisure that I never before thought possible for myself. I feel a pang of guilt when I think of Marilee and my sisters back on Earth.

They deserve a life like this, not me. They are decent and kind; they should be here surrounded by such ridiculous wealth, not me.

"Kowan, can I ask you something?" I speak quietly. This room is so richly furnished that I feel out of place, even in this fancy dress they gave me. Inside I still feel like the pauper dressed in rags that I was when they met me on my planet.

"Of course, Eleanor." Kowan looks at me expectantly.

"Why did the king choose me? I mean, look at me. How did he even know about me?" I desperately want to know the answer to this question. While I am working on accepting that I am to be his queen. I do not understand how this came to be. When and how did the king learn about me and decide I would be his queen? "What about me could possibly be what he was looking for in a mate?"

"I am afraid that is something only the king will be able to tell you," Kowan says to me apologetically. I feel my face fall in disappointment. "If I could tell you, I would. But it is not my place to have this discussion with you. It is a matter that should only be discussed between mates."

My heart falls, I can read between the lines. Even Kowan does not understand why I would be chosen to be a queen. I just feel that there must be a mistake of some kind.

"Can he be wrong? Maybe he claimed the wrong person?" I whisper. "What if he needs to send me back?"

Terror is racing down my spine—if I were returned I would be shunned on Earth. My return to the planet would be a blatant sign that I was unworthy and that I failed to uphold the treaty. I may even be accused and charged with neglect of female responsibility. If they tried me and found me guilty, they would stone me. Terror turns into panic. No, he can't send me back!

"He did not make a mistake, it is impossible. You are his mate."

"You are sure?" His calm, confident words do seem to help me breathe easier once again. My breaths are only coming in small gasps now instead of feeling like I am on the verge of hyperventilating. Kowan walks to me and grasps both my shoulders firmly in his hands.

"Yes, I am sure. We know our mates upon sight. He would know if he was wrong." He squeezes my shoulders briefly before he drops his hands and takes a step back. "Now, Eleanor, unless you need more of me I will take my leave of you. You need to relax, let your mind come to terms with everything you have experienced in these last two days. Now rest until Danion comes for you." Kowan takes a bow and turns toward the door.

"Kowan..." I trail off. There is no reason to ask my question. It has been made clear that some questions they refuse to answer, instead they delay relaying the answer until their king can provide it. There is no need to ask him anything else. "Thank you for showing me to my room." He gives me one last barely there smile before his face is expressionless once again, and with a nod of his head, he is gone.

I turn slowly back to face the lavish chamber in front of me. I do not know where I can even sit in this room, let alone rest. Everything is so exquisite. I look over at the massive bed. It must be at least three times the size of any bed I have ever slept on. My small bed on Earth is barely large enough to fit me and a pillow. This bed though? This one is larger than the entire apartment that I had on Earth.

I do not know why I, or anyone, would ever need a bed this size. I long to lie down for a little while and try to sort through and process all the information I have been given these last few hours, but I hesitate to touch this piece of art. That is what that bed feels like, something to be admired but not actually used.

And it is not just the bed—this entire room feels more like art than a bedroom. The bed has massive posts on all four corners, so thick across when I put both my hands out I can't wrap them both around the posts. They are decorated with fine details, almost like small floral patterns interspersed throughout the design.

I lean forward to study it closer, they look like jasmine blossoms. How strange, those are my favorite flower. How would they know to design my bed with my favorite flower? If I can gather the courage, I will ask Danion about it.

I run my hands over the posts, they are smooth and cool to the touch. They do not appear to be made of wood. It looks and feels more like a type of marble than anything else.

"What!" I jump back and then study the bed frame again. The color changes from a deep brown to a more yellowish appearance with brown still swirling within it. The longer I stare at the marble, the more it moves. It appears as if it is actually alive. How bizarre.

I step back and shake my head in denial.

Great, just another piece of confusing information I do not want to deal with right now. If I have one more surprise, I am sure to burst. I resign myself to putting this new mystery out of mind until later.

All I need to do now is rest. Everything will make more sense if I can just sleep for a bit. I move closer to the bed and tentatively sit down.

If I had new clothes to wear I would wear those. It feels wrong somehow to be sitting on a bed so stunning, surrounded in all this splendor, wearing clothing that is not mine. I feel like an imposter. This dress feels so smooth and so fine that it is actually uncomfortable against my skin. It is so foreign.

I am not someone who dresses in finery, I am a low Area Three girl who wears coarse rags that chafe my skin. I look around the room in dismay. I am not the girl they think I am. I never thought I could miss my drab clothing, but I do. I crave to have a layer of familiarity to hide behind.

I open my tote and pull out my old clothes and clutch them tightly to my chest. I know I can't wear them again, but having them close still helps me feel comfortable.

I move my hand along the bed and marvel at how soft and elegant the blanket is. It is also gorgeous, just like everything in this room. It is black with delicate patterns of what looks like liquid diamonds woven into it. As I stare at it, it reminds me of the night sky. It is the most beautiful thing I have ever seen.

I look sadly down at the clothes in my hands, such a sharp contrast to this bed. So different from everything in this room, really. I cast a wary stare at the bed. I want to lie back, but it looks too fine for something as mundane as sleeping.

I am so exhausted I decide that if they didn't want me on this bed, they would not have put me in here. Feeling justified I lie back. The bed moves gently underneath me, cocooning me. The bed must be made of some sort of memory device. It seems to be adjusting to my body all on its own.

I meant to only lie back and think about all I have learned before I am to dine with the king, but before I know it I find myself drifting off into an uneasy sleep. My sleep is filled with dreams of myself in front of an enormous congregation where I keep tripping and falling flat on my face while Danion stares at me with utter disgust. I do not belong here.

Chapter Six

Ellie

I wake up with a start. I am unaware as to what woke me up, but I did not intend to go to sleep. I try to shake the images that plagued me while I slept. Laughing faces and a disappointed Danion swirling throughout my mind. A small shiver runs up my spine, and with a final shake of my head I finally sit up and ignore the mocking images of my subconscious.

I have no idea how long I slept; there is no clock that I can see anywhere. I cannot acclimate myself to what time it is since there are no windows in this room. I quickly realize that would have been no help either since we are in space.

Many people on Earth are familiar with space travel, but I am not one of them. No one beneath Area Seven is ever allowed in spacecrafts unless they are claimed.

It is surprisingly normal, nothing like I thought it would be. I had expected it to feel claustrophobic, like being stuck in a small metal box in the emptiness of space. I expected to always be stressing that something terrible will happen and that I would suddenly be sucked into the vast vacuum of space. But this ship is so extensive it does not even feel like it is a spaceship. It feels more like a castle.

As I come to my senses, I hear a faint knock. I train my ear and determine that it is coming from the outer door. I get up and head toward the sound. I look down at my gown, and there are only a few wrinkles in the cloth to show my sleeping in it. It will have to do, but I still run my hands down it self-consciously. My hands fly to my hair as well and attempt to smooth it down.

I pause outside of the door and take a deep breath to attempt to get my bearings before facing Danion again.

"I can do this, I can do this," I murmur to myself. Taking one last deep breath, I brace myself and open the door. Standing outside is none other than the king himself. Not that I expected anyone else—he did say we were to dine with each other.

"Greetings, my Eleanor," the king says with a bow. "May I come in?"

Mutely I step aside and allow him to pass into the room. With a wave of his hand, he indicates for me to join him in the sitting area I admired earlier. I am eager to feel this luxury, but I do wish that I was alone so that I could actually enjoy it.

Danion takes my arm and pulls me down to sit with him on the couch. I try to put some space between us, but he shifts closer to me. So close that our knees touch.

"Eleanor, I wanted to...apologize for my behavior earlier." Danion seems to be a little hesitant for a king, almost as if he is unsure of what he is saying. It is very different from how he behaved before. "I have been acting like a small boy instead of a full grown male. The male I am, one who is capable of guiding you through what I assume is a complicated time in your life, yes?" He pauses and stares at me, making it apparent he is expecting a response from me.

"Yes, this is a complicated time." I avert my eyes from him as I say this. "But, not...that is to say...not that I am not pleased to be your...mate." Recalling his earlier anger when he thought I rejected him, I hurry to make sure he knows I am not displeased with him.

Honestly I am not unhappy that I am to be his, just that I have no idea what is expected of me. In truth, I find myself drawn to him. Almost as if my soul knows his, and it is desperate to get closer to him. It is the uncertainty of all of this, and the worry about my planet that is causing me such distress. Well, his volatile temper is not helping either.

"Are you not? I was worried after my deplorable behavior before that you would be unhappy with me. That you would want to return to your planet. To hear you say that it is not your desire is... pleasing news indeed." Danion pauses at the end, as if searching for words.

He slowly reaches out and places his hand over mine. "But if it is not me, I would request you let me know what it is that is causing you discomfort. It is clear that you are uncomfortable, and I would like to fix this. I want you to be happy here. Happy with me." For the first time since I met him yesterday, Danion seems hesitant. Vulnerable.

I decide to be nothing but honest with him. I see no other way to move forward. I need answers to my questions, and no one seems to be able to answer me other than him.

I always try to be honest when possible. My mother was notorious for lying to cover her indiscretions, and my stepfather just seemed to enjoy lying for no other reason than the pleasure he got from fooling someone with his lie. That was just his deceitful nature. I have never wanted to be anything that even resembles them.

"I suppose the biggest thing that I am worried about is what you expect of me. I have never known what being claimed meant and you seem to have expectations of me that I have no idea about. To be mated to you is completely foreign to me, I don't even know what that means to you. I know what mated means on Earth…" I trail off as I realize what I have said and I feel my cheeks warm up with my blush.

"Oh? And what does mating mean on Earth, *aninare*?" He smiles at me. A very satisfied smile, if I had to put a name to his expression.

"Well…it means… Umm… That is to say…" I trail off in embarrassment. He seems to take pity on me.

With a chuckle and amusement rife in his voice he says, "You are most precious, never doubt that." Then his voice evens out, and he continues. "Yes, mating in itself is the same to us as it is to humans as we are both humanoid, but being a mate does not mean that you are only expected to perform that one physical act. It is so much more." He is smiling at me.

I do not know how to respond. That does not actually answer my question at all. So mating is the same but not the same. As a mate, I am expected to do that, but at the same time, I don't have to do that? In my frustration, my firm control of my attitude slips and I let out the sarcasm my mother always said would be the death of me.

"Oh, well, thank you, you have answered my question completely." Once the words are out, I instantly regret them. I flinch and prepare myself for his anger. But Danion's response surprises me.

He throws his head back and laughs. A full body laugh. I am mesmerized. It is so uniquely male. I feel like he has given me a gift. I get the distinct feeling that he rarely laughs. I just know it is true, his life has not been one of merriment. Watching him so joyous makes me want to ensure he laughs more often.

"Some spirit, I am very pleased. I knew my mate could not be only a meek female." He leans back and smiles at me. I would never have expected my sarcasm to please him so much. But to hear that he thought me "meek" before dampens my mood.

"You are happy with me being rude?" I am compelled to ask. I just can't leave well enough alone.

"It is not the rudeness that I am happy with, it is the strength. There is nothing that Gelders respect more." He reaches out and smooths my hair down, tucking it behind my shoulder. "You speaking out like that shows me that while you may be reserved for now, you have a strong spirit within you."

"Oh." I do not know how to respond. He is going to be disappointed when he learns how wrong he is. If I was strong, I would have stopped my parents' abuse, but I never did. I could never bring myself to ever act against them. I was weak. I struggle to think of something to say but it seems Danion needs no response.

"To answer your question, I feel that I need to go back to the beginning and explain the role of us claiming mortal women. If it is acceptable to you, it would please me to feed you while we talk." The smile that accompanies these words causes a warm feeling deep inside me. Wiping away all my worries. For now. What harm could come of throwing myself into this?

"Then it would please me to have you feed me," I say with a returning smile. His own face seems to burst with joy at my answer. When he is not angry, he really is something special. I cannot explain it, but I am drawn to him. I want to learn everything about him, his past and his future.

He stands and offers me his arm which I gladly accept.

He leads me down several maze-like corridors into a dimly lit room that I can scarcely see the walls of. The only light is around a single table that is placed on the far side of the room. It is set alight by floating balls of fire. They encircle the table, which is set with tableware that I imagine are of exquisite, and lavish, design. They are transparent with no color to them except for some magnificent sparkle they give off. I do not know what they are composed of but I am beginning to see that everything aboard this ship is disgustingly expensive. Royalty has its perks I suppose.

Upon the clear serving dishes, I see a feast. I have no idea what kind of food this is, back on Earth Nueva my family never could afford anything more than the nutritional food squares. Tasteless but they provided you with the needed nutrients to avoid starvation.

Of course, for most of my life, I was given only the weekly squares. How I hated those things. I can still feel the constant hunger pangs I experienced for most of my childhood. Once I was able to work, I made sure that I never had to live on those again. But food is so expensive, so only once in my life have I had real food. If I was lucky I got to enjoy the daily squares, but even those were considered a luxury after living on the weekly sustenance cubes. The daily ones are at least large enough to give the illusion of being full.

But the table in front of me? It is covered in food, from one end to the other. This is a luxury beyond what I have ever experienced. My mouth begins to water at the thought of eating real food.

We are facing a wall that appears to have some sort of artwork on it. It is gorgeous. It is large, taking up the entire far wall. It too has flames that appear to levitate to showcase it.

"This art, is it a stellar cloud?" I ask Danion of the beautiful art of deep swirling purple and red. The flames seem to reflect on the painting itself, allowing the portrait to appear to be moving. It is wonderful.

"You have a fine eye. Yes, this is a depiction of the formation of the Gelder home planetary system. The very birthplace of my people." I can hear the pride in his voice as he looks at this piece.

"History is very important to you then?" I find myself asking, curious about this warrior before me.

For all intents and purposes, I do not know this male. From what I can gather he is much more than the battle-scarred and bloodthirsty warrior that he is made out to be on Earth. It will be nice if we have more to talk about than how much he likes to do battle or wage war.

"Oh yes. History to me holds the answer to the many mysteries that are all around us. To the Gelder race, only pursuits of science are held in higher regard." He looks at me with a smirk. "Well, in an academic sense. We are, after all, a warrior race. So the highest rank is, of course, a warrior, but every warrior has to have their hobbies."

"Really? I knew you were warriors, but I did not know that you valued academia." This is a surprise to me, but one I find very pleasing. History was my passion back on Earth. Maybe I will have some place here after all. Maybe I'll find a way to carve out a little happiness here.

"We are more than just a species at war. We have the most advanced knowledge of science and medicine that we have ever found in the galaxy. No species we have come across is more advanced."

"Which do you prefer? Science or history?" I cannot help but ask. I am finding myself curious about this male.

Now that his anger is gone I can start to feel like we are just two people sharing a meal and getting to know one another. He looks like a man, but I have to remind myself this is a being that has lived for more lifetimes than I can count. Still, his relaxed air allows me to feel comfortable around him.

He seems to enjoy my questions though. He smiles gently at me, and I realize that leading up to now I had never seen him sincerely peaceful. It is a good look for him. It softens his looks. Turning him from an untouchable tribute to masculinity to something a little more human. Ironic as that is.

"You ask a difficult question. This is one I have had to give great consideration. For within one you can design innovation, and the other can divine the very reason for our existence."

"Which is which?"

"That is the question, is it not?" He chuckles at my frown. "Truly I do not mean to jest with you. I am in earnest. There is a great question I have been attempting to answer for well over two thousand years, and for the first time in my existence both science and history are failing me." I hear the bitterness in his voice. Whatever this is it must be difficult indeed if he has been trying to solve it for so many years. "So I would say, whichever one I eventually find the answer in will be my favorite." I can tell he is trying to bring some lightness back into our conversation.

"Well, for me it is history. There was not much science taught in my area level, but I thrived in history." I try to steer the conversation back into familiar waters and away from whatever issue has Danion looking so desolate.

"What do you mean, science is not taught in your area?" Danion's words are hard, his eyes turning angry. It seems I have failed in salvaging this conversation—he now has an even greater frown on his face. The colors that swirl around him, while a second ago they were calm, are beginning to whip around in a growing frenzy.

"Nothing bad, really. It is only that on Earth what type of education you receive depends on your area level. I lived in a bottom tier area, not the lowest, mind you, but below anything that would produce a scientist, so I was not taught it. But history was well covered. Many of my schoolmates also went on to pursue studies of the past." His frown is getting even worse, looking more like a scowl. "Is anything the matter?"

"I am afraid I do not understand what you mean by these areas, and what this has to do with you not being taught science." His words feel forced. Maybe he is merely confused by our customs.

"Well, see, on Earth Nueva you are born into an area. This is not like a location, but more a social class. Yeah, that is a good way of putting it. Social class. And at the top, you have world leaders, the ambassadors and such that interact with our galactic relations.

And at the bottom, you have the servers' class, like people who serve others in some function or another.

"In between these two extremes, there is a whole spectrum. I come from one of the bottom tier areas—you could name us as 'the thinkers.' We are allowed to study literature and history or other similar fields, but it would be several areas above of me before hard science is taught in any real detail."

As I am talking, his scowl seems to be getting blacker. He seems to be in a dark mood now. Like when we were in his chambers when his powers were out of control. I have said something wrong again. Why can't I just do something right for once? We were so happy just moments ago.

"I do not mean I am stupid in the sciences. I could talk with you about them if you wanted me to. I do know a little. They cover the basics of the disciplines." He is probably upset that I will not be able to discuss science with him since his people so value it.

"Tell me, what are these basics that these *fiefling* infers deem acceptable to teach my queen?" I can hear the rage behind his words.

His face is locked in a fierce scowl. I avert my gaze to the table and whisper, "Have I done something wrong?" I am hesitant to speak with him now. Why can I never say more than a handful of words before I anger him?

"No! I. Just. Want. To. Know. What. Basics. The. Humans. Have. Deemed. Acceptable." The words are bitten out. He is furious. He is staring at me with barely banked rage.

"Biology, physics, chemistry...things like that." At my words, he seems to relax minutely.

"I see." His words are tense, and he is silent for a full minute before he speaks again. This time, he sounds almost civil. "But not in great detail? What of genetics do you know?"

"Um, I know that it is the study of our genetic code and things like that, but I never learned very much about it." His scowl is back. "Please, can we discuss something else? Or I can return to my chamber if you..."

"No! You are not leaving!" His voice thunders in the room.

I feel my face whiten in the face of his anger. It seems to have some effect on him, because he closes his eyes and his body stills. He takes a deep breath and the rioting mass of color around him begins to retract, being pulled back into himself.

Then he speaks again, "I mean, no it is fine you do not need to leave. It does not matter if they did not instruct you adequately, I will teach you all you need to know. But let us eat and discuss happier topics." His tone is much less harsh.

"OK. What is a good topic for you?" I am leery of picking a topic as I do not know what will set him off again.

It seems my mate is volatile in his moods. In his anger, the color that surrounds him almost blasts out of his body, and I feel like I'm being suffocated. I prefer to keep him calm as much as possible. But he seems to have little control over his temper, and the littlest thing can set him off.

"First, let us eat." He grabs a bottle and pours a light amber liquid into my glass. "This is a drink that is sweet yet bitter. It is similar to what I believe humans call wine, but this is made from berries only found on a small moon in a star system that is otherwise lifeless. I am sure you will love it." I have never had wine, but I know it is popular among the wealthy and higher area classes. Not wanting to anger him again I decide to omit this fact and I merely smile and take a sip.

"Uh... It is lovely." I say around a cough.

Ugh, it is not. This is disgusting. It burns, and I want nothing more than to spit it out. Not wanting to be rude, I manage to swallow the vile liquid. Why people choose to drink this is beyond me.

"My dearest, you cannot hide your emotions that well. I can tell you hate it." He is so joyful again. It is such a difference—his smile and laughter transform his face. He takes my glass and moves it to the center of the table and hands me another one and fills it with water. "Here, you can have water instead."

"No, I would like to continue with the wine. I just have not had this much. On Earth, I hear it is an acquired taste." I try to bring back some of the laidback smiles we shared earlier with some humor.

"If you so wish." He has a soft smile on his face again. He places my wine back in near my plate, but also keeps the glass of water within arm's reach as well. "Now while you seem to be easily distracted, which I will file away for later use," he says with a grin, "let us get back on topic. What would calm your mind most to know about your fate here? I would not have you so uncomfortable."

The look in his eyes is so earnest, so open I am able to muster up the courage to ask him with complete honesty.

"Well, truthfully, on Earth we don't know why you claim us. I do not know what is expected of me and I fear that without knowing what you want me to do I will fail. If I fail, I am worried it will break the treaty and my entire race will be left to face the Erains alone. I am afraid my people will suffer due to my ignorance." I can hear my voice starting to break, but I cannot help this. This is the moment. I went out on a limb, and I am hoping that he does not get angry and push me off, leaving me to fall into the abyss.

Danion's face makes no noticeable change. But in the colors surrounding him, I can see the shift in his feelings. I don't know what kind of change this has brought, but it is severe. There is a maelstrom of power flowing from him. Again, it seems I am always angering him.

"You fear that I will break the treaty with your planet and let billions of souls perish? Billions of souls die just because you don't do exactly as I say? Why? Have the Gelders given some sort of indication that this is at risk? That this is a punishment we will enforce?" His words do not match his tone. His tone is completely blank as if we were discussing something innocuous, like the weather. But his words seem to fall flat without the anger behind them I can tell he feels. "Do you think me a monster?"

"No, I don't think you are a monster. I don't know enough about you to think you a monster. It is nothing that you have done, but this is what I have been told. That if we are claimed, we must be sure to do whatever is asked of us because if we fail, we are breaking the treaty agreements."

His look seems to be growing darker now. His mask is cracking, and he is failing at hiding his black mood. "Please, do not be angry with me again. I only wanted to be honest with you," I beseech him. "You asked me to be honest. I am always making you angry. I don't know what you want me to do." His anger toward me, when I did nothing but what he asked me to do, fuels my own resentment. I am getting a little tired of always being worried about his reaction. He wants me to speak, but when I do he lashes out.

His face seems shocked. The wild inferno of color swirling around him calms.

"Young one, it is not you that I am angry with. Merely the circumstances. It would be difficult indeed for me to be angry with you." He gives me a small smile. "But I find I must correct you on the falsehoods you believe to be true. But first, I will have you eat. I know you have not had anything since you were brought here." His soft smile melts my growing anger away.

With a wave of his hand, the covers on the serving dishes float away, and my plate levitates to him. He begins to fill my plate with what looks like a bright blue meat of unknown origin—it seems like it once had wings—and a selection of what I believe to be root vegetables.

"Now I will have to start at the beginning since I do not know what lies these humans have been passing off as truth," Danion says the word *humans* as if it is an insult of some kind. "Are you aware that we, the Gelders, have several mortal planets under our protection? Just like what we have with Earth?" He raises an eyebrow to me as he sets the plate down in front of me.

"No, I did not know that. I thought we were the only one."

"No, you are not the only one. Your planet is one of eight that we have under our protection."

"You protect eight different planets?" I question.

"Actually we protect many more planets than that, hundreds in fact, but only eight that are inhabited by purely mortal people." He takes a drink of his wine.

"What do you mean by 'mortal people'? Are you not mortal?" I ask.

"Eat." He is staring at my plate. "Eat, or I will answer no more questions." I reach for the cutlery—it sparkles and looks like diamonds. Based on the extravagance I have seen it would not surprise me that it is indeed made of pure diamonds. It seems my king is fond of shiny things.

I decide to test the meat, and I am glad that I do. It is absolutely delicious. It is juicy and falls apart in my mouth. The taste is like nothing I ever had on Earth, and it is easily ten times better. Danion mouth turns up into a small smile while I try the meat.

"Before I answer your question, I need a promise from you, my Eleanor." His look turns deathly serious. "The information I am about to trust to you is some of the Gelders' most guarded secrets and our most esteemed scientific knowledge. This is not meant for any other people to know. Can I have your word that no one will ever learn of these secrets from your mouth?" He is giving me that look again, the one that feels like he is looking into my soul.

"Yes. I am able to keep a secret. I give you my word that I will not disclose any information you give to me." I respond in a staid manner as well. I see his body begin to relax slightly.

"Good. You must understand in our enemies' hands this knowledge would be ab-solutely catastrophic, and in the hands of the mortal worlds, it would plunge them into war. They are simply too young to handle such knowledge without greed corrupting them." His tone is so forceful, I can tell he wants me to understand what he is saying.

"I understand. If you do not feel comfortable with me knowing you do not have to tell me," I say forlornly. I have never been anything remarkable.

I always knew that my path was meant for nothing extraordinary, but since I arrived here, I have begun to think that I might have more. With him. But I guess I am not meant for that. I am merely a king's mate, not a partner.

"No, sweet Eleanor, you are destined to be my partner in this life. I have been waiting for you for more years than you could ever know. I will trust you with anything and everything that I know. Only then will you be comfortable in my world." His words shock me—it is almost as if he read my mind and knew what concerned me.

"Alright," I say with a shy smile. He is staring at my plate again. That's right, he will only talk as I eat. The food is much better than I first thought when I saw its strange colors so this is no hardship. I have not eaten in over forty-eight hours, and I am just realizing that I am ravenous. I continue sampling the food he placed on my plate while he starts his conversation.

"First, I must start in the very beginning, with the basics. Have you heard of evolution?" He pauses, and since I am chewing, I merely nod.

"Good. Now all life evolves, we can observe this every day. I do not mean species turning into a new species, I am talking about life surviving, of life finding a way to prosper even in the harshest of places. We have traveled all over the galaxy, and we have seen life in all stages. Observed firsthand the diversity of life throughout the cosmos.

"But despite all this variation, there is one thing that all life has in common. One aspect that every single form of life that we have encountered all possess. One thing they all have that allows them to survive tragedies and natural disasters. One thing that is absolutely essential for life to thrive. Can you think of what it might be?" He is looking at me with patience. I want to please him, show him I am capable of being his partner.

What must all life have to survive? I think back to my basics, what we called the sciences in school. I remember that in biology the most basic unit of life is a cell. So I imagine all life at least has something that resembles a cell. I know that we have single cell life and that it can cause diseases on Earth. On Earth, anyone who travels galactically has to be quarantined to ensure that no one brings an alien contagion onto the planet.

I wonder why I did not have to be quarantined when I arrived here. That is...wait. One thing that every life-form must be able to do is have the ability to fight off infection. Or heal itself.

"Is it like an immune system? We all need to be able to heal ourselves or recover from infection?" Danion smiles at me, a smile that lights up his whole face.

"Excellent, young one. It is something that no advanced life-form has ever been without. A way to heal itself. By us searching through all of the galaxy for so many millennia we have determined a...system, if you will, of categorizing life on the mortal scale. And this is all based on the effectiveness of the immune system." He pauses while he takes a bite of his food.

While he is eating, I look back on this. It makes sense. I know that when you get sick on Earth, you develop an immunity to that same illness because your immune system recognizes it. I suppose if one's immune system became so efficient you would basically be impervious to any type of disease. But how this would make you immortal, I do not know.

"Is everything to your liking?" he asks me with a gentle smile.

"Oh yes, everything is so delicious. So much better than sustenance cubes. I have never eaten anything so good." I realize suddenly that I am comfortable, more than I have ever been in my life.

I never would have thought that Danion would make me feel so content, but he does. He makes me feel...cared for. Something that has been severely lacking in my life.

"I enjoy seeing you smile, *aninare*." I was not aware I was, but now that he has mentioned it I realize I have been sitting here smiling like a loon. I feel myself blush deeply. I have no idea how to respond, but luckily he does not seem to need a response.

"So to continue, we have met hundreds of different races of people and then studied them. Through these studious methods, we have come to a very startling conclusion. Would you like to know what it is?"

"Yes." I am transfixed by what he is saying. This is information that is only provided to members of much higher area classes than my own. I feel like I am being gifted with the knowledge of life.

"All species of life that are of a certain intelligence level are all evolving on similar paths biologically. Do you understand why this was such a revelation?" I give his question serious thought.

I would love to be able to tell him the answer like I did last time but I cannot think of why it was so huge.

"I don't know," I say with a shake of my head.

"While in truth there are many reasons, but on top of all of those is the simple fact that they were similar. We are searching the galaxy to understand the variety of life and see that every single one, no matter how different from us, had similarities. They are all working to the same end result: to be impervious to harm. To live longer, to avoid death. This makes sense as a people, but even biologically they are being driven this way. How is it that all life is evolving to do the same thing?"

"I hope you are going to tell me because I don't know," I say this with a smirk. I don't know what has come over me. I have spent the better part of two decades learning to smother my attitude, and two days in the presence of Danion it is starting to emerge again.

"Quite right. I will tell you, my sweet." Danion says this with an indulgent smile. "According to our beliefs, this is the very reason of life, the very purpose of our existence. It is the answer to philosophy's most basic question: What is the meaning of life? It is simply that, to live." With the way he says this, it clicks. Why this is so important. This is world-shattering.

"So you're telling me, that even though species never come into contact with each other, all are evolving to be able to do the same things?" I know enough about hereditary genes to realize that we get our traits from our parents, but this would mean that there is a larger force at play. Driving all living things to the same goal. "This is incredible." I am in awe.

"Quite, it is very incredible."

"What exactly are the traits that they are developing?"

"This is a very complex topic, but to be simplistic, the ability to pass on immunity to disease hereditarily and to slow down the aging process." He says it so calmly as if we are not discussing something that changes the way I look at the world around us.

"Where do the mortal races come into play? You still have not answered the question on what you meant by eight mortal worlds." I realize that while everything has been interesting, he has yet to answer my original question. "Are the Gelders not mortal?" This opens up more questions.

"This information was necessary for you to understand how we classify worlds into mortal, emmortal, and immortal." He is speaking patiently.

"You see, all races of people we have come into contact with can be categorized into one of these three classes. A mortal race is a race that cannot pass immunity down by genetic means. An emmortal race is one that is able to pass immunity down genetically but is not able to regenerate their cells for the purpose of slowing down aging. Additionally, the genetic immunity is generally not one hundred percent effective yet. Either the race suffers from an illness they cannot naturally heal, or they have some diseases they are not immune to yet. Finally, the immortal races can do both. All known diseases have immunities that they are born with, and they have developed a way to slow aging so effectively that the species will never die of old age. They are in truth, immortal. Only death by unnatural means can claim their souls from the living world."

This is so much information I have to take several moments to process it. I stopped eating in the middle of his speech, and I didn't even realize it. My mind is whirling.

"So humans are mortal, and there are seven other mortal races. How many emmortal races are there? How many immortal?" I am so alight with curiosity that I have completely forgotten about being afraid of this dominant warrior across from me.

"There is only one true immortal race that we have ever discovered." He looks at me intently, almost challengingly.

"You mean you? The Gelders? Your race is the only immortal one?" This must mean that they really are the most powerful of all races. No species of people are anywhere near their strength and force. It is intimidating, and a little frightening, to realize that I am literally sitting across from the single most powerful being in existence.

"Yes. We have never come across another species as far along on the path as we are. We are the only true immortals."

Chapter Seven

Ellie

As the dishes are cleared away as if by magic, I reflect on everything I learned over dinner. Once we discussed the classifications of races, we moved onto less intense conversation. Danion seemed very interested in my likes and dislikes. He wanted to know my skills, and what tasks I like to occupy my day with.

He seemed to realize that I needed time to digest everything that he told me earlier. In truth, I am still processing everything and coming to terms with what this all means.

Once the table is cleared away, and I am staring at the now empty marble top, I realize that I do not want my time with Danion to end. We have had such an enjoyable time over dinner, and I wish it could continue.

"Would you like to take a walk with me through the Hall of the Ancients?" He is standing by my chair with his hand outstretched.

"What is the Hall of the Ancients?" I ask while I look at his hand before taking it. The thought of walking hand in hand with him is sending small shivers down my spine. What is wrong with me? I have never reacted to anyone like I do with this warrior.

A peculiar, almost disappointed look comes over his face, and he drops his hand.

"Must you know the destination to wish to spend time with me? My presence is not satisfying enough to warrant you desiring to share it regardless of where we are?" His question baffles me. Throws me entirely off guard.

I merely wanted to know what the hall was, I didn't mean to imply that I didn't want to spend time with him. My feelings are actually the exact opposite, but I know that he is a king and probably has a million duties he is neglecting just to humor me.

"I meant no disrespect. I really only asked because I did not know what the hall was and was curious." My words have no effect on his stony expression. "Also, I don't want you to feel that you have to entertain me. I would be fine on my own if you have duties to attend."

As soon as I say the words I know I said the wrong ones. The pleasant and relaxed look he had on throughout dinner is gone. His face was so warm and full happiness then. Now that happiness is gone. Replaced with a decidedly colder emotion.

Could he really want to spend time with me? Plain old me?

"If you have no other duties though, sire, I would like...that is...I would like it if you wanted to walk with me and we could talk more," I say to him again, in the hopes that I can bring his happy look back. I fail. He has a look of resignation.

"Please, call me Danion. Please, just say my name." His head drops for a moment, his shoulders moving slightly in a half-hearted and dejected shrug. "If you wish to be alone you do not need to feel obligated to spend your time in my presence. I can show you to your room."

His face looks very forlorn. So lost and lonely, a complete contrast to the warm grin he wore while we were dining together. It stirs within me a desire to fix whatever I have said to cause this.

"Truly, I would enjoy learning more about my new role. During dinner, we only got through a minimal amount of my new life. Did you not promise to tell me about my role and function as your queen? I do not think we got to that, do you?" I tease him. I cannot explain it, but I very much would like to see him smile again.

"You are right, I have neglected my duty. Come, I will escort you to my council chambers, and I will correct my failing." I take his hand this time when he offers it. The plan of teasing him backfired.

I blow out a sigh. What did I do this time? And more importantly, how could I fix it?

Danion

As I silently escort my mate through my ship to my private war room, I am lost in a sea of emotions. My only anchor is her hand in mine. For millennia I have known precisely how to move forward regardless of the situation, never doubting my decision once I commit to it. But with my mate? For the first time, I am truly lost. I have no idea how to move forward with her.

I do not know how to make Eleanor desire my presence. Her words say she wants my company, but her actions say otherwise. And her actions are what reveal her heart's true desires. Anyone can give lip service.

The only time she has wanted to come with me is to get more information out of me, or because she is obligated. Dining with her, and providing her with food and conversation was the highlight of my century. *Sheit*, my entire existence. I have never had a more enjoyable evening.

I have never before felt as rewarded as when I made her smile. It was as if I was being given a great gift. Then when she laughed with pleasure over the flavored sweetbread? My eyes couldn't look away from the simple yet pure joy on her face.

I would give everything I have if it meant I got to spend the rest of eternity with her, sharing meals just like that one.

Yet as soon as the meal was done, she was anxious to be rid of me, to be alone.

At least she came to me to learn about her role in my world. That is something. She did seem genuinely interested in the state of the galaxy. Maybe upon more detailed conversations, she will slowly become more receptive to me. We are at different points in our relationship. I have known of her existence and who she is to me for twenty years; she has only known me for two days.

I must have patience.

But it is harder than I thought it would be. Mating is sacred, a binding of our souls. I am ready for our bond to be complete.

I long to be able to feel her emotions as my own, to hear her thoughts within my head, but I force myself to remain patient. Only a mate that is content and has accepted the bond will have the privilege to share these intimacies. I crave this a thousandfold more than physical intimacy with her.

Though her body is perfection itself. The idea of burying myself so deeply within her that we are never parted is a potent drug. But this pales in comparison to the craving I have to feel our souls merging. I have lived long enough to not doubt the truth of souls.

I know many of the young races think they are merely a myth—our own race went through the same phase. I have read of these dark times, when war and death were little more than games to our people, never considering what the actual price they were paying was. Much like the humans and all other mortal races are currently experiencing.

They have not lived long enough to truly experience pain and loss and understand that without a soul, eternity is a vast and horrid punishment.

This is why the Gelders have always considered a mate to be the highest gift a warrior could ever be given. To make the endless years a joy instead of a life sentence.

I remind myself that I have known about her for twenty years and have awaited our joining with anticipation. She is new to this and, as Amell informed me, she had no knowledge of what claiming was. She has absolutely no comprehension of what she is to me. Or what I expect of her or what our people expect of her as well. I must be patient and take joy in what has been gifted to me.

I turn to look at the small woman walking beside me. Her hand feels warm and soft in my own.

"Would you like me to tell you what it means to be a mate? And why you are so precious to me?" She seems shocked by my question. Is it the volume of my voice? Or...?

Does she truly not know how precious she is to me? Even after my actions over dinner, and my words in my public chambers, I can still see the wariness lurking behind her eyes. She is unsure of my intentions. If I want to forge a lasting bond between us, I must make her realize how important she is to me. Let her know that she does not need to fear me.

"I would like that, sire...I mean Danion." She corrects herself with a small, apologetic smile.

The sound of my name on her lips is heaven. Just one word, but powerful enough to send blood rushing to my shaft. I discreetly shift myself to avoid embarrassing her.

"As I told you, the Gelders are the only true immortal race. We became this way many thousands of years ago, before my time. Our lead science officers were tracking our paths in great detail. We have entire libraries completely dedicated to just the study of when we were transitioning. But the time itself is missing. We do not know exactly when, or how, we evolved as we have."

As we approach the doorway to my war room, I keep moving past it. I am enjoying the sensation of her hand in mine too much to stop and risk her pulling away from me. "We had already begun our travels into the stars before this time." The look she is giving me as we walk is rapt. As if she is hanging onto each word, committing every word to memory. It causes a strange sensation in my chest. I have never felt anything like it before.

"You have a nice smile. I wish you smiled more often." Her soft voice drifts around us in the empty corridor.

"Am I smiling?" But as I ask, I realize I am. I have a large, pleased smile on my lips and now that I am aware of it, I am also made aware of how unnatural it feels. How foreign. I have smiled only a handful of times in my life. "I guess I am," I answer my own question. Before we can follow these thoughts to uncomfortable tellings of my past, I steer us back to the topic at hand.

"Looking back, it is incredible that my ancestors set off into unknown areas of open space in such crude spacecraft. Before they were immortal even, they still dedicated their entire lives to exploring space. Many never made it home, but they still managed to send information back. Our knowledge then was minuscule compared to what we know now." I shake my head in bemusement.

"What do you mean?" Her eyes are so open and curious when we talk. I could get lost in them. This is certainly the best way to get to the close bond I crave. Sharing experiences like this, and forming memories together. Merely speaking with her calms the madness that tears at me from the uncompleted bond.

"Well, you may not know this, but some of our ships can travel quite fast. For instance, this one. It is my personal ship and the fastest one my people have ever created. It can reach and maintain a speed that is over three hundred times the speed of light. Do you know what this means?" I want her to understand the distance that we will be traveling to secure the Gelder territories. It is no small distance.

"I think so." She looks at me quizzically.

"For instance, if we were to travel to the edge of our territory, where the Gelder homeworld is located, it will take us, on this ship, roughly five days on the Earthen calendar to arrive. That is because it is many, many light-years away from where we are here. And we can travel at record-breaking speeds."

Eleanor looks dazed, which I understand. We have just recently developed highly advanced propulsion systems that have revolutionized our space travel. We have not shared this new information with any races outside the Gelder though.

"Is that where we are going?" Eleanor asks me.

"We do not travel there often; in fact, we rarely travel to any planet. This ship can sustain itself and the crew for nearly a hundred of your years before needing to stop at a base."

"You live on this ship?" She asks with her blue eyes round with disbelief.

"Yes, almost our entire population lives in ships or star bases. As a warrior race with trillions of lives depending on us, we have to be constantly moving. We have a massive territory to protect."

"Explains the lavish accommodations, I suppose." She mumbles.

"What was that?" I ask her with a smirk.

"Oh nothing, please continue." She is quick to respond. I find myself smiling once more, but with a gentle tug on her hand, I continue with my tale.

"Back when space exploration first began for my race, they traveled in vessels that barely did half the speed of light. It would have taken them hundreds of years to cover the distance between our two planets. And yet they did it. And thanks to their sacrifice, they provided the knowledge that laid out the map of the galaxy for us." I hold my hand in a diagonal line across my body as a sign of respect for those males.

"Without this dedication from my ancestors, we would be thousands of years behind where we are today. We very well may have never been there when your planet needed us."

"Then I am very honored by their sacrifice."

I smile down at her. Even though she is young she holds herself with a dignity I understand well.

She values those around her and lives in the moment as if she does not take happiness for granted. Her life should have been so much easier than what she had to live through. Someone from the Earthen government failed to do their duty. I have to purposefully distance myself from thinking about it, or I am afraid of what I might do. Lower social class indeed. She is worth a hundred of these humans' highest-ranked members. She is a queen for eternal's sake!

"Is everything alright, Danion?" She is pulling at her hand, and I realize that I have tightened my hold while I was in thought. I must be hurting her.

"*Aninare*, I am sorry." I immediately relax my hold. "I apologize, I was merely lost in thought. I sometimes forget my own strength."

There is a tense pause. I am not sure how to get us back onto the more comfortable ground we were sharing a moment ago. Luckily my mate once again surprises me by instigating conversation. It is a simple act, but her speaking with me brings pleasure to my soul. Sating a hunger I have had for twenty years.

"Weren't you about to tell me about my role as a mate?" she asks with a tinge of awkwardness. "I don't think we have got to that point yet."

"You are quite right, but for you to understand your importance, and how special you truly are, you need to know the entire history leading up to it."

I lean in, wanting her to understand I do not stall to avoid telling her, I am merely making sure she has the information needed to truly understand what she represents to our people. "As I mentioned, the lead-up to our transition spanned thousands of years and is well documented. It is because of this documentation that we can trace when our race started down the path to our death." I let this hang in the air. I still cannot believe that the great race of Gelder is dying.

"What!" She lets out a gasp of disbelief. "You just said that you are immortal. How are you dying?"

"I do not mean we as individuals are dying, but as a species. There are more of our warriors falling in battle during this forsaken war than being born every year. We are becoming fewer and fewer, and in a mere few dozen millennia, maybe a few hundred, we will be but nothing but a memory." The idea of our death is like a *scimtar* through my heart.

"How is this happening?" she asks me with force.

I again am astonished by my mate. While others of her race would be short-sighted and may think that a problem that will not occur for thousands of years is not to be worried over, she understands that without immediate proper correction, our population will never recover. Much like her tiger that she gifted to me.

"It has taken centuries of study, but we have discovered that at the very point that we turned truly immortal, we reached a point of no return. When no illness could befall us, and when our bodies reached our prime the aging process stopped. It is at that time that our race began to die. Our genes began to be more and more difficult to reproduce with one another and now..." I trail off. It is hard to speak of my people's fate.

"Now none of you have children?" She tries to finish my sentence. She is close but not quite.

"Did you know, my Eleanor, that Gelders are able to sense their mates? That we can detect our perfect match and these mates are the only beings we can produce children with? They are the ones who complete us, who make us whole.

"Since we underwent the transition we have stopped mating with each other. We are no longer compatible with one another. There are a few mated pairs out there that still produce children, and they are under our most heavy of guard. But the numbers are too few. Our population is shrinking at an alarming rate." I look at Eleanor deeply, willing her to come to her own conclusions about what it means that she is my mate.

"Wait! Are you saying I am to be some sort of breeder for you? That I am to have your babies and replenish your population? Like some sort of baby factory?" Her indignant words echo down the hall.

Ellie

Did I really just say that? Why do I not have a filter around him? I have been narrowly avoiding insulting him since I arrived and now, I basically tell him I don't want his children. Perfect. His hair-trigger anger will surely handle that well. I allowed myself to become comfortable with him, relaxed my mental guards, and let my inner bitch out. Letting my true emotions take control before I was able to think about the response.

I know I should try to say something to make it better, but there is nothing I can think to say. I am in shock. But as I look at Danion, I realize that he is livid. He has a dark scowl on his face.

"Does the thought of carrying my child fill you with disgust?" His words are growled at me.

"Uh..." The ability to speak is still beyond me.

"Well? I asked you a question. Or is there some little human back home whom you wished to fornicate with and bear children?" The last bit is yelled at me. Where did that come from?

As his anger climbs higher, I am finally able to speak again.

"It is not that." This is all I can get out before he is on me again. I cannot imagine what has provoked him so much. He is in a dark rage.

"Then what is it? You are obviously distressed by even the thought of having children with me." With these words, I can see through his anger to the hurt it attempts to conceal.

My thoughtless outburst has wounded him deeply. He wants children, desperately so, and if I trust all he has told me, which I do, I am the only one he is able to have them with. I just acted as if the very idea of having children is revolting. He must be crushed. Me and my stupid mouth. I feel like I just told a child Santa isn't real.

"Truly it's not that. I like kids. I always helped with my little sisters and would love some of my own." His face is guarded, and now I realize that my words probably reinforce that it is him personally I dislike then. Man, I am really screwing up here. Communicating has never been a strength of mine.

"I never really gave thought to children. I am young, barely living on my own, and I do not have any romantic interests with anyone I know...so it just surprised me. That's all. I didn't know you needed me to be some kind of broodmare..." I trail off. I spoke so fast that the words ran together. I try to take a moment and compose my thoughts.

"Broodmare? I do not know what this word is. Define it for me." Danion demands an answer from me. His words are clipped and sharp, his rage once again is boiling beneath the surface just looking for an escape.

"Oh, it is a female horse that breeding farms use. You know they use them to give birth to horses with good bloodlines, specific traits that they want to reproduce, and things...like that." I taper off when I look up at him. His scowl is getting ever blacker with each word I utter.

"I will ask you not to speak of yourself in such a manner ever again. I will not stand for my mate to be disrespected. Even by yourself. You are to be my wife not some faceless incubator for my children. And you will be happy to bear my children! My children, no one else's. Do I make myself clear?" I try to pull my hand from his as he is beginning to clench his fists so tightly that the bones in my hand feel like they are being slowly crushed.

I am beginning to really dislike this habit he has of bruising me just because he can't contain his anger. The more I tug, the tighter he holds my hand. "Now you wish to not experience my touch? Is the thought of some tiny mortal man more appealing?" This last word explodes out of him and I can feel it in my bones.

"Please! No, it is not that, I swear! Please, you are hurting me! Please let my hand go." My hand is released almost as if I burned him.

He flings it away so vehemently that it snaps back and hits the wall behind me. He turns his back on me and strides to an observing window across the room.

He leans against it, his one arm placed over his head with his face pressed up against the window. His back is tense. The colors that fly around him are violently whipping down the hallway. I am so terrified of what he will do next. While I wish I could run away, I know that is not an option. He is king on this ship, to not only his people but mine as well.

No, the only option left to me is to try to assuage his anger toward me. While keeping my distance, I begin to speak quietly.

"Danion, I do not mean to offend you. And I promise, there is no other man I covet. I am not wishing I could be with anyone but you. But with that being said, I don't know you. Can you not imagine that I am struggling with the news you have given me?

"For the last twenty years, I have been nothing but an ordinary girl. Just a plain girl, with no real talents that made me stand out, and now within only two days you have told me I am to be some sort of queen. To a race of people that I know nothing about. Worse than nothing—I am beginning to realize that the little bit that I was taught is false.

"To top all of that off, you are now telling me my purpose is to have your children. Becoming a mother should be my decision, and it is one I have never even given thought to yet. I don't even know you, let alone thought about having children with you. I just need time. Do you understand what I mean?" As I have been talking, I can see that his back is slowly relaxing. I take this to be a good sign.

"Your purpose is so much more than to have children," Danion says quietly as if his words are not meant for me. Then louder, "Yes, I know what you mean." Danion sighs.

"You are shocked because you are confused. But be honest with me on one thing." He turns back to stare back at me unrelentingly. I can see flames in his eyes.

"What would you like to know?" I cannot hold his gaze. I lower my stare to the intricate tiles on the floor.

"Is there or has there ever been someone you thought you might join with? I know what you have said, but I want to know if there is anyone you ever knew that if they asked you, you would have joined with them?" His words have no emotion.

"Afraid of some competition?" I attempt to tease him, but as soon as I say the words, I know it was foolish. His previous actions have proven that he can rise to anger unbelievably quickly. The level of rage that I can sense building in him has me yelling at myself inwardly. I should know he wouldn't find humor in that. I'm beginning to realize that he is very possessive. Bordering on obsessive. Oh, who am I kidding? He flew past that border a long time ago.

"There has never been anyone that I have ever felt a strong emotion for. Never have I been tempted." This is something that I have always been ashamed of. Worried that there might be something wrong with me. While everyone my age was dating men in our area, I never felt anything romantic for anyone. I don't even bond well with women, so I had no desire to attempt a connection with a man. Back on Earth Nueva, I am close with only my sisters and Marilee. "I have worried that there is something wrong with me, honestly. Maybe I am just not meant to have someone." I don't know what causes me to admit this to him.

I feel a hand cup my head. I look up, and he is looking at me with a somber smile on his face.

"There is nothing wrong with you, my *aninare*. It is as it should be. You were made for me, you are my perfect mate. No one else's. An exact match for me. Just me." He smiles. "You would be too good for any human. It is as it should have been."

His words make me feel conflicting emotions in my chest. I am not sure if what he says is true, but it is clear that he thinks it is. And it is clear he feels that humans are inferior to him. How am I to believe he is pleased with me if he looks down upon humans?

I am a human, and he is a legendary warrior. He will grow tired of me when he realizes how inconsequential I am. When he realizes that I am nothing more than what my mother has always said I am. This is too close to my greatest fear, so I decide a change of subject is in order.

"Do you think we can go back to talking now? I enjoy listening to you speak. There is something pleasant about your mouth while it moves." I blush furiously when I realize what I said. I cannot believe I just admitted to that aloud.

"Yes, I enjoy listening to you speak as well." He has a gentle tone in his words. "Would you like to learn more about what you will be to me?" I am transfixed by him.

"OK." It is all I can muster in response.

"So as I was saying, we Gelders are unable to mate with one another for thousands of years. Our youngest child that was born to a marriage of two Gelders is only a few centuries old, but they bonded two thousand years ago, and he is their only child. Recently a few of our mated couples have had children with mates that are from races from the mortal worlds we protect, like your Earth.

"They are all from mortal-only races, and the children do not seem to favor their Gelder heritage much at all. No mates have been found within the emmortal races to date. Many of us have begun to lose hope that we will ever find our mate. I never thought such a gift would be given to me after so many thousands of empty years." With those words, he cradles my face in between his hands. He pulls my head to his chest and places a small, chaste kiss on my forehead. "It brings me much pleasure that you were brought to me, Ellie."

It was the first time he has ever called me by my nickname. It is incredibly intimate sounding on his lips. I raise my head and stare into his eyes. I feel that I am caught within his gaze. I try to pull my eyes away, but Danion holds me tight, his hands moving down to my waist to grasp me gently but firmly in his embrace.

As I stare up into his beautiful gaze, I feel an almost surreal sense of safety and warmth. As if this is where I have always meant to be. This is what I have been missing in my life. I have been searching for something that I didn't even know I was missing. Without conscious thought, I press myself forward until there is no distance between us. We are so close that I can feel his body heat.

His stare now visibly burns. I can see a swirling flame in the depths of his gaze.

"Eleanor, you cannot look at me this way." His words hold a note of pleading.

"What way?"

"Do not tempt me. I intended to give you more time, but if you do not stop this now, I will not be able to contain my hunger."

"Who is asking you to?" For the life of me, I do not know what has come over me. But after a lifetime of feeling unwanted, this warrior looks at me as if I'm the most important person to him. I am overwhelmed with longing for this male.

"Forgive me, I cannot control myself." Then his lips are on mine, and I finally know what all the songs and books described.

I feel like I am burning up—heat is expanding out from my core and settling in my breasts and low abdomen. With more enthusiasm than skill, I kiss him back with abandon. Nothing has ever felt as good as this.

Danion

I once witnessed the birth of a star. I came across it in its very final stages of creation and stopped to watch it come to fruition. One of the rarest events in the entire cosmos, and I was there to witness it. Watching the explosion of primal, raw energy that occurred as that star first began to burn filled me with wonder.

Seeing the star produce its first energy, being there to realize that one day this star might actually provide the heat and light needed for new life to survive, gave me the motivation to keep going forward through the endless years ahead. It renewed my appreciation for the beauty of the universe and how it works. Afterward, I was left with a new sense of gratitude for all that surrounded me. So I left that scene with hope and an invigorated determination to continue down my path as the warrior king.

That feeling is totally eclipsed by the feel of her lips on mine. The taste of her is so sweet, there is nothing in this universe that would tempt me to stop tasting her. The taste of her ignites a fire within me. At first, her lips are unmoving on mine but only for a moment. Suddenly, she seems to come out of her shell, and she is like a wild tigress in my arms. She has such passion in her that it overwhelms my senses. An equal, uncontrollable passion rises within me to match hers.

My hands move from her waist to her back. I run them up and down, around to her sides, and back around to trace along her spine, eliciting a moan of pleasure to fall from her lips, the sound driving my desire to even newer heights.

My hands are beginning to shake, moving faster and faster down her back as they are becoming more animalistic in their quest to touch every inch of her. I can't get enough of the feel of her. Her back feels lean and fit, and yet her skin feels soft, so soft it is like an aphrodisiac to my senses. She is so much softer than my own body. A perfect balance.

My hands fall down to cup her luscious, pert bottom. The globes of her ass are perfect handfuls, and I can't help myself from squeezing them. While the rage of passion is consuming me, somehow I manage to keep my strength in check. I have bruised her too many times. I refuse to let my power get away from me again.

With my grip on her bottom, I lift her body into the air and back her up to the wall for better leverage. The feel of her body against mine is so erotic, I ravage her mouth with new vigor. Her arms come up around me in answering passion. They move erotically to explore every inch of my back and neck.

I need to feel more of her, so I forcefully pull her legs up around my waist. The skirt of her dress has ridden up, so only a small amount of the fabric hangs between her legs. Only the leather of my pants and that thin, practically nonexistent layer of her skirt is keeping us apart. Letting my throbbing shaft nestle against the heat between her thighs.

I trail my mouth down to her neck and realize nothing has ever tasted so decadent. Every lick of her skin is like ambrosia on my tongue. I could become addicted to her taste with no trouble at all. Her skin is the sweetest nectar I have ever had, and I will happily lose myself within her. Letting my lips and tongue caress everywhere, relishing in every gasp and moan she gives. I lead my lips behind her ear and gently suckle.

"Oh! Oh! That feels so good!" Her exclamation draws me to her other ear where I am met with another euphoric gasp. Her legs tighten around my waist, and she begins to ride my shaft through our layers.

I can't stop the triumphant smile that comes over my lips. It seems I have found a way to please my mate. I want to drive her crazy. I want her to feel the same level of erotic abandon as I am feeling. My mouth migrates down to the base of her neck.

Her arms and legs tighten around me. She is pulling me in closer. I thrust my hard cock into the junction of her thighs. My action is met with more moaning. She is perfection, soft and warm in all the right places. I bring my hands up to cup her breasts.

Even with my large hands, her bountiful breasts fill them perfectly. They are not overly large but perfect for me. Such a contrast from her delicate and slight frame. My mouth gravitates to her breasts, and I take her nipple into my mouth through the fabric of her gown.

"Oh!" Her gasp is so loud that it echoes down the corridor. That echo reminds me that we are in a very public place and that we have yet to perform the joining ceremony to bind us. Under different circumstances I would have no issues with the location, knowing that every crewmember on board would know to give us privacy.

I would punish anyone foolish enough to dare to look upon my mate while she is in the throes of passion. But if we were to be discovered in such a situation before the ceremony has been performed, it would bring shame to my mate.

Above all else, I must protect my *aninare*. Even from ourselves. That thought is the only reason I am able to gather the discipline to pull back and let her drop to the ground. I reach behind to unlock her legs from my waist.

"Eleanor, my sweet, delicious Eleanor. We cannot continue. Not until after the ceremony tomorrow evetide," I pant to her. "Then. Then we can finish what we have started here. Then you will be mine."

Her gaze seems clouded. Then a look of confusion comes to her face.

"What? Oh! I am so sorry, I don't know what came over me." She quickly tries to back away and is stopped by the wall. Her face and chest are now bright red with embarrassment. Her reaction surprises me.

"Why would you be sorry, *aninare*? This has been perfection, you and I. I would not wish it to be any other way." I run my hands over her hair. "What we just shared is no cause of shame. As much as I want to finish this with you, we must wait until after tomorrow's joining ceremony."

"What is this ceremony you are talking about?"

Her face looks like she is slowly gathering herself together. I am so pleased that she is so affected by me. Her question takes a moment to sink in as I am basking in the contentment that this realization fills me with. Once it does, I realize that I have failed to explain to her exactly what she is to me and the steps that she will be needing to take in the next few days.

"It is I who needs to apologize. I have again allowed myself not to successfully inform you of what has changed in your life. Correct?" As I talk with her, I cannot stop myself from running my hands over her hair.

"Can you please stop? I cannot focus when you are doing that." She tries to shrug off my hands.

"Is it distracting to you, my *aninare*, to have my hands on you?" I try and fail to keep the satisfaction out of my voice.

"Yes! Now please, stop." Her eyes are full of fire. I love to see this spirit in her. She seems to try to hide it most times, but I love when her passion refuses to be controlled and breaks free. I am tempted to keep needling her to see how much fire she has locked inside but decide against it. With one last tender caress, I lower my hands.

"Very well, though I would much prefer to be touching you," I say and show my hands in the air in front of me.

"What did you ask me earlier? Something about you telling me what I am doing here?" She seems to be trying to change the subject from our passionate exchange. "Yes, I would like to know what I am to expect and what it means to be claimed." She looks at me expectantly.

"Alright, have it your way. As I said, you are my mate, which is very rare. There are so few left who are mates to us. A mate can be thought of as a spouse on your world of Earth." At this, her eyes open wide. "Yes, it is much like a marriage. You could think of it as our version of marriage though a much more permanent kind. Once we are joined in the way of my people, there is no way to dissolve the bond."

I pause to let this sink in. "It is a bond of the souls, not just a verbal and written contract like you are aware of. We know our claimed on sight, and if we are strong enough, we can sense them over great distances." My mind drifts to how it felt when I was aware of her, the sensation of longing that filled my chest. My mood darkens as I think of how the leaders of Earth failed in both protecting my mate and reporting her welfare to me.

"So you are saying, you are going to be my what? My husband?" Her words are high-pitched, frantic even.

"Yes," I answer her cautiously. I am not sure why she seems so distraught over this notion. "You said that there is not another male you prefer. And it is apparent that you are well pleased with me physically, given those lusty moans you were delighting me with only moments ago. Why then are you so upset over the idea of being mine?" I attempt to keep my voice even, but my frustration is coming through.

I call upon my control I honed on the battlefield to remove any trace of my emotions from my words. "You are the one that is my other half, no other would suit me. Be it for that reason I claimed you, as is my right. Do you wish to deny me this? Are you refusing to accept the claim?" I await her answer with trepidation.

I genuinely fear her response. Never before have I felt genuine fear. Not even when my life was in danger on the battlefield have I felt this terror. If she forsakes me, I will not have another. The upcoming centuries will be bleak with no hope.

It is cruel indeed to be given a glimmer of hope only to have it taken away from you. To almost touch the reality of spending eternity with the one soul that is an equal match to my own, only to have it snatched away. But her response calms me slightly.

"No, of course not. I just did not expect to be granted such a position. I never dreamed that I would be a wife to such a strong male." Her words are spoken with almost no tone. But I take her words at face value since I am so relieved to have heard them.

"No, it is I who is the bearer of luck. You will make a fine wife and an even finer queen." I offer my arm to her again in the fashion of humans. "Now tomorrow we must join officially in the ceremony. This will start the process to have our minds, bodies, and souls bound to one another for all eternity..." I trail off at the look she gives me. "Is something amiss?"

"I just wondered how exactly we get, well, bound. How is that even possible? To bind myself mentally and physically to you?" Her face seems forlorn.

I imagine she is afraid that she will not be able to perform this ceremony since she is but a human. Humans often feel threatened when they realize they are so different from us. So unevolved.

"Do not fear, my dear, even as young and simple as your people are we are similar enough to be mated to each other. In all the ways that count you are my equal and more than capable of being bound to me," I assure her.

When this fails to clear the frown from her face, I attempt to pacify her further. "Many primitive people, such as humans, are upset by this notion of binding souls. It is understandable. You incorrectly worry it interferes with your religious beliefs. Reasonably, you think that it undermines all you believe in about how you came to be. However, the steps life takes to evolve into sentient beings, like myself and you, are more similar than they are different. Be this because of divine intervention or because the building blocks of life are all the same is completely your own belief. They truly are not mutually exclusive, both theories complement each other. One speaks about what started us on the path, the other is the study of how the paths diverged from there. Does this make sense to you?"

"Oh, I guess I had not thought about the implications it has to religion before. But I guess it does make sense. So you are saying you believe in God?" Humans are so funny sometimes.

"Me, myself? I believe that a higher power must have laid the groundwork for life in our galaxy, yes. But that is not the belief of all of my people. It is their right to believe whatever they want and it is not my place to judge it, let alone seek to change it. The action to force your beliefs on others, as opposed to accepting them, is a failing of lesser races. My intention was merely to assure you that your belief system is not to be challenged.

They work together." I pause and contemplate her words. "But if this is not what you were referring to, what then was your question?"

"You stated that once joined, we cannot break it. And then you said that we will be bound in mind, body, and soul. I don't understand how that is possible. How do you bind people's souls?" She looks at me with such revulsion my stomach clenches. I now know what she fears.

"I do not mean the divine soul that rests between you and your God if you are a believer. But the Gelders refer to our energy state as our soul. Your spirit. I believe you will be much more comfortable with the idea if I explain the entire ceremony. Will you permit me to do this?" I ask.

"Yes." Her answer seems short, but I am so content in the thought that soon she will be bound to me that I pay it no mind.

"Wonderful." I guide her to a bench near the observing platform nearby. "In the ceremony tomorrow you will begin the joining process that will bind you to me for all eternity.

"First, we will join our minds before a congregation of my highest-ranking warriors and officers. This is done both literally and figuratively. We possess technology that can join minds to one another so that we can feel each other's emotions, hear the other's thoughts, and always sense where the other is. But only mates are able to do this and not suffer mental harm. And the mind is wily—it takes willing participants to result in a successful joining." I know how overwhelming all of this information must be.

There will be time later to explain that only pleased mates possess the necessary trust required to open their minds to one another. I am not worried. I have every intention of making Eleanor very, very happy.

"This is the first part, and the public part, of the joining ceremony. After we publicly perform the mind-sharing ritual, we will move on to the joining of our bodies. Where we will be able to finish what we started here in this hallway." My voice deepens with the memory of her hot, tight body in my arms. Her sweet skin in my mouth. Her sexy gasps and moans filling my ears.

"You mean sex. We will have sex with each other after the ceremony?" Her words again have a lifeless sound to them.

"Does this displease you? I am sure you will be satisfied. The actions we shared in the hallway should be reason enough to suspect that we are quite compatible with one another."

"Yes, I am sure. What we did—" She breaks off as a blush creeps over her skin. "But must we do it right after the ceremony? So soon? We only met yesterday." Her hesitancy is apparent, and it sends shockwaves reverberating throughout my body. She does not wish to share her body with me. Hearing this while my body is still hard and straining to get to hers is particularly challenging to handle.

"Why should we wait? We are to be mated. Joined in every sense of the word, we cannot experience the joys of fulfilled matehood without completing this step. Why would we want to delay this?" Why does she resist me? Does she not want to be my mate despite all that she says?

Her hesitance serves to only drive my desire to claim her even higher. The instinct to claim her, join with her, is as primitive as it is powerful. "Even among mates it often takes several years to have physical joining result in a child. This is a great concern to our people. If we delay the ceremony, who knows how long it will be before your loins will bear fruit." She sits in silence, refusing to meet my eyes.

"Answer me, Eleanor. Why should we wait? To wait on the physical bond is to wait on the entire thing. In my people's ceremonies, you are not truly joined without the fusion of physical bodies on the same night of the ceremony. To forgo this step will compromise the melding of our minds. The only reason we would wait is if you do not wish to be my mate." I stare at her.

She is still sitting mute, staring at her hands clasped together in her lap. I have been fighting the bond madness for twenty years, every day is harder than the last. Now that I have seen her though? That drive to mate with her is almost unbearable. I must have her, and have her soon or I will lose every ounce of control that I possess in my body.

"Eleanor, I need an answer. Do you not wish to mate with me tomorrow?" I wait for her answer.

"I do want to be your mate. It is just that...sex is not something I have experienced before and on Earth...well, on Earth a lot of girls wait a little while before they...well before they do it." She lets out a small chuckle at her own words but I cannot see the joke she thinks she made.

"I do not see the humor in the contemplation of joining with one another." My words are harsh, I know this, but I am beyond frustrated. Everything I have longed for is within my grasp, and she seems to be resistant to letting me claim it.

"I am sorry, the phrasing just made me chuckle. 'Do it,' literally, I am talking about doing it." I stare at her blankly, and her laughter slowly fades away and she lets out a long sigh.

"I do not understand your reference. I personally do not find anything humorous in this situation. There are steep consequences for rejecting any part of the bond. Maybe you do not grasp the severity of what is at stake." I have explained to her that my entire race is on the verge of collapse. That without mates we have no children. Even knowing all of this, she still does not wish to fully meet her duties as a mate. The never-ending drive to claim her pummels into my sanity every moment, I long for the peace only she can bring me. A warrior of my power losing control is dangerous, the longer we delay the greater the risk.

I open my mouth to explain this to her, but she speaks first.

"No, I do understand." Thank the Powers for that. "I'm just nervous about the act itself. Not you or what it represents." My mind settles with this. If her words are once again cold and toneless, I do not notice.

"Ah, of course, you are worried about the pain." My whole body relaxes back into the seats we are in. This is a common fear for women on their first times. If she knew me better, she would realize that I will ensure she finds her pleasure long before I find mine.

"I do apologize for not realizing sooner. Yes, women are often nervous their first time. It has been a very long time since I was with a virgin and I forgot the little fears females have. I give you my solemn oath that I will bring you pleasure before my own. I will hear you scream thrice the level you did in this hallway. By the time I sink within your tight depths, my name will be the only thing you are able to speak." I am lost in a sensual dream, picturing our naked bodies joining together finally.

"Oh. Well, thank you. My little fears are put to rest now." I am so lost in my thoughts I miss the biting sarcasm in her words. "I am sorry, but what else do you expect me to say?" Her voice brings me out of the dream where I am experiencing the magnificent sensation of her tight sheath surrounding me.

"You do not need to say anything." The time dial on the screen shows that it has been several hours since I escorted her from her rooms. It is very late indeed. We only have merely half an Earth day's worth of hours until the ceremony. "Come, I must see you to your room. It is very late, and you have only twelve hours to rest and prepare for the ceremony." I stand and offer my arm to her again.

She stands and takes my arm silently. I really do love her hands on me. I am anxious indeed for her hands to be on my naked flesh tomorrow.

I guide her back to our rooms in comfortable silence. She will have them to herself just this one night. After tomorrow they will be our rooms. If I have my way, this will be the last evening that I sleep without her.

"Here we are, *aninare*. Do you need me to help you locate your gowns or do you wish to go to sleep alone this evening?" I ask her.

"No, I will be fine on my own," she responds quickly. I'm awash with disappointment, if I am being honest I have to admit I was hoping to steal a few more kisses. Perhaps even a few caresses of her soft skin.

Beginning early tomorrow she will have her maid help her prepare for the ceremony. I inform her to expect her there early in the morning.

"But, how am I to know what to do? Do we rehearse it?" She seems nervous.

"I will send for Liam to review what is expected of you. Do not worry, the ceremony is guided by our highest spiritual officer. We merely follow the steps he lays out for us," I assure her. "You will be magnificent, my queen."

"If you are sure..." She trails off and looks unconvinced.

"You will have to trust me, I am quite sure." I smile down at her. She is an enigma. Confident one moment, shy the next. Fierce and full of fire, then quiet and withdrawn. I lean and place a kiss on the crown of her head and then open the door to her outer chamber. "Sleep well, Eleanor."

Chapter Eight

Ellie

I awake slowly. I have never slept so good or so deeply before in my life. It is remarkable what a soft, comfortable surface to sleep on will do. As a child, I slept on the hard, cold stone floor in our family hut. In my apartment, I had a bed, but it was just a sack filled with a thin layer of straw and grass that I grabbed from the forests near where I lived. That lumpy bed was nothing like the luxury of this thick, full cushion that I am now resting on. I take a rare moment to lounge in bed before I start to get ready for work.

Oh, it is all coming back to me now. Dread settles in my stomach.

I am not going to work today, I am going to be married today. With none of my friends or family there to witness it. Just me and a bunch of warriors I hardly know.

I am not ready to be married. At home, women are not allowed to marry until after they have completed ten years of open claiming days. That way we remain eligible. In my head, I had ten years before I was able to even contemplate getting married, so I never gave it much thought. I just barely got out from under the control of my stepfather and was looking forward to discovering who I am on my own.

Now I wake up on my wedding day, all alone. Marilee would have loved this. I can see her squealing now, unbelieving that I have found a man. Except I haven't. Not really. He found me, and after talking with him I suspect he doesn't actually want me. He only wants me due to some obligation to help save his people. Evolution is driving him to mate with me. It actually has nothing to even do with me as a person or a woman.

He doesn't even like humans. His words betray his true feelings. I can tell he thinks very little of my 'primitive' race.

And yet what choice do I have but to marry him? If I anger him or deny him anything, he could seek revenge and decide not to defend my planet or my people. He is a powerful warrior. And he seemed so hurt, betrayed even, when I expressed concern over this happening so fast.

My stepfather and my mother were most dangerous if they felt they had been slighted. They could do the very cruelest of things when their feelings were hurt, striking out where they knew it would hurt the most. And the only power they had over me was physical punishment and withholding food. I shiver to think what Danion, a king, could do when he felt vindictive.

I have to go through with it today. I wish I could have a little more time to come to terms with giving up my virginity and binding myself to him, but really I saw no way out last night. Even a few days would allow me to feel like I have some semblance of control over my own life.

I try to bolster my spirits. It will not be that bad, from what we shared in the hall I am sure I will enjoy it. In truth, I'm looking forward to the sex, it is the irreversible marriage I'm more worried about. To know that I am binding myself to someone I have only known for two days. That I am binding myself to a warrior like Danion, who has lived for thousands of years and fought countless battles, is terrifying.

How am I supposed to please him? I am nothing but a small, weak human. He has made no qualms over his distaste for humans. If it was not for this weird biologic mate thing, I am sure he would never have picked me. His people need children, and I am the only one able to give them to him.

I am actually looking forward to having his children. Especially the physical act of making them. I feel heat rush to my cheeks as I think back over the pleasure I felt in his arms last night. Boys stole a few kisses from me while in school, but I never felt anything like what Danion made me feel. It is not the act itself that makes me worried, it is the timeline. Ever since my birthday, my life has been nothing but a whirlwind of shock after shock.

I couldn't make Danion understand what I meant about it feeling too soon for us to join together. I never expected this, but he has. He has been waiting for me. So of course, he is anxious to have it done.

When he reminded me about the consequences, I remembered what is truly at stake. This marriage is more than just me joining with him, I am serving a higher purpose. After having a night to come to terms with this, I realize that, as far as prices to pay for the safety of my planet, having fantastic sex with a hot warrior king is not so bad. It could be quite a bit worse in the grand scheme of things.

Then I am brought out of my musings by the familiar sound of my inner voice speaking to me. She has been oddly silent since by birthday.

Don't you think you are being unfair? He did assure you that he would protect the world even without you.

Oh, there you are, you have been remarkably quiet these last few days.

I was merely giving you time to work out your own decisions. Now don't avoid the question. Why do you think he would forsake Earth when he said he wouldn't?

I know what he said, but he is a king. A king who has no qualms about showing that he doesn't like humans very much. He has so much power, and I don't know him, let alone trust him. My sisters are on Earth, so is Marilee. The stakes are too high for me to take a risk.

I am interrupted from my inner discussion by a knock on the door.

"Come in." I raise my voice to be heard through the door.

The door opens, and I see a beautiful woman enter. She is tall, graceful, and serene. Her black hair is the same as all of the other Gelders that I have seen. Her eyes are a golden brown and very open and kind. She towers over me as she approaches. She must be at least six feet—everyone here makes me feel so tiny. Her bone structure is elegant, and her mouth appears dainty and full at the same time. I study her and I have never seen someone look more perfect. There is no fault that I can see.

"My lady, I am so pleased to meet you. I am Rowena Halsi, and I will be your maiden of ease. I am so excited to get to know you better." Her words have a lyrical sound to them. She is so happy. That is the only word for it. She carries herself with so much happiness, joy practically bubbles out from her.

"It is nice to meet you as well, Rowena," I respond in kind while my mouth involuntarily stretches into a matching grin. Her joy is infectious and makes me relax marginally.

"Oh, my lady, you are so kind. Our king is lucky indeed."

"Ellie, please. Or Eleanor at least. I am uncomfortable with so much formality." I murmur quietly.

"Ellie then." She has a smile while she talks. "Now, we will get to know one another more later. Right now we must get you ready for the Cerem Fuse today. I have brought your gown, and once we get you dressed, I will summon Liam. King Danion has asked that Liam come and explain what is expected of you in the ceremony. I thought to offer myself up to talk to you instead but truly Liam would be much better suited for it. I will do your hair as he talks and explains everything you need to know. We are a little pressed for time." She is all efficiency and still managing to be so happy. I find myself envious of her inherent goodness.

She has white fabric draped over her arm and leads me to a vanity table along the far wall. Along the side of the table is a type of paneled room divider. Rowena leads me behind it and hangs up the...uh...the dress. If you can call it that.

"Are those strips of fabric supposed to be my dress?" I manage to squeak out. The dress barely covers the private parts.

"Of course this is." She gives me a funny look. "This is the ceremonial gown for the joining."

"I understand it's traditional but isn't there something a little more...modest? Everyone will see...well, everything." I cannot believe this is the dress they expect me to wear. "I don't think I could wear this in my own room let alone in public."

"But, Eleanor, you must wear this. This is the only dress that would be allowed, to refuse the dress is to refuse the joining. If I was to go and tell the king that you refuse to wear the dress he will be most unhappy with me." Rowena's persistent joy seems to have vanished. She appears truly distressed.

"It is not the joining that I don't want, it is the dress itself. It will leave nothing to the imagination." I try to reassure her. "Isn't there some kind of compromise that could be made?" I plead with her.

"I do not know, my lady. Everyone always wears the ceremonial gown that is connected with their mate's rank." She still seems upset, but at least she is not frantic. "To not adhere to the tradition would be an insult to your mate."

"Is there someone who would know? Can I talk with Danion about this?" There must be something that can be done. From what I can see it is closer to lingerie than anything I would call a dress.

"No, not the king. He has much he is doing in preparing for today's ceremony. But...perhaps Liam? He would know better than anyone the intricacies of our ceremonies." She seems to be lost in thought for a moment. "Yes, I will go and bring Liam. I will return to you shortly, my lady." With that, she hurries from the room.

Once she exits the room, I realize that she called me "my lady" again when she was upset with me. It seems that I have a lot of adjusting to do in my new life. I look around the room.

Back on Earth, my apartment was the size of this changing area. Seriously, the bathroom I have here in these chambers is at minimum twice the size of my small studio apartment. It was all I could afford. I was slowly climbing myself out of the hole of poverty that my mother and stepfather were in.

They should not have been so destitute. Both of my parents worked and should have been able to afford certain luxuries, like a roof that didn't leak and a door to ward off the cold. They were just horrendous with finances. I always helped them scrape by. My young sisters were the only the ones that I worked for. I wanted to ensure their lives were better than mine. They are several years younger than me because my mother said that once my father abandoned us after my birth, she took six years to love another.

I mentally scoff at the notion of her loving anybody but herself. From what I have seen, my mother doesn't possess a caring bone in her body. There is no one she truly cares for. Unless they could be of some help to her, she would be more than happy to let a stranger drown right beside her without offering so much as a hand out to help them.

My mother never talks about my father, but I like to think he is nothing like the man she now insists I call Dad. The only good things that came from that marriage were those four girls. Two sets of twins. Jessica and Jaime are the older pair, they will be thirteen this next year. And then Samantha and Savannah are turning ten in a few months.

They would love to have rooms like this; they deserve so much more than to share one bedroom between them. I was working so hard and saving everything I could so that I could bring the girls to come live with me.

I feel my eyes begin to water as I think of them and Marilee, whom I will never see again. I hope my mother is not being too cruel to them. She reserved cruelty for me alone, the twins merely got indifference.

Oh, how I miss them all. Their absence stabs at my heart. No matter how pretty this room is, or the extravagance my soon-to-be husband has, I will never be full again. I will always have a hole where they will be.

My back is to the door, and for that I am grateful, when I hear it open. I wipe my eyes discreetly before I turn around and greet my guests. I imagine that it is Liam and Rowena returning, but when I turn around, I see Arsenio.

"Oh. Arsenio, I wasn't expecting you." I pull my robe a little tighter around myself. I know that it covers me from shoulder to knee, but the material is thin and soft. I am acutely aware of how every curve of my body is highlighted under the silky covering. My memory is full of the comments he made yesterday and the consequences that came from them. How angry Danion got when he believed him to be flirting with me.

"Eleanor, I know. I did not mean to make you uncomfortable, but I just wanted to speak with you in private before the ceremony. If you would permit me?" he asks.

Something about the way he talks puts me on edge. There is an underlying meaning to his words.

"Of course, we can sit down." I awkwardly motion to the couches that Danion and I sat on yesterday. I sit down, and I can sense the tension between us. I know I am the cause. I feel a little uncomfortable, and I know he can feel it.

"Your reception of me is the reason I am here. I wanted to apologize for my behavior yesterday. I meant no disrespect. Truly, it had nothing to do with you and everything to do with past resentment."

"What do you mean?"

"Danion"—he way he says his name is full of disdain—"and I have a wealth of history behind us. Very little of it is good. When I met you and realized how generous the Powers have been to him, it filled me with jealous rage. He does not deserve you, Eleanor. He will never deserve you." He says those last words so passionately.

"Well, um...I am not sure what to say to that." I taper off awkwardly.

"I expect nothing from you, my queen," he says with a fond smile gracing his lips. "I would like you to know that I will always be here. He may be your mate but I hold the position of your *ignis* protection, and I will always be there in any capacity. I know that you will feel isolated here. If you need someone to talk with you may always come to me for an unbiased shoulder. I have no love for your mate so you can be assured to find an ally in me." He says the last bit with a smile.

I sit stunned as the true meaning of his words hit me.

This is no small gift that he is giving me. I understand that he is saying that, if needed, he will stand with me against his king. That I have someone to turn to if I feel isolated. He is giving me a gift so profound it leaves me speechless. In this new place, I am surrounded my people I know nothing about and in a relationship with an extreme power imbalance. I have never known what it is to have unconditional support from someone. Even Marilee often is too focused on her own life as well as being concerned for her own survival. Arsenio though, he has the power and the ability to watch out for me. And he is pledging to do just that.

Relief floods through me. I did not realize until just this moment how isolated I was feeling. How trapped. Having someone I can turn to means the world to me.

"Thank you, Arsenio, that means a lot to me. More than you can ever know." I reach out and clasp his hand briefly in mine.

The door opens, and Liam and Rowena walk through at that precise moment to see us sitting close together with his hand over mine.

"Arsenio, I did not expect to find you here." Liam's eyes are focused on our hands. I pull my hands away and fold them in my lap.

"Maybe one day, Liam, you will finally understand that you will never be able to predict my actions." With those words, he stands up, turns to me and gives me a small bow. "My queen, I bid you good ceremony." And with that, he leaves with not even a glance toward anyone else in the room.

"He just came to speak with me about his behavior yesterday. That's all." It technically isn't a lie. It just isn't the only thing he came to talk about.

"Yes, yes, of course, my lady Eleanor." He looks at me intently. "With that in mind, if that is all he came for, it may be best that you do not mention his visit to the king before the ceremony."

"Why? It was perfectly innocent visit," I ask, affronted. If he is trying to insinuate that I am being unfaithful, he has another thing coming.

"The king has a short temper, which is understandable. There are some very...primitive instincts that he has when it comes to you. Of this, I am sure you are aware. As if that were not enough, the king also has a, let us say, strained relationship with our little firemaster." Liam comes to claim the seat Arsenio vacated.

"If he were to hear that Arsenio came to you, alone, in your chambers while you were not clothed, he would have him removed from his position in your guard. Once the ceremony is over and you take to your throne, you, and you alone, have final say in who fills your *praesidium*. The king will have no power to demote him. Of course, unless you do not wish him to fulfill this role, then, by all means, let us summon Danion." He looks at me with a sly look on his face.

"Of course, I will not be the one responsible for costing him his position, but I don't like secrets. In my experience, they only breed more of them." I am leery of starting our marriage off with deceit. Liam's next words show me that he understands my reticence.

"Yes, I understand how you feel. If it suits you, we will merely not have time to inform the king. You are not to see him until the ceremony, and then you will be too preoccupied. At the very first opportunity I will inform the king on your behalf, informing him that you wished him to know that Arsenio came to make peace. With the proceedings, I expect that to be sometime on the morrow?"

Liam's words slowly begin to relieve my apprehension. We are not hiding anything from him, merely not distracting him with unnecessary details.

Sounds like a rather thin excuse, if you ask me.

Well, no one asked you, did they?

Wow, someone is a little defensive.

Fine! Yes, I am aware I am justifying lying to him, but really he will know soon enough. No harm will come of this. Now shove off!

You are wrong, there is always harm when a lie is involved.

I said be quiet.

"Now, Rowena mentioned that there are some pressing concerns about the dress you are to wear?" Liam continues, ignorant to my inner struggle.

I wonder idly what they would do if they knew their soon-to-be queen talked to herself. The thought brings a small smile to my face. Once I realize Liam is waiting for my response I focus on what it was he asked me.

"Yes, it is very revealing. I am not used to exposing so much of my body. I was hoping that there is some sort of compromise that I can make since I am human and our cultures are obviously a little different?" Liam's face gives him away. He does not wish to make any changes to the dress. "Please, I know Rowena mentioned it is a sign of disrespect to not wear it, but I really would be uncomfortable with so many people looking at me," I beg him with both my words and my eyes.

"My lady Eleanor, I wish that I could change the attire for you. But it is not possible" His words deflate me, but he continues on, "However, I might make it easier to bear by explaining the traditions behind this type of dress?" He looks at me inquiringly.

"Sure." I feel like there are more pressing concerns, but I am fascinated by their culture. It is so different from our own. Additionally, the little that we were taught I am realizing is completely false.

"Let me start with a question—do you know what we use for currency among the Gelders?" he asks.

I search my memory trying to recall the answer only to realize I have no idea.

"No, I don't," I admit. I am not sure where he is going with this, but I can't believe I don't know something so simple.

"Simply put, strength. Power. We have no metals that we hold dear or paper we exchange, it is power alone that we respect. That we crave. The ability to provide protection that is revered. Our entire civilization is ranked on power level.

"It is like a pyramid. Your strength is measured, and then you are ranked in our people's hierarchy. Anything that is placed in the level beneath you is yours. If you can hold it. The less power you wield, the lower you are. The top, our king, is the strongest. There is no bloodline to the throne, we respect the discipline of character. Only through this can you be strong enough to hold the throne.

"The strongest warrior claims it in battle, and will reign as king until someone challenges him, and then wins in a feat of strength. Danion has been our king for over two and a half millennia and I am sure will continue to hold it for two and a half more. There is no one who rivals his power." He takes a slight pause, and I take advantage to ask a question.

"How do you purchase food or limited resources? There must be boundaries of some kind on what the top levels take. How is food rationed appropriately if everyone takes whatever they want?"

"In a way yes, every rank can only take so much, but it is limited by our powers. We do not purchase food as you think. Our powers and knowledge allow for it to be gathered with no great hardship, so all food and necessary nutrition is freely provided to all Gelders regardless of rank. The king is responsible for ensuring the protection of everyone beneath him, so food is always in abundance. If you are higher ranked than someone next to you, it is your duty to ensure they are being well cared for. It is a fairly complicated system to understand in one sitting, but I can always show you the archives which showcase how the system was designed at a later time?"

"Yes, I would like that." Even with everything going on, I admit to being fascinated by this culture.

"Once you are settled into your role, I will show you then." He has a small smile on his face. "But as I was saying, our social classes are determined by power and strength. The physical body is not viewed the same in our culture as what you are used to. A naked body is not thought of as a sexual thing, it is just our natural form. In fact, the body itself has held many important roles in our society. For instance, in formal gatherings the amount of bareskin exposed is a status symbol, if you will. It showcases that you do not need to rely on weapons or shields to defend you and yours. As our king, it is expected that both himself and his wife are the most exposed. If you refuse or add layers, you would be inviting someone to challenge the king for the throne. Do you understand?"

So it is more than just a ploy to see me scantily clad, it has a real social bearing. I admit I am very curious about this class system they have. It seems so foreign, nothing like back on Earth. Though it does resemble the feudalism from ancient times back when we were still Old Earth.

"I understand. But understanding does not make me any more comfortable wearing it in front of strangers. I scarcely want to wear it here in my private chambers." Now that I realize I must wear the dress, that there will be no getting out of it, my panic from before returns.

"But how would you know how you will feel in it if you have not even worn it yet?" His smile is that of an adult humoring a small child. I scoff, no need to be insulting about it. Seems Danion is not the only one who earns the name of an asshole here.

"Fine, I will go put it on." I stand and head to the changing room, while Rowena follows from her silent post. Once we are behind the barrier, I remove my robe.

"You may remove your undergarments that contain your breasts, but you may leave the lower ones on if they make you more comfortable." She says this with a shy smile.

I find I am drawn to Rowena, she is a kind soul. I can tell from her smile that I usually would be bare under the gown, but she knows that it will make me more comfortable and will do no harm to the display of power. I smile and give her my thanks. Such a small act of kindness is what helps me get through the act of disrobing.

Once I have removed my bra, I stand in only my panties. Rowena helps me into the dress and moves me in front of the mirror.

The dress, while revealing, is divine. The material is softer than anything I have ever come into contact with. It is like I am wearing silk and Egyptian cotton combined. Or what I imagine that would feel like, since I have never been in contact with either. The extent I know of fine fabrics is that it is not even for sale in my area, as they are the symbol of wealth thus reserved for higher classes than me.

The top half of the dress is designed with a single band of white fabric that just barely covers my breasts. By some adhesive I cannot see the dress sticks to my breasts, leaving my entire back exposed. The band is the only covering on the top, my entire abdomen is left bare.

Attached is a short white skirt barely long enough to cover the junction of my thighs. There is a translucent overlay that trails down my right side, providing a comforting sense of cover, even though you can see through it. My left side is completely bare from my upper thigh down.

The pieces are connected by a length of corded fabric interwoven down my right side. This cord is the only color in the entire ensemble. The connecting material is a mixture of bold colors. Dark blue, deep red and dark purple all swirling together as if the fabric is a living thing. As I stare, new colors begin to appear—yet another color-changing object. One day someone is going to explain to me what all these materials mean and why they possess a mixture of colors.

The dress feels almost like a swimsuit. While it is very revealing, it does cover everything important. Depending on what you deem important. But rather than feeling embarrassed or exposed when I wear it, I feel a sense of belonging. As if I was meant to be here, in this room, at this very moment. As if this is something I have been working toward all my life and I didn't even know it.

"So, my queen. How does this dress make you feel?" Liam asks me from the other side of the barrier. I ponder his words and try to sort out my feelings about the dress. I must be honest with both him and myself.

"Empowered." It is the only thing that feels right. Something happened to me as I put it on. This dress was meant to be worn by me. I cannot explain it, but I just knew that it was. It even feels warm to me, as if the dress is providing me with the confidence I need. I slowly walk around the barrier and stop in front of Liam.

He stood up some time since I left him and he is now waiting near the divider. Once he sees me, he drops into a heavy bow.

"My queen, you are exquisite. The perfect match to our king." And for the first time since I came on this ship, I feel like it.

Chapter Nine

Ellie

I stand outside the binding hall alone. I know what to expect since my talk with Liam. I am to walk by myself to join Danion at the foot of a stairway. I do not enter the room accompanied by anyone, this solitude is supposed to represent that I alone choose to bind myself to Danion. That I alone take my soul and give it to him for safekeeping. That I alone accept his in return.

It is a lot of pressure for a girl from Area Three to carry.

I was told that I must voluntarily complete each step of the ritual. If I am not committed, it might not work. This part worries me. I feel committed, I want to be committed, but how do I know? I never expected to be entering into something like this. Part of me always felt like I would be eternally a spinster. What do I have to offer anyone?

I am afraid that I will mess up this ceremony. That the part of me that has always felt defective and useless will somehow ruin this.

Liam assures me that that is an impossibility. As long as I want to be bound to him, and I complete the steps without being forced, the binding process will occur. Liam told me that unlike marriage ceremonies on Earth, these are performed in complete silence, with the exception of the officiant speaking the ceremonial words after each step is taken. No music, no chatter from the audience. Complete silence to respect the importance of what is occurring. The binding of two minds that can never be undone.

Liam assures me it will only be a small gathering of the highest ranking members here to witness the ceremony. How my knowing that the most powerful beings in the known universe will all be in one room witnessing me getting married, most likely judging me, is supposed to make me less nervous is beyond me. But that is neither here nor there.

The clock on the wall near the double doors flashes once. I know this signals the doors are about to open. I stand dead middle of the doors and wait. I can feel my pulse in my head I am so nervous.

Before I am fully ready, the doors open. I guess I am ready now then. No more time. No more second-guessing. Time to face the most prominent beings ever to be and then marry a male whose power dwarfs theirs. I take a final moment to ask myself one last time: What am I doing?

With a deep, fortifying breath, I walk barefoot into the room.

As I walk down the aisle, I am amazed at the image before me. Even though Liam described it to me, words cannot express the serenity of this room. While the rest of the rooms I have seen are ostentatious, this room is the opposite. The walls resonate with peaceful thoughts.

At the front of the room is the stairway with seven steps. Each step has two pillars, one on each side with a single goblet on top. Each step is a different color. In ascending order, the steps are brown, blue, red, purple, gold, a combination of the five, and then white. I remember Liam's words as I stare at them:

"Each step symbolizes one of the great lineages. On each step you will pick up your goblet, drink half of its contents, and then you bow and offer the rest to your mate. He will do the same, and you then finish his while he drinks yours. This is a process to bind you within each of the great lineages."

Floating above the steps are two orbs of power. They resemble a pair of stars. Each star has six orbiting balls of color that match the stairs. There is a missing color—white. I think back to what Liam said each color represents:

"The lineages have always been known to possess a distinct essence. For those strong enough you can see them as colors. Therefore, these colors have extreme significance to us. Blue, the line of aniun. Red, the line of ignis. Brown, the line of terra. Gold, the line of vim. Purple, the line of caeli. A combination of them all is the line of simul. And lastly, there is the most powerful of the lineages: the original. From this one line, they all were created. It is also known as the dead lineage. No known Gelder can weave this, it died out thousands of years ago. Lacieu, or as you would know it, ice."

I am walking very slowly down the aisle to where Danion waits. On either side of the walkway are two identical pools of water. They are supposed to be healing waters. The few attending guests are standing atop floating stones that do not touch the water. It is never to be disturbed except by the highest soul officer.

I am now approaching Danion. His attire is also designed to show off skin. He needs no help in defending what is his. He wears nothing on top, exposing his chest and stomach. The intricate markings down his chest and arms are proudly on display. His pants are two strips of white cloth tied together with wide laces down the sides. Most of his thighs are exposed. I notice the laces themselves are a matching color to the connecting band I wear down my side.

I reach my soon-to-be husband and feel my shoulders drop slightly in relief. I managed to not embarrass either myself or Danion on the walk down the aisle. Now he can guide me through the rest of the ceremony. As I finish my stride I let out a faint sigh I did not realize I was holding.

When I am abreast with him, I place my hands how Liam instructed. I wrap my hand under his and reach around to grab the top of his forearm, and his hands mirror mine. We stand facing each other, arms entwined.

I hear the officiant begin to speak, but I am unable to hear anything that he says. I am lost in Danion's gaze. His expression is so...triumphant. So pleased. So primal. I cannot help but feel a little pride that I am the one causing his happiness. I don't know why he is pleased to be stuck with me. But for now, I am just glad to be the source of his pleasure.

Before I know it, we are ascending the steps. Each step I do as I was told—I grab the goblet on my side, drink, hand it over to him, drink again, place it on the pedestal again, return to our stance, and then repeat. As we get higher and higher up the steps, everything begins to blur together. I am so aware of Danion's hand on me that I soon forget where I am, and the significance of what we are doing.

I let him lead me through steps, and we stand at attention while the officiant speaks again. The next thing I know, Danion has guided us to the base of the steps again where all of the goblets now stand together.

A little distractedly, I wonder how they got there. But I am quickly diverted by Danion's hands. They are ensconced in flame. Before my eyes, he is sending fire around the goblets. As they melt the liquid metal runs down little divots on the stands that I did not see before.

The metal seems to pool together into a little reservoir and then slowly starts to shrink. Liam did not explain this part, and I am not sure what the purpose is. I look over at Danion with a question on my lips. Right as I open my mouth, he makes a quick movement with his hand.

That's right, I am not allowed to talk until we are alone. I watch patiently as the metal is soon no longer in the bowl, it has all disappeared.

Danion opens a small container under the bowl revealing two crowns and two rings. He has created rings from the joining goblets we used. I can't help but feel that this is a very romantic gesture. It makes me feel a little less like an actress playing the role and more like a woman marrying a man she loves.

Love? Where did that come from? You have only known him two days.

I know, but there is something about him. Something intoxicating. When I am with him, he is the only thing I can see.

Because he is dangerous.

No, is not that. His danger is appealing. Sexy.

Yes, his rage and bruising embrace are very sexy. You're an idiot.

Oh, shut up. I don't know why I talk to you.

Because I am you?

I mentally shake myself and focus on the ceremony again. Purposefully shutting out my inner voice. Danion places one of the crowns on my head and then stands back and looks at me. I take that as my cue to lay his crown on his head. I take the remaining crown and hold it up to him. He is going to have to bend down if he wants me to place this on his head. He obliges me and lowers his head, which I then fit the crown around.

I look over at the rings. I did not know that Gelders also observed the tradition of wearing a wedding ring, but I am pleased. The small touches of familiarity go miles further in putting me at ease than the two-hour discussion with Liam.

As I watch, Danion picks up the rings, keeps one, and then holds the other out to me. He extends his left hand and indicates I should as well. I understand what he wants us to do. At the same time, he guides the ring onto my finger, and I guide his ring onto his.

With that, he takes my left hand, entwines it with his, and leads me from the room in complete silence.

I suppose there are worse weddings.

Danion

I almost do not believe this good fortune could be mine. Finally, I have her. My gaze moves lovingly over the delicate features that grace her face. Eleanor, my bound mate. It actually came to pass. Finally, she is mine after twenty years of waiting. And within moments I will join our bodies in the final step of the ceremony. Lust fills me. I am beyond ready to consummate this joining.

It has been two decades since I have had a sexual appetite of any kind. A bonded male desires no one other than his mate, and only since meeting her has sexual urges begun to surface again.

Ever since our encounter yestereve, I have anticipated this very moment most ardently. It is not every day that a warrior gets to conquer their most esteemed adversary. I came, and I conquered. She is mine for all eternity. From this night forward she will be my mate, my wife, my everything, my entire world.

Now that I have seen her, tasted her, I am quite ready to mark her as mine. I want to hear her screaming my name. The desire to pleasure one's mate is one of the most instinctive drives a Gelder has. Only when we are bound entirely to one another will I know peace at last.

I guide her into our chambers. She believes them to be hers, but in reality, they are the chambers we will share. For her peace of mind, I designed them for her comfort.

Every item was chosen carefully, debated about countless times. I poured over the reports I had of her—what her hobbies were, her favorite things, her color preferences. I even had the flower she seemed to favor added into the décor. I glance at her to see if she is pleased with the surroundings.

But as I lead her to the bedroom, the only expression visible on her face is apprehension. She is literally shaking, and I know it is not from the cold.

"Do you need any time to prepare?" I ask her. "All you need do is tell me what you require, and I will provide it for you. I want you to be comfortable, anticipating our joining, not fearing it."

"I am not afraid per se. And, no, I don't need time to prepare. I am as prepared as I can expect to be, given the circumstances." She blushes and ducks her head. "I mean, you are my husband, I know we need to finish." She bites her lip and averts her gaze. "Oh, that came out wrong. I am messing this up, I knew I would. I didn't mean I think of this as a chore that I need to finish, just that it is something that needs to be finished." She seems to be becoming more flustered by the moment.

I place my arm around her shoulders. "Shh, everything is fine. Calm yourself, all is well. Here, come sit with me." I speak to her in quiet, soft tones. I guide her over the bed, and we both sit on the edge.

"Now, there is nothing additional we need to do to complete this bond, outside of the joining of our bodies and each finding our individual pleasure. I have no other expectations and neither should you. We are learning about one another and this first time will be about discovering what we like and do not like. Nothing you do will displease me, nothing ever could."

I hope this will help her. I am anxious indeed to have this claiming done so that our minds are one and I will be able to stop having to guess what she is thinking. I crave to hear her thoughts as my own, but I will not let that allow me to ignore her feelings.

As I stare at her, I can see the thoughts whirling in her mind. The worry, the questions, and the disbelief of what I have said. She is overthinking this and adding too much unnecessary stress.

"I know, but—"

I cut her off with a kiss. I think the time of the spoken word is over; it is now time for the physical words our bodies will make when they unite into one.

Ellie

The second I feel his lips on me my mind goes blank, just like in the hallway. The heat inside is exploding from my center. I cannot seem to control my limbs as they circle his head to pull him closer.

Danion's arms come up around me, and he pulls me to him. Our bodies are pressed to one another's, and our arms are fighting to feel as much of the other as we can. I open my mouth wide, trying to take in more of him. He is exquisite. Everything but what is inside this room falls away, and I can recall nothing while we kiss. If someone asked me what my name was, I would have to ask them, "What is a name?"

All I know is a profound pleasure that sinks inside of me and permeates through every inch of me.

How long we kissed for I do not know, but I find myself being pushed back by Danion until my head is cushioned on the pillows. He holds himself over me, his eyes staring at me so hard it is as if they are penetrating my very soul. He slowly fans my hair around my head on the pillow. A small tentative smile graces his lips, and his eyes are warm with tenderness. He leans and places a soft kiss to my lips.

He raises his head, and the small smile slowly shifts into a devilish smirk. His hands leave my head, sliding down my body to caress my breasts through the strap of fabric they call a dress, and I can't help but moan at the exquisite feeling.

I writhe beneath him, trying to place more of my breasts in those glorious hands. He happily obliges. His hands grip the material and peel it off of my breasts.

"Eleanor, in all my years I have never seen anything more perfect. These mounds, they are perfection. They were designed for me. My hands, my mouth."

With those words, his lips trail down to my chest and I am lost in a haze of sensation. I don't know what sounds I make, only that they are loud and rapturous. I am gasping for air; the room feels so warm I can't catch my breath.

Danion slowly slides the fabric down farther, removing the minuscule skirt easily. Before I know it I am wearing only my panties. I have a brief moment to be embarrassed about my plain white, cotton briefs before he dives back to feast on my breasts.

"Danion, oh Danion!" I scream. I never knew anything could feel this good. "Yes, please!" I don't know what I am begging for, all I know is that I need it. Desperately. Fortunately, Danion can read my body like a book, and his fingers find their way under the waistband of my panties. Giving me what I so desperately need when I myself didn't know.

His fingers move through my folds and leave a fire raging in their wake. Never before have I ever felt something like this. If sex always feels like this, I can't understand how anything ever gets done. I never want to leave this bed again.

"That's it, *aninare*, build for me. We both must reach the ultimate pleasure in each other's arms. Build. I need you to build." His words are frantic, sounding almost desperate. I am not sure what he means, but I think I have found the ultimate pleasure. I can't imagine it can get any better than what I am feeling.

Danion's fingers soon begin a steady rhythm at the top of my slit, and I realize how wrong I was. This feels so good it is almost painful. Suddenly I hear a ripping sound; Danion has ripped my panties with his free hand. I am now naked, and he roughly grips my upper thigh in his other hand and spreads me wide before him.

I always felt that this would be exceedingly difficult for me to do. I have always been a little shy, but the look of stark appreciation in his eyes makes everything better. I feel no embarrassment. I can tell that Danion is as much in this moment as I am.

Soon I can feel a persistent ache deep inside. It pulls from my very center, almost like a little buzz that slowly gets stronger and stronger.

"Danion? Danion, something is happening. I don't know what it is, but I think I might die from it." I hear the note of fear in my voice, but I can't contain it. I am frightened. I have no idea what is happening. I can't control what is going on, but I think I may explode.

Danion laughs, laughs! How can he think this is funny?

"Yes, *aninare*, yes! Go with it, give it to me. I want it. I need it. Give. Me. It." Each word is accompanied by a harder and faster stroke, and soon I am falling to pieces. My entire body tenses up in supreme pleasure, and I wrap my arms around him tight. I see flashing lights behind my eyes as wave after wave of pure bliss crashes over me. For one brief, perfect moment everything is right in my world.

I slowly start to come down, but before I am fully relaxed Danion is pushing my legs even farther apart and moving between them.

"Yes, I have thought of little else, my *aninare*, and I am afraid this may hurt. But only for this one time." I don't know why he thinks it will hurt; I have never felt better. But as he lines up and enters me in one hard, long thrust, I realize how wrong I was.

"Ow!" I scream out. Danion does not move.

"I know it hurts, it is unavoidable." His hand comes back to rub me where everything felt so good as he starts to slowly rock back and forth. "Tell me, does this feel good? Tell me, I need to know."

"It is...pleasant." It is the best word I can use. The pain is fading, but it still is nowhere near as good as what he did before.

"You wound me." Danion looks down at me and smirks. "Pleasant? I need to do a hell of a lot better than *pleasant*." He begins to rub faster and adds a rotation to his hips. "I like it when all you can do is moan." His thrusts become sharper, more forceful.

"Oh! Oh, right like that. Don't stop," I mumble to him. It feels fantastic.

"I wish I could hold off longer, but I am sorry. I must. Have. You. Harder." His thrusts pick up in speed and begin to lose the fluidity, his body now rocking in sporadic bursts. And with a guttural roar, he is spent within me.

Danion collapses and rolls onto his back by my side. He gently pulls me into his arms, and we curl around each other. For minutes, hours, maybe days we pant intertwined with one another. I have lost all sense of time.

"Are we bound now?" I ask.

"We are as bound as we ever could be," he answers after a brief pause. "Now close your eyes, you should get some sleep before I take you again." He kisses the top of my head and then wraps his arms tight around me.

I love his gentle caresses. I received very little in the way of tender touches throughout my life and I find I could easily become addicted to these.

"Go to sleep, my precious *aninare*." I feel my eyes grow heavy and I start to drift off to sleep.

Chapter Ten

Ellie

I wake up slowly, enjoying a few extra minutes beneath the covers. Something I rarely have experienced in my life. Actually, I've never had a morning to sleep in. Or covers that actually keep the cold out. Thinking back on my time on Earth, I suddenly realize how dismal my life was. And I never did anything about it. I have always just accepted whatever was given to me and never looked for more. I never held resentment or unhappiness over my lot in life. It is just the way of the world. I was dealt my hand, and I would play it as best as I could.

But something feels different now. Something has changed inside of me. Whether the ceremony or the fabulous sex afterward is the cause, I don't know. Maybe it is Danion himself. He seems to be this untouchable force, an undefeated warrior, but I have seen him be gentle. I have experienced his desire, and now I want to be someone worthy of being his queen.

You know him for three days, and now you are changing everything about yourself to match him? Typical.

You can shove it. Why am I cursed with you?

Well, I am you, so you are cursing yourself. But maybe you should check with that big, strong, orgasm-giving man and see if he wants a woman who talks with herself. Albeit silently. Might be one more thing to change for him.

I am not changing because of him. I just...I just want a chance to be me. Whoever that is, and I think he might be the one who will finally let me figure out just who I really am.

Why? Do you think he respects you? You're a human, and you heard him, humans are tiny and weak.

Why do I even talk to you anymore! I should have shut you up years ago. Sane people don't talk with themselves.

Classic evasion, so typical.

Ugh! OK, yes, I think he respects me. Or at least he could. The real me, the one I have never even met before. I always lock her up. Maybe he could like me. Maybe even love...

"Eleanor!" I am interrupted from my internal argument by a bellow from the anteroom. The door to the bedroom explodes open, and a very angry Danion is in the doorway. I jerk up and grab the sheet to cover my naked chest. "What in the Powers' name were you thinking?" he yells at me.

"What do you mean?" I question him. My mind is blank; I can't think of a reason he would be so angry with me.

"Why am I just learning now that that *infer* came to see you before our joining? In this room, our private bedchambers? Before you were dressed in my gown. How could you entertain that *berat* and not tell me a word of it!" With those last words, he takes a beautiful vase on the vanity and sends it sailing violently across the room. In shock I watch as the vase explodes against the wall, leaving a pile of jagged shards on the floor.

With this, I catapult out of bed. However, it seems there is something out to prevent me from making a graceful exit from the bed. The sheet is still tucked under the mattress, refusing to come with me. My foot is wrapped in the material, and I trip, falling to the floor at his feet. Naked.

"He has no right to be anywhere near you unless he is performing his duty of protecting you. For no other reason! None! If he were not the strongest warrior gifted in *ignis*, he would never have been recalled from his banishment." Danion continues to rant above me while I try to untangle my legs enough to stand up. "That is a mistake I intend to correct. He proved himself without honor before, and he has done so again. For the last time." He begins to pace, talking to himself more than me.

"He resented banishment? I was too easy on him last time. This time I will give a true punishment. If he wants something to resent, I will give him something to resent. Death is too lenient for that sneaking, blasted...!" Danion stops abruptly as he turns on his heel and heads out of the room. Fearful of what this means I jump up and run to follow him.

"Danion! Wait!" I chase after him. I am clad in nothing but air, but I am so concerned with what Danion plans to do I barely notice my naked self. Danion keeps walking, refusing to stop at my plea. I grab his arm and attempt to pull him to me. He pivots so quickly, I once again go careening for the floor. If not for his warrior reflexes I would have hit the ground once more.

"Eleanor, release me. You would not like to witness what I am about to do." His words are nothing more than a growl.

"No, you cannot. He is my protector, not yours, and I don't want him harmed," I plead with him.

His eyes go from light gray to jet black so quickly I almost let him go from shock. His face is as hard as granite. Anger is pulsing off of him, and I mentally prepare myself. Refusing to back down. Not this time.

"No, he *was* your protector. No more. He will not hold the honor of *ignis* when he covets what is mine." His last word is imbued with so much power that it is slithering up and down my spine.

Yesterday, I would cower before him. Yesterday, I would leave Arsenio to face his wrath. Yesterday, I was weak. Today, I stand tall in defiance to him. Today, I will not allow someone else to fight my battles. Today, I am strong.

"No. I may be ignorant of a lot of things, but this is not one of them. As your joined mate, I am queen. As queen, I control my *praesidium* and every member on it. Not you. You cannot remove him without my permission, and I do not grant it." My words are the epitome of calm. I deliver each word with precision. I stand a little taller with each syllable.

"You would choose this male over me?" His words are incredulous.

"That is not what I am doing. I am defending an innocent man. I am refusing to let you punish a man who did no more than apologize to me." Technically he did say he would betray the king, but only upon my defense, so I don't feel it is strictly necessary to mention that right now.

"You think you defend an innocent man? You do not. He is no warrior, no man of honor. He fell from grace over a century ago when he betrayed his race. Only because no one is stronger in his lineage did I permit him to fill your *praesidium*. That is a mistake I intend to correct. Right now." He once again turns.

"No!" I scream. "You will not. He is my guard, and he is under my control. He has done nothing wrong."

"He lusts after what is MINE! He is no gentle human who needs your protection. He is a Gelder warrior of the Elite class. He knew the risks in seeking you out. He must face the consequences."

He is being beyond stubborn. I now wish I had listened to Liam's first plan about not informing Danion about this at all. I can't make him see reason.

"Danion, you are angry over nothing. I am your mate; we shared something amazing last night. Something beautiful, at least it was to me. We are one. Does it really matter if

Arsenio came to apologize? Isn't that enough? I am right here with you, aren't I enough?" My voice is unintentionally small on my final words. Hesitant, when I want them to be powerful.

"It is not enough!" Danion roars, ripping my heart apart. I am not enough, and I never will be. "It will never be enough until he is punished. Do you think a little physical pleasure would make me forgive his betrayal?" His forceful words shake the room, but they are nothing compared to how they shake me. I can feel his words reverberate into my very soul, leaving painful holes where I thought he would be.

With his words, I realize how foolish I have been. I thought marriage and some sex was enough to make him care for me. How could I be so stupid? He is a warrior. A king. They do not care for small, weak humans. I am no partner to him. His actions speak louder than his useless words over dinner.

He is not in love with me, not like I am with him. He claimed me as his mate only because biology forced us together. It wasn't fate or destiny. I am nothing special to him, just the one female who can carry his children.

For the first time in my life, instead of feeling acceptance over yet another disappointment, I feel anger. Righteous anger that I take and embrace wholeheartedly. Anger is preferable to the terrible grief that is threatening to crush me.

"That's right! Why would I ever think that I could speak to someone without your permission? I should have had him removed from the room to protect him from your anger because you would never trust your so-called *mate*." I put as much disdain as I can into that word. "Your so-called partner!" I scream this, lashing out as the anger consumes me. I turn and grab the nearest thing to me, a pitcher of water on the table in the sitting area, and I throw it with all my might.

"I have lived in the shadows my whole life but not anymore! I will not just stand idly by and observe my life happening. I am done with you. You can get the hell out of my room, or you can damn well banish me too." With those words I turn and return to my bedroom, slamming the door as hard as I can. Only then do I realize that I had that entire argument in the nude. I'm so angry I can't muster any energy to care.

Later that day I'm dressed in what I am told is Gelder casual wear. The pants are a loose design, but tight at the hips and ankles. The top is nothing more than one long strip of fabric that winds around my chest forming an X before looping around my stomach. It covers me decently enough, leaving only a small amount of flesh exposed between the two. I step into a pair of slippers, a deep maroon color to match the clothes, and leave my chambers.

After the explosive fight this morning I find I am craving exercise to help me sort my feelings. On Earth, I would walk to my riverbank, the very one where I carved my gift to Danion. Here I have no such haven, but I hope to find one. I am determined to find one. A ship this blasted big has to have a quiet corner for me to claim as my own. As I enter the hallway, I see that Amell and Malin are standing on each side of the door.

"Am I a prisoner then?" I challenge.

"Of course not. We guard against those who would enter, not exit," Amell answers.

"Is there any way I could be left alone? I desire some privacy to be with my thoughts."

"We cannot leave you unattended, but we can walk separate from you. You will not even know we are here." These words come from Malin this time. I sigh but decide against arguing. I give them a brief nod of acceptance and begin my walk.

I set off with no exact destination in mind. I merely want to lose myself in my thoughts. I need to think about what this fight means for our relationship. Do we even have a relationship? I let out a forlorn moan. I can't escape a relationship with him. For better or for worse we are bound, we are mated.

I may not be Gelder, but I can tell that the ceremony was more than just a public showing. I am different today, more assertive, more...just more. I am who I always have been but held inside. I refuse to knuckle under tyranny of any kind for one more second. It's as if something last night raised a blindfold I didn't know I was wearing. I am not useless, or worthless, or any one of the many hurtful accusations my mother hurled at me.

I may not know why she hates me, but I finally realize it isn't something I did. The fault is on her, and I have no desire to fix it anymore. The young girl who desired her mother's approval is long gone. It is something she must correct, not me. This morning I thought Danion was the cause of my newfound and surprising self-worth, but that cannot be so. After his heartless words I don't care if I never see the asshole again.

I don't care what I thought I felt earlier, I do not love him. I could never love someone like him. So selfish and arrogant. With no concern for me or my desires.

144 E.M. JAYE

If the ceremony is supposed to bind us in mind maybe this ceremony allowed me to borrow some of Danion's strength, just as he gained power from me. Maybe this new power allowed me to overcome a lifetime's worth of feeling inadequate.

I know I can be more, and I have now been given a chance to find out exactly who I am. I am going to treasure that chance. I would have been happier if I was able to take that chance with Danion by my side, helping to guide me and support me, but I do not need him. After a lifetime of solitude I can function just fine on my own. Just fine.

Danion

"How many of those *starskies* have you had?" A most unwelcome voice intrudes upon my attempt to forget the abyss my life just became.

"Go away, Golon. I desire solitude." I raise my glass again. Of course, Golon doesn't listen and takes a seat across from me. Stinking *infer* that he is.

"Why would you want solitude when your mate of one day is here, wandering the ship alone?"

I refuse to answer him. While I know it is pointless, I hope Golon will leave if I don't acknowledge his presence. I hear him settle more comfortably in my lounge and brace myself for the coming lecture. Why I put up with his insubordination is a mystery. I am a king, he my subject. I should put a stop to his antics. However, I know I won't. A king who refuses to listen to council is a dead king.

"Could this drinking binge, something you have never done in all the years I have known you, be connected to why Ellie is wandering the halls, dampening the spirits of anyone who sees her woeful eyes?" I was right, he isn't going anywhere. *Sheit*. His intimate use of her shortened name causes anger to rise in me. Not that I can do anything about it; my mate doesn't even want me.

"It does not concern you, cousin." I pour myself another glass, but as I raise it up, I stare into its shining, golden depths. I recall Eleanor's glowing body and her last words as she stormed away from me. With a curse, I fling the glass across the room and enjoy the sound of it shattering.

"Cousin Dane. Share with me your burden. Let me help shoulder this pain." With those words, I realize I am witnessing one of Golon's rare moments where he drops his playful façade.

Where he is nothing but absolutely, stone-cold serious. I gaze at him, and I realize he is indeed sincere. It is times like this that I remember why he is my second in command. He is unflinchingly loyal and dedicated to our people and me.

"We have had a...disagreement." He merely waits for me to continue. Not rushing me or offering useless platitudes. "Before we were joined yesterday Arsenio went to Eleanor. He was found in her chambers, alone. Had his hands on her while she wore nothing but a robe. And she did not tell me any of this. She. Did. Not. Tell. Me." As I think about Arsenio and his desire for my mate I feel rage building again. "She chooses him over me. Refusing to see him face any punishment for his actions. Defends him to me, banishes me and rejoices in his presence." The table between us bursts into flame, and the air around us begins to swirl. It takes several moments for me to bring my power under control.

"Danion, she is your mate. She did not choose him over you." Golon speaks slowly, carefully. "Did it occur to you that she is right? As her guard, he is allowed to speak to her."

Did I say he was loyal? I was wrong. "You dare too much this time. Leave now before I banish you in his place."

"Now Dane, listen to me. Eleanor has not accepted the bond yet. This is straining your control. Not only control over your power but control over your emotions. Until she has accepted it, you have to be aware that your feelings are amplified. Making it difficult to see reason—"

I cut him off, I care not for his platitudes. "I said go." With that, I release the tight hold of control on my power and thrust him out the door. That blasted rat needs to realize I am king for a Star-loving reason. If I want him gone, I can make him be gone.

His words stay with me where his body doesn't though. The words echoing in my head are much harder to banish.

Could it be true? Does she not accept the bond?

Of course, she doesn't accept it. Three days. That is how long she has been here. In an unfamiliar place surrounded by warriors she doesn't know.

I reprimand myself for acting so rashly. In my haste to bond with my mate, I failed to give her what she most needed. What she most needed and failed to ask for: time. She should not have needed to ask. As her mate, I should have known she needed more than a couple of days to come to terms with me. One of which she spent locked in a trance. That I caused.

I recall her hesitancy to join in a new light. As desperate as I was for her I pushed and now face a mate who desires another. She must resent me. And she has reason to—I have not been a worthy mate.

Worse still, I resent Arsenio and his bond with my mate. No matter what they say, she is choosing him over me. Maybe not physically but she is still taking his side against me. Choosing to defend him, respect him, show affection... With a bellow, I lose all contron over my power.

With nothing left to hold it back, I channel all my raw power into the room. Matter blasts around the space, and as the dust settles, I see that every physical item in the room has exploded. They simply disintegrate, even the chiar I was sitting on. I am left sitting on the floor.

I look around at the now barren room, shocked. Well, that is new.

Ellie

I look out into that vastness of space through the viewing glass on the solar deck. This deck has become my new haven. It replaced my riverbank back on Earth. I come here every day and lock myself away while cursing big, vain, and too powerful for their own good kings.

He has not spoken to me since the day after our wedding. I refuse to call it by their stupid name. Everything about my new life is stupid. I seem to be in perpetual anger since Danion has refused to speak to me. I now am at the point where I do not wish to speak to him either. He would have to come crawling, begging on his knees for me to talk with him.

He is a liar and a barbarian. His words of devotion from our first meeting have been destroyed. I hate him!

Truly? You think you hate him?

Not you again. Go away.

We have been through this. I can't go anywhere, I am you.

Whatever. I'm not talking to you.

Again, that's a hard sell since I am you. Me talking is you talking.

Ugh, I really do hate you.

Does the male you love know you have such self-hatred problems?

I don't love anyone.

On the contrary, you do.

No! I don't love him. I don't even like him. I barely know him.

You know his character. You know his heart. Love has no timeline. You feel even more drawn to him since he left. That is why you are so angry he has not come to talk with you.

I don't love him!

I am interrupted from my argument by a knock on the door.

"Come in." I look up as Arsenio enters. I feel a sharp pang of disappointment. I was hoping he was someone else. Someone with gray eyes and a ferocious temper.

"Oh my queen, your face betrays your emotions too easily. You will need to learn to mask your inner thoughts better than that. It pains me to see you so upset. Especially when I am the cause. Had I known that my actions would bring such pain to you both I would not have sought you out that day," he says with a grimace.

"Don't feel bad, this was inevitable. When a warrior like him marries so far beneath himself, he is bound to regret it."

"He has not—"

"Arsenio, stop," I interrupt him. "Tell me your reason for being here. Let us not discuss him."

"I am here to ask you to speak with him." I stare at him with no words. I cannot come up with any response. He hates Danion. I am in this current state due to him assuring me he was on my side. Now he wants me to talk to him. His betrayal runs deep. "I can tell you are confused and I assure you I have not had a change of heart. I still take your side on all things, but I can tell this disagreement has made you unhappy as well. This is not something I can stand idly by and not try to fix."

"Thank you for your concern, but it is not necessary. I refuse to apologize to him, and he is too arrogant to make the first step. I refuse to be just another pretty thing for him."

"He has pardoned me, let me know that he will not be removing me from your *praesidium*. He would not have done this without you asking it of him. This speaks of how highly he values you. For no one else would he allow such a crime to go unpunished." I scoff at his words; it is apparently a crime to talk to me. "Don't shake your head, I performed a great offense to the ways of my people. I am unmated." He says this with a forlorn, hungry look upon his face. "And I sought you out, in your chamber while you were alone and unclothed. That alone is a crime worthy of banishment. The fact that I touched you? It is punishable by death. It is one of our highest crimes, to touch another's mate before they are bound."

"Why are you defending him?" I question him.

"To be honest, I was forced by the rest of this *praesidium*. As it is my fault you are so desolate, they decided it is my duty to help bridge this gap."

"Well, thank you for your concern. But while I cannot explain what caused this change in me, I refuse to just sit by as a spectator in my life anymore. I will not apologize, I will not make the first step," I say with finality. "I did nothing wrong."

"I am not asking you to, just be receptive if he comes to you."

"I doubt he will," I say sadly. But the look he levels at me causes me to say, "But I will be open to him if he does." Even though I know he won't.

Chapter Eleven

Ellie

"Eleanor?" I hear the familiar voice through the door, but I refuse to open it. "Eleanor, I know you are in there."

I sink lower into the tub and ignore the persistent voice outside. My promise to Arsenio rings in my ears, but I can't bring myself to speak with him just yet.

"Don't you think we need to discuss this? Eleanor, we cannot just ignore each other indefinitely."

Through the door, I can just make out the sound of a sigh. "Alright, enjoy your bath. We will speak later."

Yes, later. I will go find him later and try to speak with him. Just not now.

"My queen?" I look over from my book and see Malin standing at the foot of the lounge I am sitting on.

"Hi, Malin. Come on in." I gesture for him to enter as I mark the page I am on and set the book aside. "What can I do for you?"

"I wanted to see how you have been. It has been almost a week since..." Malin's voice tapers off. I know what he is referring to though.

Since Danion reached out to me and like a coward, I avoided him. After I refused to speak with him, and later actively hid from him for the rest of the day, Danion could be heard ranting for hours.

He has been in a horribly tempestuous mood since. Easily angered and continually snapping at everyone around him. I have been wondering if someone would be coming to me soon trying to convince me to reconcile with him.

"I am fine," I answer flatly.

"I am not here to convince you to speak with my king, Eleanor," Malin assures me, "only to see how you are doing."

His words do little to calm me, only make me feel more guilty than I already do. Here is a warrior who is being subjected to rants and rages from his king, which are caused by his queen, and he comes to check on how said queen doing.

"I am alright, Malin, thank you for your concern," I mumble, while steadfastly studying the hard leather cover of the book in my hands.

"What are you reading?" Malin asks me, his hand reaching for the book.

"It is an accounting of Gelder history that Golon gave me. I am trying to learn a little bit more about your world. It helps keep my mind distracted." I have said too much. I rush on hoping to gloss over my telling admission. "I really like this room, though I do miss my river back home."

Try as I might, I could not disguise the wistful tone present in my words. I miss my river so much, not only would I walk along it, but I would wade in and even completely submerge myself in the deeper areas. With nothing but cool, crisp water around me, I felt revived. Rejuvenated even. It was the one place I felt truly at peace.

"Did you like to swim?" Malin asks me, a contemplative look on his face.

"Oh, yes. Yes, I love to swim. Do you enjoy it, Malin?"

"As water is my power, I find that there is little else that I enjoy more."

I give him a small smile, and we enjoy a pleasant day reminiscing about all the best places that we have swum. Malin has a considerable amount more stories than I do.

I really wish I had somewhere to swim here, a place to lose myself in the tranquility of water.

"Eleanor, would you walk with me?" I freeze as the voice over my shoulder approaches.

How did he sneak up on me? I have been so careful to avoid areas that he frequents. After Malin and I discussed our love of water a week ago, I have felt even more unsettled. Craving the peace that only water can give me.

"Eleanor?" His large, warm hand falls onto my shoulder sending delicious shivers down my body. How a single hand can elicit such a feeling, I have no idea.

Unnerved by the sensation his touch evokes, I step out from under his hand. "Did you need something?" My voice sounds shrill and harsh.

I see Danion's expression harden, cold distance wiping out the hopeful smile it had a moment ago. I wish I could take back my words, but I am fighting a battle within myself. The strong woman beating back the subservient girl I always have been.

If I give in to Danion, would I revert back to that weak little girl? It is too much to risk, better to maintain distance, at least for a little bit longer.

"No, nothing. I just wanted to escort you to the new addition that was built a few days ago."

Without touching me, he shepherds me across the ship in complete silence. He hardly even glances at me, just stares resolutely ahead of himself.

Finally, we come to a gold-encrusted door, and with a wave of his hand, he indicates for me to enter first. With an uncertain glance in his direction, I put my hand on the door and open it.

All the breath leaves me, and my eyes stare not comprehending what I am seeing.

"How?" I am speechless. So touched by what I see before me. "Did you do this for me?" I whisper in awe, but my question garners no response. I turn to Danion, only to see he has left.

I pivot and gaze at the beautiful pool in front of me in disbelief. It is perfect. There are rocks and artificial flora all around to make it feel like an oasis. The edge of the pool by the vegetation has a stream of water flowing through them. The current looks strong enough to gently move me along. I could float on my back and imagine I am back on my riverbank. It is precisely what I have been craving.

I stare out the door in confusion. Why would he do this for me?

Amell and I are walking the hallways like we enjoy doing when he is on guard duty. Usually, I either sit in my observation deck alone so that I don't have to face the repercussions of my actions or swim in my beautiful pool. The pool given to me by my mate whom I have yet to thank for it. But I am not ready, and the guilt from that is almost too much for me to bear.

But with Amell, I can relax and enjoy our time together.

Just like when I arrived here, Amell provides me with companionship that feels comfortable and safe.

"Are you enjoying your pool?" His words pull me out of my own thoughts.

"Yes, it is wonderful. Malin, Arsenio, and I swim together almost every day," I answer him.

Something in my words seems to interest him. "Really? And how do those two get along?"

"Malin and Arsenio? Oh fine, but they do not speak much to each other. I get the sense that Arsenio is not well-liked."

"You would be correct in that regard."

I have to hold myself back from questioning him further. No one seems willing to discuss what Arsenio did that has left him with so much animosity toward him.

Amell is silent, if he is aware of my curiosity he ignores it and we continue to walk side by side.

"Have you told Danion how much you appreciate his gift?" Amell's words shock me. He has never brought up Danion before.

I don't know how to answer him, so I say nothing. Just keep walking.

"Eleanor, he deserves to know. I understand your reticence with him, but you are being unfair to you both. It has been close to a month since you have come here."

I know he is right, but the concerns I have run far deeper than a mere argument with Danion. Until I can sort through all the emotions that have been surfacing, I cannot face my mate. It is all I can do to get up every morning.

Each day is harder than the last. It is as if emotions and feelings that were locked away all my life are emerging, insisting that I deal with them now all at once. I can recall each painful memory with crystal clarity as if I am reliving the hell of my childhood all over again.

I can't share this with Amell. We have grown close, but that is the problem. He is too close, I don't want him to know what happened to me. I long to share this burden though. I fear I am going to be crushed under the weight of my own pain soon, and there is no one I can turn to.

"Hiding again, I see." A chuckle from behind startles me.

"Etan, oh it is you." I put a hand over my chest, trying to calm the rapid beating of my heart. "You scared me."

"Did I? What a shame," he says with mirth evident in his eyes. "What are you doing, peeking around corners?"

I flush, embarrassed to be caught. "I wasn't."

"Really? What would you call tiptoeing down this entire hall? Exercising your toes?"

"Etan! No, I—" I break off. I am not going to get out of this. "Fine, you caught me. I am trying to avoid Danion. I heard he wanted to dine together again."

"Yes, yes he did. That was three hours ago. Are you afraid he has been searching this whole time?" Etan asks me knowingly.

"No, it is not that." I stop when I can feel the tears rise. "This is so hard, Etan. So much harder than you can know."

Like a switch, the humor in Etan's gaze disappears as if it was never there. Replaced with somber intensity.

"How about we go and discuss it then?" He holds out his arm for me, and tentatively, I take it.

Silently, Etan guides me through the ship heading toward the docking bays. Once we enter a large hangar filled with ships, he keeps walking until we are in a small room off to the side that is furnished with comfortable chairs and a cabinet full of supplies.

"Now, no one should be coming anywhere near this part of the ship. Tell me, what is troubling you so greatly? What causes these tears? I can sense a great struggle within you. It has stolen all the joy out of your life."

That causes me to chuckle without humor. "As if there was any to steal," I mumble.

He ignores my self-deprecating joke and continues to stare at me. I am desperate to share my story, and unlike Amell, I do not feel as close to Etan. Or perhaps we are close in a different way. I feel compelled to open up to him, I know he would be able to handle my past and not pass judgment. His eyes are nothing but sincere, giving me the confidence to confide in him.

"Have I told you about my mother?" I ask him, knowing full well that I haven't.

"No, but I did meet her. Vile woman, if you ask me."

His words shock me, but I keep going. "Yes, she is. My whole life she has told me how worthless I am. How much of a burden I am. How no one would ever want me. And I did nothing, I just took whatever she threw at me."

I pause to look at Etan, expecting to see agreement or judgment on his face. But I see nothing of that. Just calm expectancy—he is simply waiting for me to continue. I release a breath I didn't realize I was holding. This is what I needed. An unbiased ear to just listen.

"I don't want to be weak like that anymore, and I don't want to hate my mother anymore either. It is exhausting. Really, I just don't want to be me anymore. Everything I am feeling is too much. I am being bombarded with all the emotions I suppressed throughout my whole life, and I am afraid." I stop myself, unable to go on as the words begin to quiver. Tears are filling my eyes.

"You do not want to be weak anymore. You are afraid that if you let Danion in, you will let him treat you as your mother did. That is understandable. You do not need to be ashamed of your emotions, Ellie."

With those calm, simple words, Etan gives voice to my inner fears. I feel relief. I was so worried that he would not understand, or more worrisome, that he would not agree with my position.

"I have such anger inside me. Until I learn to deal with that I am not sure how I can bridge the gap that has grown between Danion and me."

"I don't think you can." Etan's words shock me. Is he telling me I need to let Danion go? My rejection of that idea is fierce and tells me quite a bit about my feelings toward my mate. "We need to work through your anger first. I can do that with you."

"Really?" I ask him breathlessly. My heart is beating so fast that I am afraid my chest will get bruised from the inside out. I am desperate for relief from the anger and pain.

"Yes, together we will go over everything that hurts you. Every memory, every scar, and we will heal you. One moment at a time."

Tears fill my eyes, but this time they are not tears of pain, but tears of gratitude. I take his hand in mine, and I thank him.

Then, I do something that I never thought I would do. I bare my soul to someone and let them see the pain. If it were anyone else, I would be ashamed of the weakness that I am exposing. The pathetic girl that I do not wish to ever see again is brought to light.

I realize this is why I do not want to share this with Danion. I know that he respects strength. If he knew how weak I really was, he would shun me. Cast me aside and hope to never see me again.

"Well, in my earliest memory, I am about three years old, and I am hungry. So very, very profoundly hungry..."

One week later

"That was a great session, Eleanor." I wipe the tears from my eyes as Etan and I stand up.

Over the past week, we have met and spent countless hours working through my past. Handling each abusive moment independently. Slowly, Etan has helped me focus on the moments of happiness in my childhood, rather than the pain.

The birth of my sisters.

Marilee.

My riverbank.

Today we have been focusing on my mother, and how she is a woman drowning in her own misery. If I let her make me miserable, I am no better than her.

"Thank you, Etan, for everything. I never thought that after one week I could feel so much better. So much more settled."

"It might have only been a week, but we have spent more hours in this room than out of it. You have made remarkable progress."

"It is all thanks to you. You have shown me how to focus on the bigger picture and let go of the smaller pieces that bring me pain. I can never repay you for your kindness," I tell him with a smile.

I reach over to hug him, but he stiffens. That's right. As a mated female, hugging another male is frowned upon. I imagine if Danion and I were on better terms, Etan would be a little more comfortable with it.

I take his hand in between both of mine instead, squeezing it warmly.

"There is one thing you could do for me, Ellie."

"What? I would do anything."

"Danion has asked you to start dining with him in the evenings. Please accept his invitation."

"Etan..." I whisper. I am still hesitant to face Danion, but I know I can't avoid him forever. Our bond is not going anywhere. He has been trying to mend our relationship, and I have been everything I possibly could to damage it even more.

"Eleanor, you are ready. You do not have to accept him or even speak to him. But you need to start being around him. Just share your meals with him." He asks of me.

"I will think about it," I promise him, but I have no idea what I am going to do with Danion. Am I ready?

Chapter Twelve

Danion

Eleanor is swimming again. She loves to swim, and over this past month, she has swam often, her and Malin getting in and enjoying the water for hours. She never asks me to join her. Though why should she? I put in this pool when I was told she liked to swim and missed her river back on Earth. I was hoping this would bring her pleasure. That this would show her I would like to try to make amends.

It was an obviously failed attempt to bridge the gap growing between us. I do not know what to do to close this divide. I caused this coldness, but I have no idea how to make it up to her. While she has begun to take her meals with me again, it is only because I have forced her. In a particularly desperate attempt to bring her back to me, I refused to let her eat if it was not with me.

Not my best decision, I admit. It only fueled her anger. But what could I do? I asked her politely, and she still refused to eat with me. I actually was surprised that my threat worked. I would never let her go hungry; it was an empty threat. But she did appear at dinner that night, being escorted by Etan.

I know that I am handling a mate all wrong, but I can't seem to do anything about it. The joining caused primitive emotions to rise inside me, and they have no outlet. The only thing that would calm the inferno inside is Eleanor. But alas, I cannot find a way to win her affection.

During dinner, she barely speaks to me. She only makes brusque, one-word responses to my queries. Her presence alone brings me some small amount of peace though. I have tried to have her join me more frequently in her day, but I am met with stone-cold refusal. When I ask her to walk with me, she always has another activity planned and quickly disappears.

I am beginning to wonder if she truly wishes to be rid of me. I hold out hope that one day the physical enjoyment we shared will cause her to come to me. That her body will crave the pleasure it knows I alone can bring to it. That hope has been in vain though; she never comes to me. I am beginning to suspect she never will.

There are times I will come upon her when she has been alone in the observatory she likes to frequent, and I swear she has been crying. Or she is walking with Etan by the docking bays and her eyes are red. But then whenever I question her, she makes a speedy exit. Rarely even uttering a single word to me. If I am lucky, she will nod to acknowledge my presence.

The morning after our first joining I was worried when I did not hear her voice in my head and was unable to sense anything from her. I can feel the connection inside me where she should be, but I can get nothing out of it. It is like an empty wall. I was worried that the joining failed, destroyed due to our anger, so I consulted with Golon.

"Dane, that only happens when a mate is...for lack of a better word...happy. Or more accurately, in love. Her entire being must be trusting of you. It is common for males to think it happens immediately, but trust must be earned. Give her time, and you will have what you desire."

Of course, since that morning was the same one we had the argument that shook her fledgling happiness with me, I still am missing her presence within me. Not having her inside my head is like having a piece of my soul missing. With no known course to follow, I did the only thing I could think of. I have given her space, hoping that she will come to me.

But I have given her time, and it has all been for naught. I have given her nothing but time, and still, she refuses to spend any with me. Malin, Amell, and Arsenio are all in the pool with her today. As her guards, they are duty-bound to accompany her everywhere. They also informed me that our separation has been hard on her as well. The logical side of my brain knows that she needs friends and guards she can count on.

But as I look down upon my mate and her guards, it is not the logical brain in control.

As I watch them receive the smiles only I should get, I feel my fury build. She is so relaxed and open with my warriors and so reserved and cool with me. They see her wet and glistening body. Why did I even put in that stupid pool on this ship?

As I hear her laughter travel up to me from my position on the balcony, the deep chuckles slithering up and down my spine, I decide I have had enough. I jump the railing and use my command of *caeli* to slow my descent and land gracefully on the ground.

"Eleanor, a word. Now," I bite out. I can see her jump and all traces of merriment disappear from her face. My mood darkens further. She moves toward the edge of the pool and climbs out.

I turn my black scowl on the men in the pool. "My mate will be with me for the rest of the day and evening. You may leave us." If they are smart, they will hear the threat and know it is a command. I want them gone. "Now."

"Oh, if it is alright I would like them to stay." She cuts off her speech when I turn my fury on her. She takes a step back and, for once, I do not care that she withdraws from me. She deserves my fury. She has been nothing but open with other males while I, her mate, her *deim* mate, get nothing but icy indifference. She should be cool with them and open with me. I can feel jealous rage coursing through me.

"No, they need to go. They will be in the way. It will be you and I, Queen. I intend for us to spend some time in each other's company, mate. It is long past due, do you not think so?" I do not take my eyes off her, daring her to argue with me this time. I can see Amell and Malin giving a bow and making polite noises.

I have no concern about them as long as they leave. Arsenio and Eleanor share a long look before he too makes his exit, something private shared between them. It fuels my anger to witness this obvious connection between them.

"Alright, Danion. What do you want?" she asks me so quietly I have to strain my ears to hear her.

"I want to know why you avoid me. You are my mate, bound to ME. We shared harsh words in anger, yes, but we must move past this. There is no escaping our bond. You do not get the luxury of taking a lover. We need to mend our bond, not drive it even further apart." My words are full of barely leashed anger.

I would never admit it aloud, but the anger stems from insecurity. In all my years I have never been unsure of myself. But this tiny imp of a woman makes me so nervous. She holds my entire future happiness in her hand, and she could crush it if she so desires. I have no idea what else I could do to make her desire my presence.

"You can't just come in here and demand I forget what you said." She tries to challenge me. She will quickly learn that you do not become a king of a warrior race without being able to rise to any challenge.

"Oh no? You don't know your mate very well," I challenge her.

Her shoulders stiffen, and her eyes harden. I prepare myself for battle, finally something between us. I will take more arguments; anything is better than the silence of the last month.

But then her shoulders drop, her eyes soften and she lets out a forlorn sigh.

"I...I do not know what to say." Her lack of response causes my spirits to fall. I cannot seem to reach her. I can't force her to open up to me, and even anger can't draw her out. "It is true. I don't know you, and I don't know if I ever will. You clearly look down upon me. I really just don't know what you want me to say."

"The truth, Eleanor. The truth would be nice." I stare at her. "We cannot move forward as mates if you refuse to open up to me." Still, she makes no move to answer me. "Please, Eleanor, we have to move forward." I wonder if she knows that I have never said the word *please* before meeting her. Or if she would even care.

Her eyes turn hard for one brief moment, her gaze running over my face as if looking for something.

"You want the truth, Danion?" Her words cause me to stiffen, might I finally get an answer?

"Yes, I would like to know you the way mates should. We have to learn to forget the words we both said." While I admit I am to blame for the distance, she too contributed to it. I can admit to my failings, but I will also force her to admit hers as well.

"I will try to explain myself then. But I need a promise from you." She is wringing her hands together nervously in her lap.

"Anything," I assure her. I will give her anything to close this cold chasm between us that I caused. To end this desolation that I feel. If I have to go one more day without her companionship, I fear I will finally succumb and the mate madness will claim me.

"I want you to promise me that you will not become angry and take it out on my people." Her people? I am her people. "And you have to know I won't be just a pretty little thing you possess."

"What do you mean your people? Do you mean the people back on Earth? I am your people now, not them. You are Gelder. And I don't want to possess you. That is ridiculous. Why would I want to possess you? I want to protect you, care for you. Perform the duties of a mate."

"Yes, of course, I mean the people on Earth! I may be your mate, but I am human too. You can't remove your protection from them just because we disagree." Her words are backed with iron. She is prepared to fight. To protect people that I have already sworn to protect.

"Eleanor, I will always protect Earth as long as they need it, I have told you this. I will make sure they are safe. That is the entire mission of the Gelder warriors, to protect life. If there is a threat to the human race that they cannot defend against, Gelder warriors will always stand fast in their defense. It has nothing to do with you or our bond," I assure her, but this is of no consequence. The second part of her promise draws me in. "But what do you mean about a pretty thing I will possess? You will not disparage yourself in this way. I have warned you about talking about yourself this way before. I will not stand for it."

"I don't think I can hold your interest outside of something you put on display like this entire blasted ship. I know you don't respect humans. And since I am one, tell me how you expect me to believe that you desire me. How I am to believe that once you get to know me, you won't realize that I pale in comparison to you?" Her words, which started angry, slowly taper off into a quiet whisper. She takes a deep breath. "You are so, so large." She blushes deeply and grimaces. "I mean like your presence. You are such a large force. You are strong and fair, and from what I've seen, you're also arrogant and harsh. But not cruel or manipulative."

I cannot help but laugh at her words. After I do, I notice that she flinches. I forget that my mate is a delicate flower. I can easily hurt her tender feelings. She had been so angry I never thought she was hiding insecurities as well. It is a hard lesson to remember after a lifetime of dealing with warriors.

"I am sorry, *aninare*. I only laugh because it is such a relief to know that it is not something that cannot be fixed." I try to take her hands, but she pulls them away. I take them again and hold them tight. She will have to learn that she is not allowed to pull away from me. "No truly, Eleanor." I pause until she brings her eyes to mine. "You are more than human. Yes, humans have a long way to come before they earn my respect." She tries to pull her hands away from me, but I hold fast. "No, don't turn away from me, this is important. I have been in possession of this throne for many reasons. None of those are because it was handed to me. Humans are young, not flawed. I respect strength, and a sign of strength will never be inheriting a title like your Earth ambassadors do.

"You have to stand up and take what you want. You already stand up to me, challenge me. To me, this is what a mate does. You stand up to me and make demands, not requests. Why would I want to change that? To limit that, or possess that? So now tell me, what do you mean, this entire ship is on display?"

"Look around you, the walls are made of literal gold, and you eat on plates and cutlery that are made of actual diamonds." I can tell by her tone she does not approve of this.

"Why are you upset with this?" I ask her. I try to come up with an answer for why the décor would upset her. It is nothing but necessary.

"It is so...so extravagant. So wasteful," she answers me wearily. Oh, Stars give me strength, such a meager thing to worry over.

"The ship does use an abundance of gold to line its hull, but it is for a reason, not extravagance. It is easily shaped, and plentiful in the galaxy so it is easy to come by, and frankly, it is virtually useless for anything else. It does possess an ideal weight to balance the gravity engines, so it does have some use, so we collect it and use it in all our ships." I look at her, trying not to laugh at the look on her face. "Why is this so surprising to you? Does gold have a useful purpose back on Earth Nueva? We have never found any truly unique use for it."

"Well, your...well OK. But still, diamonds for silverware is ridiculous," she says with anger.

"Diamonds, as you call them, are just perfectly organized forms of carbon. It is extremely durable, and it is abundant in the cosmos. Many dead stars collapse in on themselves and turn into massive balls of pure diamonds. It is completely useless to us, just a mass of floating carbon. Such as the star your own Earth Nueva orbits. Once it dies, it will become an extremely dense sphere of perfect diamonds. We mine these dead stars and shape them into what we need."

"But isn't there something easier to use?" she asks with despair.

"No, neither gold nor diamonds are hard to come by nor useful for much else. They are both abundant and easy to acquire," I try to explain. "It is not something we covet. Material possessions hold very little allure to us. The one and only thing we do hold as a sign of wealth is not a physical item we can hold."

"What is it then?" she asks me.

"It is power. Plain and simple, the power to claim. To defend. To protect what is ours. This is something you give me. You give me power."

"Really?" she asks, her word dripping with sarcasm. I know it is wrong, but when she looks at me with such scorn and challenges me, I can't help but get hard. Rock hard. We need to mend our fences soon. I am getting well and truly tired of aching like this. I discreetly adjust my pants to block the physical evidence of my arousal.

"Yes, Eleanor. Physically you have strengthened me. You have brought power to me. But you have pulled away from me both physically and mentally. I would like to know you on all levels. Do you think we could try? Try to move past the words we both said?" I need to possess her on all levels. I want her to crave me as I do her. Want her to need me to function as I need her. I want to own her as she owns me.

"We can try. But I can't promise you anything." She seems very hesitant. But I will take it. I just smile at her.

Ellie

It has been over two weeks since I finally gave Danion a chance. Etan was right though, I need to try to understand him. It has been a tentative truce. It was true that I felt a little inferior to him. I still do, really. But I also struggled to trust him to keep our relationship one of equal footing and not to have him use his power when we disagree. It is not like he hasn't done it before. He tried this very thing before, the morning after when we argued so bitterly. He tried to push my desires aside to accommodate his.

But slowly I am learning to trust him. I told both Arsenio and Etan that I would try if Danion made the first step, so that is what I am doing. After a month of scorning his advances, I admit I was not ready to trust him. To forgive him. But I am willing to try now. Etan has helped me to move past the majority of my insecurities, and I can never express my gratitude for that.

I have been happier these last two weeks than ever before in my life.

For almost two months we have been bound, and since then I have challenged him. I know that it was difficult for Danion to allow me to distance myself. I always expected him to force me, to use his power to make me behave as he wanted. He has the ability, as he has already demonstrated by locking me in a trance.

My mother would have changed me if she had the power to do so and forced me to do as she wanted. His nasty little "forcing me to eat with him" did come close. I was furious when he threatened to make me go hungry for an entire day if I continued to refuse to dine with him. However, since our truce, he has relented on that, so I am choosing to let it slide for now.

Since our reconciliation, Danion has not failed a test yet. He has shown that he wants to know me, the real me. I barely know who I really am to show him. Even after all the work Etan and I have put in there is much to do. Since we joined, I have felt as if I am coming out of a fog. As if something was holding me back my whole life, dimming my senses.

Since we decided to try to move forward together, we have spent almost all of our time with one another. He has taught me about games and educated me on his history. We have eaten every meal together since that day by the pool because I choose to, not because he forces me. We actually communicate with each other now.

We have begun discussing our likes and dislikes, and he has tried to make me open up about my dreams. Since then I realize I never really had any goals, but am quickly forming some. He had me relive my best memories of childhood, few as they are. I am still struggling to trust him with the darker memories that Etan knows of. I can't shake the feeling of inadequacy toward him. The fear that he will one day see me as my mother does and look at me with disgust.

Slowly I am becoming who I have always thought I could be. My own person. I may be developing strong feelings for him, but I refuse to be dependent on him for my own happiness. As lovely as these two weeks have been I cannot trust him with my happiness. To do that would be to open myself up to dependence. Never again will I be dependent on another person. I would need to know he loves me for me to trust him.

I am not so foolish as to think that he could love me. How could he? I was forced upon him. He did not really choose me, biology did. He doesn't even like humans, so how could he ever love me? I know he is fond of me, and I know I am good for him.

He has admitted that since we have been spending more time together, he has jumped again in power. It makes me proud that I can give him something tangible. He is a warrior, and there is nothing that he respects more than power. I feel like I have something worthwhile to give for the first time in my life.

"What thoughts are running in that bright mind that brings such a smile to your face? Dare I hope it is me?" a sly voice says behind me.

I turn and see Danion leaning against the open bedroom door. I am sitting at my vanity finishing getting ready for our morning meal together.

"That is for me to know, and you to find out," I answer him with a smile.

"Is that so?" he says with an answering smile.

"Yes." I smile back at him.

"Well, now I am sorry to have to tell you that you have done your hair for nothing." He is walking toward me and removing his shirt.

"My hair?" I am distracted by the sight of his muscles being displayed as his shirt comes up.

"Yes, because you are not leaving this room today." With that, he grabs me by my arms and pulls me up. I feel his mouth pressed to mine. While his body causes a craving inside me, I can't bring myself to allow him the use of my body. Even if I know it will bring us both immense pleasure. The argument that happened after the last time we slept together leaves me leery of being so vulnerable again.

I am afraid to have him revert to thinking nothing of me but as a human pawn, as if I am just a body he can command. Maybe this has always been his plan. Make me complacent and willing to do anything he wishes. Slowly starting to act on his plans with no more resistance from me, removing Arsenio for instance.

"No, I am sorry, Danion. I don't want to," I say quickly and push against his chest.

"Please, Eleanor, I can feel your desire." He tries to pull me back into his arms. "Do not deny me, us, this pleasure. I can make you scream with ecstasy, I promise." His words are choppy and full of passion. Still, I refuse to yield.

"No, Danion, I don't want this." He stares at me deeply. I can tell he is trying to decide if he should push this. Undoubtedly if he pushes hard enough, I will succumb. We both know this. I beg him with my eyes to listen to my mind, not my traitorous body. I am not ready to open myself up this way again.

"You would deny us both?" His eyes are laser-focused on me.

"Yes, I just can't, Danion. Not yet." I meet his eyes head-on. I can tell he is trying to read my mind, though I know he can't do that yet. I see a plethora of emotions cross his face. Lust, anger, determination, and finally acceptance tinged with sadness.

"Would you be willing to spend the day with me again?" I am brought out of my reverie. "Regrettably if I cannot spend the day inside you I would still like to be in your presence." His words cause a blush; they are always so blatant.

"OK," I answer quietly. I cannot bring myself to succumb to him, but see no harm in spending time with him. "What are we doing today?" I say with yet another blush. I can't get the imagery that his words caused out of my mind.

"We are going to be spending some time in our communications center," he answers. "To ensure that I can actually leave you, I best remove myself from your tempting presence now." He smirks at me, and it is then I am made aware that I am clothed only in a thin robe. "I will take my leave of you and await you in the anteroom." With that, he gives me a quick kiss and flows out of the room. He has such grace, every movement is filled with natural strength.

I smile at the view of his buttocks in his tight pants that I am afforded as he leaves. While I can't trust him yet, I do enjoy his body. I make my way to the bathroom and begin filling the bathtub. I add some of my favorite bath salts. Once full, I use the settings dial and set it to an automatic quick body wash. One thing I have thoroughly enjoyed about this bathtub is all of these cleaning settings. I can set it, lie back, and it will wash and scrub my entire body for me. I am careful to keep my hair out of the water.

As I sink into the depths, I slowly lean back and relax. Letting the waters, bubbles, and soft sponges that fold out from hidden slats along the inside clean me.

Once it is all done, I step out and hurry through getting dressed and finish fixing my hair. I am anxious to join my husband again. I know that we are not at a perfect place in our relationship, but I feel complete when we are together. The issues in our relationship doesn't stop my body and mind from craving his presence.

As soon as I am ready, I open the door to the anteroom and see him waiting for me. He has a smile on his face as he turns around.

"Eleanor, you are ready a little sooner than I expected. I meant to surprise you." It is then that I see the table he has set up. He has all of my favorite foods to break my fast on the table.

"Are those eggs with ketchup?" I know that this is something that Danion must have requested especially for me, because he absolutely hates ketchup, particularly with eggs, but it is something I discovered I love from a dare of his. It is something he heard was common back on Old Earth, but we both thought sounded unappetizing. After I first tasted it though I found that it is my favorite meal to break my fast with.

I do believe that ketchup itself is not a very common condiment in the Gelder cuisine. He thought it would be amusing to make me eat some and watch me grimace, but shocked him when I asked for seconds. I find myself smiling at the memory. These little events are what draws me to him every day.

"Thank you for doing this," I say to him, and I really mean it. It always makes me feel better when he shows that he pays attention to me and knows my preferences. It goes a long way in making me feel that we will get to a point where we are finally able to move past these stormy days and actually share our lives together.

With that, we sit and eat our meal together. We share easy conversation, and I can't believe that just a few weeks ago I felt so nervous around him. Now I can barely stand being away from him for even a minute. A few days ago he had work to do in the war room, and I just sat around, anxiously waiting for him to be done. I am so glad that he has asked me to join him this time rather than just wait for him again.

"Have you eaten your fill, *aninare*?" Danion asks me. I nod to him as I wipe my mouth.

"Very well, then if you allow me I will escort you." He offers me his arm. "Are you excited to see the war room?"

"Oh, yes. I am so curious. Golon lent me some books on Gelder history and I am fascinated with how the Gelders have come to amass such power in the galaxy," I tell him, remembering all of the battles I have read the details of.

"Yes, what I am going to show you will explain our many successes." With those last words, he tucks my arm into his elbow, and we exit the room.

This simple gesture is yet another way that he shows how he takes special care to make me feel at ease. In one of my history sessions with Liam, I learned that warriors usually have their mates hold their shoulder so that they can quickly reach their weapons in time of attack. But Danion uses the method that humans do so I feel comfortable. Also, I don't think I could reach his shoulder, let alone walk with my hand on him. He walks me toward a room I have not been in before.

"Now, Eleanor, you are not only my mate. You are my queen. As queen, you are expected to be my equal. Able to take command, if the need ever arises. Give orders in my place. How can you do that if you are in the dark about what you are the queen of?" he asks me as we pause in front of the room. He does not wait for an answer.

"You cannot. Inside this room, you will see the true might of the Gelder people. You also will learn why the Erains have never been able to best us in battle, even though they outnumber us more than three to one." As we enter, I notice a huge holographic display rising from the floor. This hologram takes up the entire center of the room. It rotates slowly around itself, originating in the center. As I slowly walk around it, I notice that it looks vaguely like a massive grid pattern.

"Danion, what is all of this?" I ask him.

"This is a display of all of our bases throughout the galaxy. This here shows why we are the leading military force in the galaxy. The Erains have never been able to get a good fight against us because of what this represents," he explains.

"It looks like you have enough bases to cover the entire galaxy," I say as I study the grid.

"Very astute," he answers with pride in his voice. "In fact we do. And because of this, we not only monitor the entire galaxy in real-time, the bases have automated defenses in place. These outposts are also equipped with a sophisticated program that allows us to communicate across the entire galaxy with virtually no time delay. This is why we can respond to any threat quickly and fiercely. This system here can detect an event, monitor it, assess its threat level, and even take action all with no command from us. It also alerts us so we can review and step in if necessary."

"I see, so if any of your planets or outposts are attacked you can respond?" I am struggling to comprehend what he is telling me.

"More than that, we can actually see all of their attacks in real-time. Detect their movements by sensors at each station and even make predictions on their future movements. Erains are not the only enemy out there but they are by far the greatest threat in this galaxy. But they lack foresight, and they are inherently impulsive. This allows us to monitor their movements and respond accordingly. We do not waste resources. We know exactly where our ships are needed. Also, these outposts scout around on their own, gathering information and then using it to predict future attacks. It has been extremely successful so far." Something occurs to me that is worrying.

"You say that the Erains outnumber us?" I ask. I am stunned by his words. Never before did I question the power and superior strength of the Gelder. I always assumed they were the most powerful beings in existence.

"Yes, by great numbers," he answers without showing any concern. He is studying a report casually, utterly indifferent about our disadvantage.

"Then what is stopping them from conquering us? From banding together and attacking? I thought that the Gelders were the strongest power in the galaxy." I try to hide my fear, but I can hear it in my voice. Danion puts the report down and looks up at me.

"Do not worry yourself. While we are not the most abundant, we are the most powerful. Erains, as I said, are impulsive. They do not think ahead, and they do not work together. They are working in factions and constantly battling with one another as well. They see a planet that they deem inferior, and they attack. No strategy. We never have to stage an all-out war. We monitor here where they attack, and we send adequate numbers. And even if they were to band together, this network is more than just a map. It allows us for instantaneous communication among the outposts." He waves a hand at the display.

"If we have an attack here"—he points to a spot on the very edge of the map—"by the speed the waves can travel via our old system, it would take days to reach us here. But with our network, fractions of a second. This here is the lifeblood of our success. No war is won without information. This room allows us to gather all the information possible before we plan our defense."

"What if one breaks? What if the network goes down?" I am still worried. "It looks like these are all links in a chain. If one goes out doesn't it change the whole design?"

"We have redundancies in this design. If one goes down, there are backup outposts to cover the outage," he assures me. "See this? This is the central hub—everything routes through there. If it was damaged, everything gets relayed to a backup operation. It is so sophisticated it even mounts counterstrikes when threats are detected automatically. Nothing can even touch these bases. They also are very robust. They can withstand solar flares and have shields to block asteroids and other impacts. I assure you, we are safe from an attack."

"But what if they did go out?" I persist. "Nothing is perfect."

"Fear not, it will not happen." I stare at him. He sighs in defeat. I can tell he thinks I am being foolish but I am determined to have my answer. "Fine, if they went out it would blind us. We would not know where the attacks were coming from. There would be a delay in getting our old, outdated system up and running. But do not worry, Eleanor. It will not happen. Before we phased out the old communications, we made sure we had backups to the backups. We could lose over thirty percent of the outposts and still be able to fully communicate. Truly, it would take over sixty percent of them failing before it collapsed and we would know they were being targeted by that point and we would mount a counterstrike well before then."

"Do you not think this is a large weakness? With no backup system, if your enemies knew of this..." I trail off. "Would it not make sense to have a backup system? What could it hurt?" I ask him. I have read enough history on my planet alone to know that a superpower with only one line of defense always falls. It makes them too vulnerable. How does he not see this?

He studies me.

"Here, let me show you. If you will allow me?" he asks me. At my nod, he goes to an interface of some kind and adjusts the settings. Now the grid has pulsing points all throughout it, along with large spheres around them. "See this? The system in itself is a backup."

"Are you patronizing me?" I can't help but ask.

"No, I am explaining. See the pulsing points in the center of each sphere?" I nod. "These represent the outposts and relay centers. See how there is overlap in each sector?" At his words, I study the map in more detail. I slowly begin to circle the grid, examining every aspect.

"Yes, there is overlap. But some areas are more heavily covered than others. Some only have a few handfuls of overlaying grids. While others are layered so deeply, I cannot even see where the bases are."

"Yes, that is true. These are in areas in high-danger zones. Be that because there is heavy asteroid activity in the area, a star with active flares, or even just common trade routes that see a large volume of ships. With these higher risks, we need to protect these bases. This is designed so that if one goes down, the network is not compromised. It can still function while we repair the damages. Our enemies would need to take out nearly the entire network simultaneously to crash it." His words, while meant to be reassuring, only worry me more.

"But how? There are areas where they are spaced too far apart. Where only a handful are needed to be out of commission, and they would not connect," I point out to him. "If an enemy ever learned of this, it would not take very much to collapse the whole network."

"What are you talking about?" he asks me, a look of alarm on his face.

"I'm sorry, was I not supposed to notice it?" I ask him, chagrined. It would not be the first time in my life that I pointed out an error, only to be chastised for it later.

"Notice what, Eleanor? Are you saying that you see a way to weaken this grid?" His question seems earnest as if he has no idea what I am talking about.

"Not weaken it, destroy it. See these six outposts? If they were taken out, it would strain the entire system. Strain it so much it would collapse and not be able to function. See?" At his confused look, I walk into the holographic display. "Right here, see how they are in the very center? Everything runs through them, right?" He nods. "These six also only share one range of overlap with each other. If you were to take these six out, the very center would fail, which would leave nothing to route everything through. And nothing to send a backup to. So…" I trail off as I see his features darken. "Should I not have said anything?"

"No, I am secure enough to admit when I am wrong." His dark look has not gone away. "You are remarkable. How did you see this? And so quickly? You barely spent two minutes looking at it."

"I study history," I remind him.

"Yes, I am aware of that," he answers with a sharp bite to his words.

"Well, you know that in history we study remains of ancient civilizations. I have always had a knack for being able to see what the city looked like with only a few pieces given. I guess it is like a puzzle to me. I can see the individual pieces just as clearly as the entire picture," I try to explain.

"You are right, you see everything. We have had this system for centuries and never before have we seen this. Not even our computer simulations have ever caught this fault. It is a good thing you discovered this and not an enemy. We will start correcting the design immediately, but there is no reason not to have a backup system in place as well. A very intelligent female mentioned it is foolish not to be prepared," he says with a smirk. "We have plenty of resources, and now that I have you to protect, I find I am never satisfied with enough security."

I smile in response. I am pleased that he listens to my ideas and contributions instead of ignoring them. The desire to throw my arms around him is almost too much to fight. I have to work on holding myself back. Just this morning I told him I wanted physical distance, so if I throw myself at him it would only be teasing him.

I smile at him though. He never treats me as if I am merely a child compared to him when considering our age gap he would be justified in doing so. He has lived for thousands of years and fought through countless battles, so it is a real gift that he does not write off my comments as useless chatter. Every time we talk I feel a little more confident in our relationship.

I smile once more at him as he takes my arm and escorts me from the room.

Vlad-Kish

"Not weaken it, destroy it."

"We will start correcting the design immediately."

The new queen's words shake me. I have been studying the maps for months, long before she came, looking to find just such a weakness. I have been unsuccessful in trying to shut down the network. Now, it appears I have her to thank for the breakthrough that will cripple the Gelder scum's system. Unfortunately, she wants to not only improve the design, but she also plans to have them implement a backup plan so that we will never be able to successfully collapse the grid.

No, I will not stand for it. I cannot go back to our king empty-handed. Fear slithers down my spine as I imagine the king's reaction if I was to fail. I blink my borrowed eyes and fill myself with resolve.

The queen is a worthless, powerless whore who deserves to be eradicated. She thinks she is worthy of our world? Worthy to exist with the mighty Erains? It is not enough that she strengthened the swine that is their king? Her, as nothing but a mortal.

An inferior mortal who should know nothing but death and pain. She is nothing compared to me, to us, yet she will try to topple all of my plans. I am only a few weeks away from finally ridding the great Erain race from having to share a life with mortal and Gelder scum alike. I will not stand for this. I'll make plans to move up our destruction of the Gelder vermin.

Our new king will have my head if I fail. I must stop this female. In the most permanent of ways, I will stop her before she can ruin me.

I smile. With any luck, this will also send the king into such despair he will not notice our plans before it is too late.

Chapter Thirteen

Ellie

The food here is so much more than anything I knew on Earth. I savor the last few bites and wash them down with a fruity drink that I have recently discovered. Danion does not care for it, but we have it at every evening meal since I so enjoy it.

It is these little things that show me that maybe I can trust him. He is so considerate to me and pays close attention to all my preferences. As I stare at him I am awash with a feeling of warmth and his love fills me. It is almost as if there is a presence in my mind. It feels as if there is a physical connection between our two minds.

The platter of food that Danion holds while he is serving the food rattles and shakes. I study him, and I realize his hand is trembling and a look of almost orgasmic pleasure is on his face. Danion closes his eyes, and I feel a fluttering in my mind. It is not altogether unpleasant, but it is disconcerting.

"Oh, *aninare*." Danion speaks with such reverence. Such raw desire. I can feel his desire as if it was my own. I can feel a deep yearning well up inside me. A wave of arousal rushes over me and my panties soak with my excitement. The room feels like it pulses energy around me. With the very center of the energy being Danion.

I look up, slightly alarmed. This is not something I want. I feel as if I am lost at sea, adrift with no paddle to steer me home. My mind has always been the one place I can be myself. My safe haven. The one place I can be who I am meant to be with no worries about what other people think of me. If I do not have my own mind, who am I? All I can think of is one repeating question: What did I do?

"You did nothing but open yourself to me. Not fully, but it brings much longed-for peace to my soul." Danion says the words with such pride and triumph.

"Did I say that aloud?" I ask, now with real alarm. I did not speak those words aloud, I know I didn't. That means he must have been able to read my thoughts. All the color drains from my face as I realize that my most coveted place, my mind, is no longer mine alone but something Danion will share with me. Danion's face closes up.

"Not anymore. Why do you block me now?" he asks with such a look of loss on his face, I feel a momentary wave of sympathy so powerful I almost try to reestablish our link. But I stop myself in time. No, I refuse to give up my entire self for him. My mind is mine and no one else's.

"It is a little invasive, don't you think?" I can't believe I have to explain why this is a problem.

"Not at all, not when you will also be able to hear me. Just as I hear you." He is speaking to me as if I am a child who took away his most prized toy. Well, I won't be guilted into giving up the most sacred part of myself.

As a child, whenever a punishment got particularly bad at home, I could always retreat into my mind. I could always seek refuge inside myself. If I let him have my mind, he has everything. I can't just give that up without a fight.

"Oh, then I am so sorry. Why would I mind that I have no privacy as long as you have none as well?" My voice is dripping with sarcasm.

Over the last month and a half, I have become less concerned with masking my sarcasm. Just when I begin to think we can be equals in this relationship, he says something so…so condescending. He reminds me why we can never be equals. He has never worried about hiding his scorn for humans. All I am to him is a warm body that he was forced to mate with so he can father children. I am not a partner. I feel a deep rage burning in my belly, the rage is so hot that I can feel the heat climbing into my chest.

"What is it that you are trying to hide from me that causes you to covet this privacy?" He has the audacity to ask. His words make my anger climb to a new degree. He has no concern for my feelings or my desires. The heat inside continues to rise.

"It is not as if I have a specific secret, it is the principle! I should have the choice to be my own person. With no worry of judgment from you!" I scream these last words. "I should not have to defend my desire to be allowed basic privacy!" The heat is becoming too much to contain. I can't stay still. I feel that the heat will consume me if I don't do something. I stand up and start pacing.

In the back of my mind, I realize I'm making a bigger deal out of this than necessary, but there is nothing that I can do. All I can think about is releasing the internal heat. If he is talking, I don't know it because I am not listening. The only thing I can do is continue screaming at him. I try to rein in my rage, but nothing I do can stem my anger. Or the heat. It is welling up inside of me rapidly. I am beginning to feel sick, sweat is starting to bead on my skin.

"I would not judge you! As I trust you would not judge me." Danion's words sound as if they are far away. He must be walking away from me.

Why is he leaving? I need him with me. Does he not realize that I don't mean to be so angry with him? I feel that I can't control myself and I know deep down something is very wrong. When I look he is still in the room with me, he is not leaving but walking closer. His mouth is moving, but I can't focus on his questions as the heat becomes unbearable.

"Eleanor? Are you alright?" These are the last words I hear. The edges of my vision begin to dim, and then I am falling toward the floor. My last thoughts are full of relief, relief that finally, I can escape this burning heat.

Danion

"Eleanor!" I see her begin to fall and I put all my power to boost my already advanced speed to catch her before she hits the floor. "Eleanor!" I grasp her tightly to me. I put my hand to her face to try to wake her. I snatch my hand away from her face as soon as I make contact with her skin.

Her skin is blazing, it is like the surface of a star it is so hot. It is literally burning my skin. I see welts rise up where my skin comes into contact with hers. I feel terror rise inside me. Humans cannot survive this kind of heat, not even for a moment. My Eleanor is human.

I am rendered frozen by fear while my mind refuses to process the inevitable loss of her. This small human has become the most precious thing in this entire galaxy to me. I refuse to lose her. With a burst of power, I cradle her tightly to my chest and leave the room.

I begin to funnel healing waves into her small, quivering frame. Her poor features are locked in a painful grimace. I send cooling threads of water all over her body in a feeble attempt to aid her.

"GOLON!" I bellow as I begin to run as fast as I can. I use a thread of power to send the call into the ship's speaker system. "Meet me in the *hael* wing, NOW!" At the same time, I send an advance request to the medical staff. Requesting that the highest ranked and most skilled staff be ready and waiting for me when I get there.

Time is against my mate. I know if she is to have even a small chance she must get care immediately.

I race through the halls cradling her even closer to me. I feel her skin getting warmer and warmer. I pour as many cooling weaves as I can over her, but they are having little effect.

I feel real fear—humans can't handle these temperatures. I have faced my own death thousands of times before and never felt anything like this. The *hael* wing is full of staff waiting for me as I explode into the room. Good. Heads would have rolled if there would have been any delay.

"Here, sire, place her on the bed," Jarlin Clarkiel, the chief medical officer on board, tells me, motioning to one of our floating medical platforms.

I am thankful to see him, even though I am still in the viselike grip of complete terror. He is the most skilled doctor in the entire Gelder race. If it were not for Liam and his mate being stationed here, Jarlin would have been back in his lab on the medic base in our command hub, not be here to help my mate now. I am grateful the Stars aligned and brought him here. I gently place her down on the bed he indicated. "What led up to her symptoms?" he asks as he is already connecting her to monitors as well as weaving healing threads all around her.

"We were having dinner, and then we became angry at each other, and the next thing she collapsed. Her skin is hotter than anything I have ever felt." He lays a hand on her cheeks, and I have to tamp down a territorial rage that sweeps over me. I refuse to let my inherent territorial instincts risk her life. He pulls his hands away quickly.

"Yes, her skin is extremely dangerous right now. This heat is my foremost concern—it is lethal to humans. Humans, while similar to us in form, have very specific temperature needs. Their physiology cannot handle heat exceeding one hundred-five degrees on the human Fahrenheit scale without suffering brain damage. Her skin is well over double that right now. We need to get her into climate control." His words hold a trace of worry and this terrifies me. If he is feeling concerned, he truly worries about her life.

He waves his hand, and the bed glides to a unit near the wall. A glass cover descends from the roof and covers my mate, sealing her inside a glass coffin. All I can think is that she already looks like she has passed away and Jarlin has placed her in what we will seal her body in.

I cannot stop my morbid thoughts while Jarlin proceeds to interact with the controls, staring at them intently.

"What is wrong with her, Jarlin?" I ask him. I need to focus on what can be done. Only by concentrating on the small hope of saving her can I try to find some small amount of control over my raging emotions. Hope that my mate will recover is all that I have holding me together right now. She can't leave like this. We barely even got a chance to know each other. Barely began forming the mate bond. Before he can answer, Golon comes storming in.

"What has happened, Dane? It is something to do with Ellie?" He is out of breath. He must have been far away, he is in too good of shape to have a mere run to the infirmary cause him physical strain. He must have had to manifest himself here using his powers.

"Is it Eleanor?" Amell follows quickly in Golon's wake. Clearly, he has heard my call for Golon and correctly worried it was my mate in trouble.

I cannot even muster the energy to be angry with them for interrupting before Jarlin could answer me. I fear Jarlin will have bad news, and I do not know what I would do if it is confirmed that my mate will not recover. No. I refuse to accept that. She will live. I look at these two males who are the closest to me. I answer despondently.

"Yes, to both of you. Jarlin is soon to tell me what has befallen her. And the simple cure that he will perform to heal her. She will be fine." I can barely keep it together.

He has to be able to save her, he is the best healer in the entire galaxy. He will save her. He must save her. My increased power is screaming at my binds, but I refuse to distract the medical staff. Jarlin needs his concentration to heal her.

My determination is tested as Jarlin remains quiet. I begin to pace. I see Golon and Amell open their mouths and I silence them with a look. If Jarlin is not answering me, his king, he is focusing on saving my mate. My Eleanor. Finally, after what feels like an eternity, Jarlin speaks. His eyes though portray worry when he looks at me.

"Alright. There are some concerns, but I think she will pull through with some careful care. I warn you, King, it is not guaranteed. I will do the best our knowledge can provide, but only time will tell if she will survive. I have her temperature controlled for the time being. I am manually handling her internal climate, forcing it down to manageable levels. Well, to nonlethal levels. It is difficult, I will not lie to you. Her body is fighting the machines." Jarlin sighs, the lines around his eyes full of confusion. "I will be blunt. She should be dead. And if she were purely human, she would be. This poison would have killed her instantly if she were." Jarlin is immediately besieged with questions.

"Poisoned?" This comes from me. My focus is on the threat to my mate, rather than the admittedly grim diagnosis.

"What do you mean, she should be dead now?" Amell is quick to question.

"What do you mean if she was purely human? She is human," Golon asks.

"First, I need to handle my patient." Jarlin's voice is filled with impatience. He clicks a button, and a full three-dimension projection of a body rises from the floor. It is a picture of Eleanor with various vitals listed next to her. There are so many vitals and scrolling information I cannot comprehend them all. "See this? Her temperature peaked at well over three hundred degrees, no human could survive that. Not even for a moment. Yet she survived for several minutes." Jarlin motions to her abdomen on the projection. "Look at her organs. None of these should have been able to function in the temperature she experienced. Focus on her cellular tissue and her blood—they both show evidence of severe distress." Jarlin points to the data scrolling near her heart. "For example, look at these protein levels in her blood. They are lowered for sure, but not absent. If these were the proteins you would find in humans, they should have completely unraveled at this temperature. They would not sustain their shape or function in these conditions."

Jarlin waves his hand and a new set of displays pull up. "Now, this is our queen's DNA, and this is a sample of a standard human's genetic makeup. See the changes? Here and here?" He indicates the differences. "It is not significant to an untrained eye, but it is definitive. She is more than human. In fact, it looks like her DNA is still currently undergoing changes. On my first impression, this may bear a resemblance to our own ancient DNA. Before the transition into immortal beings. But it will call for a more detailed analysis before I am sure. I cannot treat her until I know more."

"She is your queen. You will treat her, and you will do it now." The threat is inherent as I speak to Jarlin. "Heal her now. NOW!" I command him but he does not move.

"Rest assured, my king, I have stabilized her, and her life is in no immediate danger. Try to understand, her DNA is changing. Into what, I do not know. I cannot administer an antidote without knowing her genetic makeup. This would only endanger her further. Greatly increasing her risk of death."

"How long?" My anxiety lowers now that I know her life is not in immediate danger, but the mate bond instincts refuse to let it leave me completely.

"I am not sure, a few days at least. More likely weeks." I scowl at him. "But, I vow I will not leave her side until she is completely healed," he rushes to assure me. Normally I do not enjoy intimidating my people, but I cannot muster an ounce of concern for it now.

"Who could have poisoned her?" I ask Golon and Amell. It is Jarlin who answers though. He opens more displays, explaining the evidence he found.

"It would be someone who has access to her food. This would not sit long before the temperature spiked. It must have been in her dinner. And since you show no ill effects, it would be something only she consumed. If you had come into contact with this, you would also experience some symptoms. Nothing so extreme, but you would know you had been poisoned, I assure you."

"The only ones who would stand to benefit from her death are the Erains. Hoping that it would damage you. We must have a spy on board," Golon answers next. "They must have heard that you have found your mate and wanted to strike back. To hurt you, weaken you. Weaken all of us."

"I will gather the rest of her *praesidium*. We will guard her room and allow no one but Jarlin to attend to her. She will not be left alone, not even for one moment. She will recover, and then we will all apologize for allowing harm to come to her. Danion, do not leave her side until I return with her *praesidium*," Amell states as he leaves the room.

I do not bother to answer him. The notion that I would leave my mate while she is defenseless and barely holding on to life is ridiculous. I turn my attention to Golon.

"What would the Erains stand to benefit from killing my mate?" I ask him. "I agree they are the only suspects, but I admit the timing is random." Golon looks deep in thought.

"Potentially. However, if the spy was able to see auras, he would know that you are gaining strength. He would see that every day you grow stronger. That every day you become a threat to everything they strive toward. If they allowed her to remain with you, to continue aiding you, you would be a force that not even an army could take out," Golon answers. "You would be unstoppable."

"That does not sound right. I am not convinced. Aura sight is a Gelder gift, and we have never seen evidence of it in another race. And if that was the intention, they would have attacked sooner, not allowed my power to continually climb. No attacks have even been made prior to this. Even unsuccessful ones. That is not the catalyst, I just know that we are missing something. Something changed today, something that caused this spy to become bold enough to try to kill her. To risk alerting us to their position on board." I try to think of what would have sparked this.

"What did you do today, Dane? Anything different?" Golon asks me. "Did you come into contact with anyone new? Were you with Eleanor the entire day? Could she have encountered the spy alone and had something we are unaware of occur?"

As I begin to think over the day, alarms start blaring all around us. The communication room's warning bells. Bells that I know should never go off, the alarm is specified for a dark attack. Meaning that we have several bases under siege simultaneously and no way to monitor them. And suddenly, I know exactly what caused the attempt on my mate's life. There was a spy in the grid room.

I stare at my collapsed network. I designed this over the course of decades. Just yesterday I assured my mate that nothing could collapse this. Yet here I stand, and it only took six outposts to be taken down, and the whole system is crippled.

"What do we know, Golon?" I ask my cousin.

"We know that all of the mortal worlds that we protect are under simultaneous attack. Our forces there are holding them off, but barely. We cannot send help to our larger warships since our system is down and they are out of range. And we do not know how many more outposts have been attacked since they collapsed our network." Golon's voice is grave. "The Erains have banded together under one ruler for the first time and have launched a coordinated attack against us. That is all we know."

"You are wrong, we know that we are at war." I look at our destroyed network. " And that I am going to kill every last one of them."

To Be Continued

Author Notes

Thank you for reading Book One in the True Immortals series. This is part of a four-book series that will feature Danion and Eleanor's journey to defeat the Erains and overcome their own faults to save one another. If you enjoyed this book, please leave a review. I love to hear from fans.

For updates on releases, please join our email list to be notified when new releases and sales are going on! Visit www.emjaye.org to sign up.

The True Immortals Series continues:

The Hidden Queen
The Lost Queen
The Mated Queen

Golon's Story

His Mate coming winter 23/24!

Gelder Warrior Stories

Etan's Hidden Pain

Other Works by E.M. Jaye

Lovers of Beverly Tennessee

Hate At First Sight- Coming Oct 27th 2023

.

Printed in Great Britain
by Amazon

30844187R00108